Dar... ...
Book #1

Promises

Of

Love

Lynne Lanning

Scripture quotations are from the King James Version of the Bible.

A sincere Thank You to Amberlyn Beach for the cover design and photography, and for your patience as I change things!

Acknowledgments

A very special word of thanks to all my newsletter recipients who helped reshape, name characters, and give details to this book. I enjoyed every minute working with you all! I also want to thank you for your encouragement to continue this writing journey.

Thank you, Lord, for guiding me and giving me the words you would have me write. I sincerely hope it honors you.

Cast of Characters

Abe Darnell – owner of a large farm

Harvey and Asa Darnell – Abe's sons

Samuel Farley – wealthy entrepreneur, founder of the town

Agnes Farley – Samuel's wife and uppity busybody

Gerald Henderson – owner of outpost/general store

Clint Henderson – Gerald's son

Preacher and Mrs. Upton

Eva, Olivia, and Amy Upton – the Preacher's daughters

Toby – troublemaker

Vince Grayson – Asa's friend

Frank Benson – Harvey's foreman and best friend

Dr. Powell and Mrs. Powell – doctor and schoolteacher

Zeb Watley – town lawyer

Preacher and Mrs. Smith – new Preacher and wife

The children: Nate, Sylvia, Ruth, Caroline, and Charlie

James Russell – children's friend

September 1847

Chapter 1

Tensions were growing as the people of the small community noticed army tents set up at the back of their one and only outpost. News, mixed with rumors, spread like wildfire. The only thing for certain, Abe Darnell, Gerald Henderson, and their sons, knew what was going on. Even they didn't know much.

Within a week, word spread throughout the community. Both the Darnells and Hendersons found they were spending much more time answering neighbors' questions than working. They assured their neighbors they had made the issue a matter of prayer and that all would work out for good.

Most of the community were good, hard-working people that liked to keep to themselves, not being too keen on what they had heard so far. The young people were much more open-minded and excited about the possibilities.

A meeting had been set for Sunday to explain everything to everyone. Excitement and suspicions grew, along with curiosity, with ladies planning to bring meals and have a day of visiting.

The preacher, who made his rounds about once a month, would be joining them, preaching a sermon that morning, and opening the meeting in prayer. He, along with Gerald and Abe would serve as moderators, explaining as best they could and keeping tempers at bay.

Gerald Henderson, owner of the outpost, stood on a small platform, addressing the crowd. "Ladies and gentlemen, Mr. Neville and Mr. Farley are men to be admired and respected. They are adventurers, businessmen, and investors. They have been scouting the area extensively for months and have decided on this location to build a town. I will let them explain."

During the next half hour, the community learned that these men had opened several mining operations within a fifty-mile radius, had several contracts with the government, and big investments in the railroads. Much to Abe's oldest son, Harvey's intrigue, these men were also helping to perfect steam engines used for farming.

"Our contacts can help turn this place into a full-fledged town." Mr. Farley looked at each one of them for their reaction.

Mr. Farley leaned forward. "The land in this area is some of the best, most fertile land within miles. Mr. Darnell's property line borders unclaimed land owned by the government. He and his boys have a great deal of knowledge about agriculture.

"Seems as though more people are moving to the cities, leaving the production of food to someone else. We need farmers to help keep these people fed. The government has agreed to extend some of the land I mentioned, for the purpose of farming. We need someone to tend it and make the best use of it."

Harvey's eyes widened. He looked over at his pa in anticipation. There was nothing he would like more than to run a big farm.

Mr. Farley continued. "We believe that this can become a thriving town and are willing to put our money behind it."

A large map of the area had been nailed to the front of the outpost. Mr. Neville began to point out where everything was now, and what they planned for the future. There was a railroad, streets, buildings, and everything you could imagine that made up a town.

"The government has granted permission for Mr. Darnell to use five hundred acres of the area surrounding his farm, with a contract to buy what is produced.

Abe looked at his two sons before addressing Mr. Farley and Mr. Neville. "I am grateful for this opportunity, but I must say, I have more questions than answers at this point. My boys and I are stout, strong, and hard workers, but five hundred acres is more than the three of us could take on. I don't want to get into politics, but I would rather not use slave labor. I think any man needs to be paid for the work he does, regardless of his skin color.

"Most of the people around here are busy with their own land trying to make a life for themselves. I don't see how we could do this and why you seem to think this place becoming a town hinges on my answer."

Mr. Farley was kind, yet all business. "It doesn't hinge on your answer, but it would be helpful and much quicker to get started with your help. This place will become a town regardless of your answer. It's a prime location between our mining operations and is perfect for expansion. This location is almost centrally located between our businesses with plenty of room for growth and opportunity to offer men with families, well," he paused and swept his hand toward the wide-open rolling hills. "Let's just say it's too big of an opportunity to pass up."

Mr. Neville stepped up. "Ladies and gentlemen, we have already set things in motion to offer incentives to people who would be interested in moving here. There will be plenty of employment opportunities for everyone at the farm, the mines, the new businesses, and of course, construction. We can assure you that everything has been well thought out and we will be glad to share our entire plan with you. This is a big undertaking, and we understand and appreciate you being cautious."

"We are not unreasonable men." Mr. Farley cleared his throat. "Mr. Henderson owns the land we would like to expand as the township. Mr. Darnell owns the biggest and most fertile farm in the area. I've also heard that both men have earned people's respect through their honest dealings and work ethic."

The meeting went well for the most part, although some of the old timers felt as if it didn't matter what they thought about it. "Progress," was muttered in disgust several times as the older men would shake their heads and walk away.

Mr. Farley was a born motivator. He wooed all the ladies with hopes of being able to shop for everything they needed or dreamed of while promising the men enough employment opportunities to make plenty of money to let their wives and daughters buy them.

"We will utilize everyone's abilities." Mr. Farley spoke with enthusiasm. "We will need farmers, carpenters, blacksmiths, bankers, lawyers, doctors, and," he smiled at the preacher, "a full-time preacher."

Cheers went up through some of the crowd before he continued to speak. "But that's not all," he paused and smiled. "We will also need seamstresses, teachers, midwives, and cooks. We have opportunities for everyone who wants it."

"When is all this supposed to happen?" someone shouted from the crowd.

Mr. Neville walked up, placing his hand on Mr. Farley's shoulder. "The first shipment of lumber for buildings will arrive next month. The building should begin before cold weather sets in."

Another man shouted out, "So you just come in here and tell us how everything is going to be? And if we don't like it, we have to pick up and move?"

Mr. Neville motioned toward Mr. Farley to take over. "Sir, I assure you, no one has to move. This is not a dictatorship. This is not my town or Mr. Neville's. We will just be seeing to the building and helping it grow. Very soon we will have another meeting to discuss the leadership of the community. I will need each of you to be thinking about who you trust to serve your interests best.

"For now, we have some buildings to plan and start building. We will start with a much bigger store and a church that will be used as a school throughout the week, for now.

"I do hope that all of us will work together as neighbors, for the good of the community. This isn't just a business venture for me. I plan to settle here with my wife and live the rest of our days right here in this beautiful place."

The crowd grew quiet with low mumblings between them. Abe stepped up and addressed them.

"At first, I was skeptical and even felt a bit pushed into something that I had no control over. Then I started thinking of all the possibilities for a better life for my sons and their children."

He hung his head and was quiet for a moment. "I can't help but believe that if we had a doctor closer, my wife would still be alive today." He sniffled, swiped at his eyes, then straightened to his full six-foot two-inch height and looked at the crowd.

"I have done some praying about this, and I believe it's a good thing happening for us. We need to take advantage of this opportunity God has brought us. We will be able to purchase things we need much quicker, instead of spending days of travel to get them. Our children will have a school, our sick will have a doctor, and our spirits will be renewed regularly through the preaching of the word of God. I think this is a very good thing."

****

After the meeting, Mr. Farley and Mr. Neville talked privately with the Darnells and the Hendersons. "There is a big convention happening in Raleigh a few weeks from now. We plan to attend and would like for you three and Mr. Henderson to join us.   There, companies will be showing all the latest machinery for agriculture, along with fertilizers, seed, and lots of printed information, everything dealing with crops.

"The government is also offering to buy the equipment needed to farm this land. I hoped you would accompany us to the convention and help decide what equipment is needed. I know how to build a machine and keep it in good working order, but I know nothing about growing crops. That's where your expertise will come into play. Think about it and let me know as soon as possible so I can make arrangements."

The men shook hands, saying goodnight. Gerald Henderson and his son, eighteen-year-old Clint, walked down the road toward their house. Abe and his two sons, Harvey, twenty, and Asa, eighteen, mounted their horses.

Mr. Farley stood as he watched them. "I have one more thing for you to consider before you make your decision."

All three sets of eyes rested on the man, waiting for him to continue. "After seven years, the land will be offered to you for purchase at a very reasonable price. As time goes on, if more land is required, I will contact the necessary officials and see about purchasing more."

****

Harvey and Asa were up before dawn, excited about the week ahead of them. It would take them two days to get to Raleigh, they would have Friday, Saturday, and Sunday there, then two days to get back home. They had never been to a big city before and couldn't imagine what it would be like.

Their pa, Mr. Henderson and Clint would be joining them, along with Mr. Farley and some of the soldiers. Mr. Neville, who was older than Mr. Farley by at least ten years, was going to stay and organize some workers while he waited for the building supplies.

Mr. Farley was good company and very practical. He was intelligent and rich, but he didn't flaunt it. Harvey was intrigued by the man, especially when he talked about machinery. Over the two-day ride, the two of them bored the rest of the group to tears with their conversations.

Mr. Farley took to young Harvey quickly. Asa was a good boy too, a good worker and conversationalist, but he wasn't near as interested in farming as Harvey. Mr. Farley could see that both were teachable, ambitious, and smart. He really was beginning to like them, wishing he had been blessed with children, especially sons like them.

On the evening of the second day of their journey, they rode into the community of Cary, right outside of Raleigh. "This is what I have envisioned for our town," Mr. Farley announced with a sweep of his hand. "Nice shops, pleasant parks, and everything you need right within your reach."

The men nodded their heads in agreement as they each looked around, caught up in their own thoughts.

They stopped and dismounted at the hotel. "I took the liberty of reserving rooms for all of us. One of you boys can bunk with me, putting two of us to a room, if you don't mind."

Harvey gladly volunteered as they untied their satchels and headed up the stairs. Once inside, they stopped in amazement at the plush surroundings. They stayed quiet while Mr. Farley got them checked in and returned with their room keys.

"Let's wash up and meet in the dining room in an hour?" After a nod of agreement, he turned on his heel and led the men upstairs.

Over a delicious supper, the boys were almost silent, speaking only when spoken to. Abe noticed they looked uncomfortable and grew concerned.

"You boys feeling poorly?" He was answered with a shake of heads as they continued to eat, keeping their eyes on their plates as if guarding their food. He glanced at Clint Henderson and saw him acting the same. "What's wrong with you boys? I've never seen you so quiet."

"Pa," Harvey leaned towards him and spoke quietly. "This place is so fancy. The people are all dressed up and, well, you know, and we are just plain old country folk. I don't know how we are supposed to act."

Abe grinned. "Your ma taught you good manners and you are doing just fine, aren't they Mr. Farley?"

"Yes indeed. I can imagine it's somewhat uncomfortable because it is different, but you are doing fine. You need to loosen up some and enjoy yourselves while you're here. Who knows when you will return."

Asa leaned forward slightly, speaking quietly as Harvey had. "But there are girls here, pretty ones, like the one that keeps refilling our glasses."

Abe tried to stifle his laughter as Mr. Farley burst out with a cackle. When he regained his composure, Abe smiled at the three boys who were mortified that Mr. Farley's outburst may draw attention to them.

"Son," Abe spoke confidently. "We have girls at home and you don't have a problem with them. What's the problem now?"

Asa shrugged. "The girls back home don't look like these girls."

Abe looked around and saw Asa was right. Most of the girls back home were worn to a frazzle every time they saw them. They had either been working the fields, scrubbing laundry, or had just come in from hunting. The only time they wore dresses was to the monthly church services.

"Yes, I see what you mean." Abe rubbed his chin. "You know, Mr. Farley, I can see some other good reasons for building up our community. These young folk could use a bit of socializing."

Mr. Farley, still recovering from his laughter, nodded and slapped Abe on the back. "I agree, and hopefully it won't take long to set things in motion."

The waitress came back over to the table with a coffee pot in one hand and water pitcher in the other. She refilled their cups and glasses, focusing on Harvey. "Is the food to your liking?"

Harvey glanced up and swallowed hard when his pa nudged him with his foot under the table. "Yes, thank you ma'am." He immediately looked back down at his plate and took another bite.

Mr. Farley responded. "Everything is wonderful, young lady. We are a bit weary from our trip, but the food is delicious, thank you."

"Oh, so you aren't from around here? Where are you from?"

Mr. Farley gave Harvey the chance to speak, but after a long moment of silence, he answered the girl. "We are from the other side of Asheville. We've come here for the convention in Raleigh, so you will be seeing quite a bit of us for the next few days."

"Well, that is good news, sir. I look forward to it. My name is Eva, and I will be glad to be your waitress every evening if possible." Another girl walked up and took the coffee pot from her as she finished speaking.

"If you will excuse me, I need to get back to business." She smiled radiantly at all of them, lingering on Harvey for an extra moment, then turned and left.

"You can breathe now, son. She's gone," Abe snickered.

Harvey let out a sigh of relief and picked up his water glass, gulping down half of it.

Mr. Farley chuckled. "Well, gentlemen, let's take a walk through town, shall we?"

They all stood, pushed their chairs under the table and turned to leave. When Harvey turned from the table, Eva passed by and smiled at him in a way that warmed his heart and flipped his stomach. He felt his face redden as he returned the smile and then quickly exited the diner.

The next few days went by too quickly to suit any of them. Harvey, Abe, and Mr. Farley were extremely enthusiastic about the machinery, talking between themselves about how things could be altered to perform better or take on more tasks.

Gerald and Clint spent most of their time looking into things to sell at their new store, while Asa enjoyed the iron displays around the blacksmith. Something about the way they shaped the iron to make it fit just right intrigued him.

By the last night in town, Harvey worked up the courage to look at Eva and say, "My name is Harvey Darnell, and it has been a pleasure to meet you, Eva."

Chapter 2

By spring, the community was starting to look more like a town. There was a wide street between two rows of buildings in different stages of completion.

Gerald Henderson had sold most of his property to Mr. Neville and Mr. Farley to serve as the town center. He made a hefty profit and used the money to construct four buildings of his own; a large general store and three buildings to rent or sell to future business owners. He was excited about stocking the place while his wife was busy planning out their living quarters in the back of the store.

There were over fifty new men in the community, most working the construction of the buildings, and would probably move on when the work was done. Several of the new men sought out permanent jobs and brought their families with them. Most of these men were taking on jobs at Darnell Farm, with some of their wives working there as well.

Abe and his two boys worked hard from sunup to sundown, thrilled with how much more they could get accomplished with the new equipment. Even Asa was beginning to like farming more.

Mr. Farley came to the farm several times a week to see how things were going and even tried his hand at the new equipment. When he arrived on this day, he had two unfamiliar men with him. They rode out to the far field before they spotted Abe.

When Abe saw them, he quickly stopped his work, mounted his horse, and rode to meet them. Mr. Farley made quick introductions, letting Abe know these men were government officials.

"Abe," Mr. Farley started. "What do you know about livestock?"

"Well, I guess I know all I need to know. Why do you ask?"

Mr. Farley cleared his throat. "Ride with us, please. We want to show you something."

Abe nodded with a look of concern, following without question. They rode past the farm and over the ridge to the other side of the foothill.

As they sat at the top of the ridge, Mr. Farley began to tell of a new plan. "Abe, the government owns all the land you see. They need to raise and keep horses here to serve the army if there is ever a need. Since the land is plush with grass, they are working together with the agricultural department in hopes of sharing the land to raise cattle for beef production."

Abe nodded as he looked over the land. "That would be a good place. It's almost blocked in between the mountains where it wouldn't be hard to keep them from wandering too far.

"So, who will my new neighbors be?"

Mr. Farley grinned. "The best kind, ones that won't give you any trouble."

Abe looked at him quizzically. "I don't understand."

"The cows and horses will be your neighbors. We were wondering if you would be willing to oversee the care of them. Of course, you wouldn't own them. You would just take care of them. Think you could do that?"

Abe rubbed his chin. "I appreciate the offer, Mr. Farley, but I'm already stretched a little thin with taking on all this acreage to farm."

Mr. Farley's smile faded a bit. "Let me explain, then you can think about it." After explaining at great length, he drew a breath and asked Abe, "What do you think? It's almost like free money. You will just be overseeing a bunch of cowpokes. Of course, you will be paid well also, seeing you will be on call at any hour an emergency may happen."

Abe's lips turned up to a quirky smile. "Once again, I find myself asking you, why me?"

"Because you are in the right place at the right time. You are already living here. We don't have to put this off while we search out someone for the job and then go through the time and expense of building a house for them. So? What do you think?"

Abe sat quiet for a moment while serious thoughts went through his head. "I would like a contract. I want it in writing, just like with the farm. I want the option to purchase the land at a good price after seven years. Then the government can lease the land from me if they continue their operation here, making my payment for me."

Mr. Farley's face lit up with a smile. "I like your way of thinking. A shrewd businessman. I will see to it your demands are met."

****

By spring 1849, the town was beginning to bustle with daily activity. Though the town itself wasn't that large, the population and economy had grown immensely. What started as approximately thirty families scattered throughout the mountainside, was now over a hundred families with more than twenty living within a mile of the town.

Stagecoaches arrived three times a week instead of once every two weeks, freight wagons made deliveries at least once a week, the mail was very regular now, and the telegraph had been promised.

There was a general store, hotel with a diner, another diner, blacksmith shop, livery, barber shop, bank, several other shops available, and a church that was a school during the week.

The men had chosen five town councilmen and the town council chose a mayor. Ordinances were drawn up and made into legally binding documents.

Mr. Neville and Mr. Farley were thrilled, except for one big problem. The railroad contract had fallen through with another, more established town winning the rights to have it routed through that town instead of theirs. Now, the nearest railroad was twenty miles away. Mr. Farley was livid.

****

Abe, Harvey, and Asa had fallen into a livable routine. All of them worked hard but were used to it. Abe couldn't keep Harvey out of the fields or off the equipment. He had even started reading about every aspect of plants and seeds.

Asa had taken well to working with the livestock. He stayed in the bunkhouse with the hired men most of the time now, spending every Sunday with the family. He attended church with them, went to the diner for lunch together, and enjoyed catching up on details the rest of the day.

Mr. Farley joined them for lunch one Sunday, brimming with excitement that he wanted to share with someone. "My wife will be here in two weeks! I am so excited for her to see this place and the house I have built for her.

"I was thinking that perhaps we could plan the first town social about the time she arrives. It wouldn't be a party for her, yet she could meet everyone in a festive atmosphere."

"That sounds like a good idea, Mr. Farley," Abe agreed while Harvey and Asa nodded and smiled at each other.

"Please, Abe, call me Samuel. I feel like we are friends now, and I would feel more comfortable on a first name basis."

"Sure, Samuel. I'm glad your wife will soon be joining you. I'm sure you've missed her."

"Yes, well, I have certainly missed her, but she was much better off where she was until I prepared a place for her. She would have been miserable in a rented room for so long.

"Now, let's talk about the social. Do we have any musicians living close by? Perhaps the women could bring desserts? I could get the diner to supply drinks. Help me plan this and let's make it a spectacular event."

They talked for over an hour, making lists and plans. Harvey and Asa knew several musicians and volunteered to get the music taken care of. Abe would ask Gerald to post a sign in the store window and talk to people about joining the fun.

The boys were excited until Mr. Farley mentioned dancing. Suddenly the excitement faded, turning to a look of fear. "What's wrong, boys? Did I say something offensive?"

"Umm, sir," Harvey stammered. "We don't know how to dance. I'm not sure if anyone around knows how."

Mr. Farley looked perplexed. "Harvey, you are almost twenty-two and you don't know how to dance? And you Asa?"

Both shook their heads.

"No sir. Our ma used to dance around with us, but that was years ago. We haven't had occasion to do so."

"Well," Mr. Farley chuckled. "Let me assure you, it comes almost as natural as breathing. As soon as you hear the music your body picks up the rhythm naturally. Then you just flow to it. Help me out here, Abe. Do you know anyone that can teach a few dance lessons before the social?"

"As a matter of fact, I do. They are older women, but they are spirited. They would probably love the chance to do it. I will ask, then set something up and spread the word. I'm going to ride over and check on Granny Bea and her sister, Miss Annie. I'll see if they feel up to teaching a few dance lessons."

****

Harvey and Asa talked casually as they rode to town for their very first social.   Since they were nervous about the evening ahead, it was decided to talk about all the changes made to their town in the past two years.

"I would have never believed anyone who said our little community with one outpost would become an actual town within two years.   It's been a lot of hard work involved, but I guess it's worth it."

"What do you mean, you guess it's worth it, Asa? It got you out of farming the fields and into working the ranch.   I thought you liked that." Harvey looked sideways at his brother.

"I do like ranching better than farming, and I like having a real store to go to, and the church. Wish we could find a preacher to stay here full time instead of just one that passes through once a month."

"Just keep praying about it, Asa. But meanwhile, think about all the good Mr. Farley and Mr. Neville have done. The kids even have a school to attend and lots of people around here are living better than ever before because they have real jobs."

"I am thankful. But don't you ever feel like you are missing out on something, and you just don't know what it is?"

Harvey smiled at Asa. "I have an idea what we are missing out on, and you know as well as I do."

"Yes, well now that we both know, how are we supposed to remedy it? We are both old enough to be married and starting our own families, but we don't get off the farm long enough to even see a girl, let alone court and marry one."

"Asa, tonight may be the beginning of something," Harvey spoke with confidence. "It's the first social for our new town, which is a big step forward. We have so many new families living here now that we haven't met them all. I have a good feeling about our future. If tonight goes well, maybe the town council will do it more often."

Asa smiled teasingly. "What was that pretty little blonde waitress' name? You know the one in Raleigh almost two years ago? The one that made you so shy that you were about to choke." Asa laughed. "You turned red as a beet and talked about her for months."

Harvey shrugged. "I don't remember."

Asa gasped and pointed at Harvey. "You lie! I bet you remember word for word what she said and even the color apron she wore."

"Look Asa!" Harvey pointed ahead, changing the subject. "We're almost there. Let's hurry." He picked up the pace turning to his brother, smiling. "Her name was Eva!"

When the boys arrived, things were already starting to get lively, even though it was still an hour before the social started. The musicians had been brought together several times in the last few weeks to practice and were now tuning their instruments and practicing a little more.

The two older ladies that had been giving free dance lessons for the last few weeks were already there, anxiously waiting to see how their students fared throughout the evening.

Women were bustling about, setting food on the tables, making sure everything was perfect. Children were running through the park across the street, keeping each other occupied while making new friendships.

Abe walked up to his sons when he saw them arrive. "Looks like it's going to be a good evening. You boys look good and chipper. Ready to try out those dancing lessons?"

"Pa," Harvey scolded. "Don't be making us nervous or we may tuck tail and head back home."

Abe laughed and patted them on the back. "It's going to be a good evening. Umm, did either of you happen to see Mr. Farley on your way in? His wife arrived two days ago, and I haven't seen him since."

"No, we didn't. I'm sure he will be here though, after all the planning and effort he put into this. I sure hope his wife is as nice as he is and likes the town he built." Harvey stopped talking as a fancy, new buggy approached and pulled to a halt in front of the churchyard.

They watched as Mr. Farley appeared and reached to help his wife out of the buggy. The couple were in their mid-fifties, a few years older than Abe, but looked stunning in their fancy clothes.

Mr. Farley spotted Abe and walked his wife in that direction. He extended his hand to Abe as he approached. "I would like to introduce my wife, Mrs. Agnes Farley. Sweetie, this is Mr. Abe Darnell and his two sons, Harvey and Asa."

She extended her hand and curtsied. "I have heard so much about all of you, I almost feel I know you. Samuel wrote about everyone in his letters, and of course, we have talked non-stop since I arrived.

"This is such a nice, quaint little town. I look forward to being an active part of the community, helping the ladies in any way possible."

"Well, thank you, Mrs. Farley. I'm sure you're proud of your husband's efforts in making our little community into a thriving town."

"Yes, I am so very proud. I hear that you are faring pretty well with all the land grants he arranged ...Oh!" she gasped as Mr. Farley grasped her arm tightly.

"Come, my dear, I want to introduce you to some other people." He led her away quickly as he spoke over his shoulder to Abe. "We will speak again in a little while. I have news to share about a preacher."

He leaned in close, walking slowly, speaking quietly to his wife. "Agnes, I am warning you. These are good, hardworking people. I will not have you making them feel beneath your social standing. Here, we are all on the same level. Don't make them feel bad about anything or feel that they owe me anything. They have all done what I have asked of them and, I will have you know, they are my friends, real friends. I couldn't have accomplished all of this without them. Don't you ever forget that! You promised and I intend to make you stand by it!"

Agnes looked at him and spoke through gritted teeth. "I understand, Samuel. Now loosen your grip on my arm!" She jerked her arm away as he loosened his grip then pasted a smile back on her face before he made more introductions.

"What was that all about, Pa?" Asa asked.

"Oh, she just wants to make sure I know that she knows how much gratitude we should have for her husband. It's fine, son. Let's see if we can help with anything."

In just a little while, the churchyard was brimming with people and the musicians began to play. Abe stood in the back with his two tall, handsome sons.

"This is a lot of people!" Asa exclaimed. "I didn't know there were this many people in the whole county!"

Abe looked at them both teasingly. "Gives you boys more choices."

"Choices?" Asa questioned.

Harvey nudged his brother, "Yes, choices." He snickered and shook his head. "Sometimes you are dumb as a rock. Choices for dance partners!"

"Oh… oh! I'm fine just watching. Besides, I'm thirsty. I'm going to get some punch."

Abe and Harvey laughed as he walked away.

"So, what about your choices? See anyone interesting?" Abe looked at Harvey curiously.

"No, not yet Pa. I wish I saw one near as pretty as that waitress in Raleigh."

"You mean Eva?"

Harvey smiled at his Pa. "Yes, Eva. Even her name is pretty. I thought about going back to Raleigh this fall to another agriculture convention and maybe see if she's still there. But as pretty as she is, she's probably married by now."

"Hmm. I didn't know you had considered trying to see her again."

Harvey shrugged. "It's just a thought. So, Pa, what about your choices? You've been widowed for six years, maybe it's time for you to take a spin across the dance floor."

Abe looked at him with shock. "All of a sudden, I'm thirsty. I think I will go join your brother at the punch bowl."

Harvey burst out laughing as Abe slapped him on the back and walked away.

"Hi Harvey!" a high-pitched voice spoke from behind him.

He turned to see two girls approaching him. "Hello, umm, Emma? Sue?" He smiled wide. "I barely recognize you all dressed up like something fancy!"

"Thank you, kind sir." Emma fluttered her eyelashes and curtsied as Sue did the same. "Isn't this the most exciting thing that's ever happened? I sure am looking forward to dancing and having a good time."

"Yes, it is exciting. The music is great and so is the food. You ladies sure put out a nice spread on those tables."

"Where is Asa?" Sue asked shyly.

"He's over at the punch table with Pa."

Emma touched his arm. "I sure would like some punch, Harvey."

"Oh," he gulped. "Umm, where are my manners?" He lifted both his elbows out to each girl and escorted them to the punch table.

"Asa, these lovely young ladies were looking for you."

Asa turned to see the two girls smiling at him. He swallowed his punch, then greeted them as Harvey had.

Emma clung to Harvey's arm. "Sue was looking for you, Asa, but I had already found who I was looking for." She smiled up at Harvey.

Abe joined the conversation. "Why don't you boys take these beautiful ladies for a dance?" He motioned them toward the dance floor with both boys taking a turn to glance back at him with a scowl as they made their way forward.

After a half hour, Harvey and Asa were finally able to make their escape, looking for their pa to make sure they thanked him properly.

"Having fun, boys?" Abe chuckled.

"You're a funny man, Pa." Harvey noticed the widow Smythe standing close by as he chuckled with his pa. He intentionally drew his pa closer without him noticing, then brought the woman into their conversation.

"Mrs. Smythe, it's so good to see you here tonight, and my, don't you look lovely, ma'am. Doesn't she, Pa?"

"Why, thank you sir. You are so very kind." Mrs. Smythe blushed as she glanced toward Abe.

At that moment the musicians started playing a familiar tune. "Pa, that's one of your favorite songs. Don't let me hold you two back from dancing, I will just make myself scarce. See you later."

He looked back, chuckling as he walked away, seeing his pa leading the widow Smythe toward the dancefloor. Walking too fast in a crowd, and not watching where he was going, he ran right into something, or someone. Looking around quickly, he caught himself as he stumbled over two young ladies sprawled on the ground that he had apparently knocked down.

"Oh! I'm so sorry! Please, here, let me help you up! Are you hurt?" He reached a hand to each of them.

When the ladies got to their feet, they began to brush themselves off. "Yes, we are fine. Why don't you watch where...?"

She stopped and stood as still as a statue when she looked at Harvey, turning pale and then blushing. "Harvey?"

Harvey looked back to her from making sure they were both steady on their feet, still apologizing profusely. His mouth dropped open, as he whispered, "Eva?" Then loudly he exclaimed, "Eva!" He lifted her off the ground and twirled her around.

"Oh, I'm sorry," he apologized again as he set her down. "That wasn't very gentlemanly of me. I certainly wouldn't want your husband to be coming after me. What are you doing here?"

"It's nice to see you again too, Harvey. Let me introduce you to your other victim. This is my youngest sister, Amy."

She extended her hand as he asked again if she was hurt.

"I'm fine, sir. But I do hope you will be more careful in the future. There are better ways to sweep a woman off her feet, you know."

"May I escort you ladies for some food or punch?" He extended both elbows and led them toward the tables where Asa stood watching his pa dance with the widow Smythe.

Asa did a double-take when he saw Harvey headed in his direction. He couldn't believe Eva was there...twice! She and her sister looked like twins. And my, what beauties they were. Both were petite, certainly not any taller than five foot two or three, standing beside Harvey who was six foot three, making him look like a giant.

"Look who I, umm, ran into, Asa." The three snickered as Harvey made his joke.

"What a pleasant surprise. Eva, how are you? It's good to see you again. And is this your twin?"

"This is my youngest sister, Amy." She smiled teasingly. "I am very surprised you remembered my name, Asa."

"Yeah well, Harvey may have mentioned you a time or two." He chuckled as he watched Harvey get embarrassed. "Amy, it's nice to meet you. Did you say the youngest sister? How many of you are there?"

Amy wasn't timid at all and spoke up before Eva could. "There are three of us, but I'm the prettiest!" She teased. "Olivia is over there dancing, I suppose."

"Yes," Eva sighed. "I'm supposed to be keeping an eye on these two while my parents mingle. I need to find her if you wouldn't mind helping me?" She looked at Harvey and then Asa.

"What does she look like?"

Eva and Amy giggled. "She looks just like us, and she is wearing a lavender dress."

Harvey and Asa looked over almost everyone's heads, searching for a beautiful blonde in a lavender dress.

"I see her," Asa pointed.

"Could you please lead us in that direction so I can get her attention? If she is still with the same young man, it's about time for me to interrupt."

Harvey offered his elbow to Eva, and Asa to Amy. They walked through the crowd until they got near the dance floor. When the song ended, Eva made her way to Olivia, asking to speak with her in private.

"Thank you for the dance, Tobias." Olivia nodded goodbye as she took her sister's arm.

"You must have been quite taken with him to have danced so long."

"He is nice, handsome and a very good conversationalist, Eva, but I'm not hearing wedding bells. He does like to talk about himself, a lot." Olivia giggled.

"Well," Eva spoke quietly. "I got quite a surprise, and I want to share it with you. I think you might like a part of it."

A moment later, Olivia's mouth almost dropped open as they approached Harvey and Asa. She couldn't believe how

27

handsome and tall they were, and there was Amy chattering away with both!

"Olivia, I would like to introduce you to Harvey and Asa."

Asa struggled to get the goofy look off his face and recapture his heart and voice. "It's nice to meet you, Olivia."

"It's nice to meet you also, Asa," she almost choked, only managing a whisper.

Harvey wanted to rib Asa but knew he would save it for later. "Ladies? Would you care for some punch?" He offered his arm to Eva and the other to Amy.

He started walking forward, noticing Asa and Olivia were standing still, looking at each other. "Umm, Asa? Care to join us?"

"Oh, yes, sorry." He offered his arm to Olivia and felt sparks fly to his heart when she took it.

After everyone got a glass of punch, they walked toward the park to talk without having to yell above the music. Amy asked Eva's permission to stand nearby with some young people her age. Eva agreed while keeping a close watch until she saw Amy join a group of girls.

"So, tell me how you ended up here tonight," Harvey quizzed as he helped her sit on the bench, taking a seat on the grass in front of her. Olivia sat next to her as Asa sat next to Harvey.

"If you don't mind, I will give you the short story now. I would really like the chance to dance before the night is over if I get lucky enough to have someone ask."

"You mean, you aren't married or engaged or anything?"

"Nope. Never came close."

"I find that hard to believe. Now, tell me the short story. Hopefully, you will be here long enough to tell me the long story later."

"Well, we hope to be here for good. Our pa is going to preach tomorrow. If the congregation likes him and offers him the position, then we will stay."

"That's wonderful, Eva. I would like that." Harvey glanced at Asa and saw him and Olivia looking at each other intensely. "Wouldn't that be great, Asa?"

"Sure would." His eyes never left Olivia.

"Shall we go back to the party and see if you ladies can find a dance partner?" Harvey flashed a smile at Eva.

The rest of the evening passed too quickly. The two couples never left each other.

****

The next day, everyone gathered at the church to hear the visiting preacher. It was a bigger crowd than usual because everyone was curious when it was announced at the social the night before. Preacher Upton spoke with authority and compassion, backing every word he said with Bible scripture. There were several "Amens" from the congregation as he preached. The congregation was enthusiastic, yet realistic about the decision to take him on as pastor.

A meeting took place that afternoon discussing hiring Preacher Upton. It was decided that everyone liked him and enjoyed the sermon, but there were some that said they would like to hear more than one sermon and see how he reacted to people in need of personal service.

"I don't think that's too much to ask," Abe replied to the request. "May I suggest that we ask him to stay for a month, taking on all the responsibilities of a pastor, just as if we had hired him permanently, and see how he feels, and we feel at the end of the month? He may not like it here. This should be a matter of prayer, not hiring from emotion or need. It's God's place to put the right man here."

Everyone agreed and sent Abe, along with Gerald Henderson to speak with the preacher.

Chapter 3

Supper in the diner that night was delightful, with lighthearted, wltty conversation. Abe and his boys were treating the visiting preacher and his family as a welcome to the community.

"Preacher, we would love to have you and your family visit our farm sometime soon. We have a lot going on out there and we are proud of it. But I'm sorry to say we can't invite you for a meal." Abe finished speaking with a mischievous look.

Asa chuckled. "Yeah, you're lucky not to be invited to eat. Harvey's cooking about killed the dog, and Pa's is even worse."

The preacher leaned forward, looking mischievous. "And what about your cooking? I sure wouldn't want you to be left out."

"Me?" Asa grinned. "I haven't had the chance to try. I stay too busy putting the fires out from these two!"

Abe shook his head as everyone laughed. "You do tell some tall tales, son. Don't know where you get that from."

Asa slapped his pa on the back. "Like father, like son!"

When the laughter calmed, the preacher took on a more serious tone. "I hear that you have met my daughter, Eva, before." He looked straight at Harvey.

Harvey put his fork down and cleared his throat. "Yes sir, a year and a half ago, when we were at the convention in Raleigh. To be completely honest, sir," he nodded at the preacher and glanced at Eva, "I haven't been able to stop thinking about her since. She made quite an impression."

Mrs. Upton gasped slightly, bringing her napkin to her mouth.

"Yes," the preacher mumbled while shaking his head slightly and looking at Eva. "Seems I've heard your name mentioned before also." He drank a sip of water before turning to Abe.

"I would love to see your farm, Mr. Darnell. I hear that you are the largest employer in this area, outside of construction and mining, and that you have job opportunities suitable for women."

"Yes sir, and I take pride in that. I believe there should be work for anyone that is willing. I also believe that work is good for everyone, it makes you appreciate what you have."

"Glad to know you have a good work ethic, Abe. But I would like to know more about the jobs appropriate for women." The preacher looked serious. "Do they work separate from the men? Are they safe from harm?"

"They are most certainly safe. We have men that ride the perimeters constantly, keeping watch for predators whether they are wild animals or human." Abe chuckled but quickly returned to seriousness when he saw the preacher wasn't amused.

He cleared his throat. "Yes, it is safe but there are a few men that work the same fields as the women. Why do you ask?"

"I have been told there are several widowers in the area, and I wanted to be sure they had a way to take care of themselves and their families. Plus," he paused and looked at Eva and Olivia, "if we stay here for long, my two oldest will be looking for employment. Young Amy is only fourteen. She will be staying in school and helping at home for now. Olivia has one year of school left.

"Eva is almost seventeen and Olivia is only fifteen," he flashed a look of warning toward Asa. "I have to be concerned with their safety while still teaching them to be productive citizens. I don't tolerate laziness or foolishness either."

"I see," Abe rubbed his chin as he took in the entire picture. The preacher was concerned about his two girls being unchaperoned around Harvey and Asa. "I assure you, anyone on my farm is treated like family. We all work together, helping where we can. My sons have been raised to respect and help others, especially women. There would be no problems, and I do mean NO problems if your girls worked at the farm."

The preacher nodded his acknowledgment that Abe and himself were thinking the same things.

****

Throughout the month, Preacher Upton excelled at everything he did. He attempted to visit every family in the community, with his wife by his side. Several people who were older or crippled needed extra care and visits, which they made sure to take care of.

They had visited the farm several times and found it to be a good work environment. On the day he was officially hired as the full-time pastor, he gave his girls permission to secure jobs at the farm.

****

Mrs. Farley was almost always in town. She made it a point to see and be seen. Although most people found her to be nice and polite, the woman had a certain way about her that made people feel a bit intimidated. Perhaps it was the way she dressed much fancier than anyone else. Or was it the way she spoke? It could have been the white gloves she wore past her elbows or the parasol she carried without fail. Whatever it was, she made herself known to everyone.

Mrs. Upton befriended the woman and found her to be a misplaced soul; torn from the life she had been accustomed to and not fitting in with the new life before her. She felt sure that with understanding and compassion she could find a way to make Mrs. Farley a more productive, happy person.

Mrs. Upton had found that when a person felt needed, it could make a huge difference, giving the person confidence and drastically changing their outlook on life. She needed to find something to give Mrs. Farley purpose.

What Mrs. Upton didn't take into careful consideration was... all it took was one bad apple to ruin the whole bushel.

****

Harvey and Asa had seen Eva and Olivia at the farm while they were working but hadn't had much time to spend with them. They had shared a few lunch breaks under a shade tree near the field they were working in and enjoyed the time in each other's company.

With July's scorching heat coming on, Abe had changed the workday hours for the field workers. The work started at six and ended at noon.

Harvey saw the new hours for Eva as an opportunity to spend some time with her during the evenings, perhaps being able to take her to the diner. He needed to talk to her privately and see if she was interested before he faced her pa, asking permission.

The next time they had lunch together, Harvey asked Eva to take a walk with him, motioning discreetly for Asa to stay put with Olivia.

Most of the workers had gone home for the day when they walked past the field. Even though no one was around, Harvey felt exposed out in the open. He wanted more than anything to take Eva someplace more private, hold her in his arms, and kiss her beautiful lips. But his pa being a stickler for propriety, and her pa being a preacher, he knew better than to even think seriously about it.

"Eva, I want to talk to you about something." He continued walking slowly without looking at her. He knew if he did, the way he was feeling right now, propriety would be forgotten. "I have feelings for you, and I would like the chance to get to know you better. If you feel the same way, I will ask your parent's permission to start spending some time in the evenings with you, perhaps even take you to the diner occasionally." He swallowed hard and felt his heart beating through pressure in his ears.

It seemed forever before she spoke, but when she did, she put her hand on his arm and stopped walking, turning to face him, making direct eye contact. He melted. His heart was hers and there was no turning back. She could ask anything of him, and he would gladly give it.

"Harvey, I would like that very much. There is so much I want to share with you and so much I want you to share with me."

"Eva, I...umm...I," he closed his eyes and took a deep breath. "I'm sorry, but I can't hold back any longer. Eva, I'm crazy about you. I think of you constantly. I want to show you that I...I love you."

She wrapped her arms around his waist and held him tight. "I love you too, Harvey."

He pulled her closer and kissed the top of her head. This little, tiny bit of a woman had wrapped him completely around her finger and made him the happiest man alive.

Just when he thought it couldn't get any better, she pulled back from him and looked in his eyes. Working her arms up around his neck she pulled him toward her. He leaned down quickly and pressed his lips against hers, which led to the sweetest kiss ever.

A magical moment later, he finally pulled his lips from hers and held her close again. They could feel each other's hearts pounding as they collected their thoughts and caught their breath.

Finally registering reality, Harvey set her back from himself. "I guess we better get on back to Asa and Olivia before someone comes along and asks us to explain."

"Yes, I suppose standing out in the open in the broad daylight, carrying on like this would be highly frowned upon." She giggled as she took his hand and squeezed it.

"I'd like to talk to your pa as soon as possible. We've got a lot to learn about each other and I can't wait to get started."

She leaned her head against his arm as they held hands and strolled back toward the others. "I look forward to it."

****

"Mr. Farley what?" Harvey almost yelled at his pa's announcement. "Pa, I just asked the preacher if I could court Eva last night! I can't just leave!"

"Harvey, just calm yourself. You aren't thinking with your head right now. You have new emotions you are dealing with, and you can't let your emotions make major decisions for your future." Abe poured two cups of coffee and sat down at the table, motioning for Harvey to join him.

"Son, this is a wonderful opportunity. It will guarantee you a successful future. You will have the connections and education to acquire your own contracts and stand on your own. One day you won't have me, or Mr. Farley, and you need to be equipped to take on anything that comes your way.

"What we have right now with the government contracts is wonderful. Being able to purchase the land in the future is a gift from God that I don't intend to squander. But what if the government doesn't want to renew its contract? We have hundreds of acres of produce in the fields with no one to sell it to. I don't know enough about business to find my own contracts and meanwhile, a year's worth of produce lays in the field rotting."

Harvey blew out a breath. "Pa, this is just bad timing. A year ago, or even four months ago, I would have jumped at the chance to go to college and learn about what I'm so interested in. But now, I have more interests than just farming."

"I understand, but this will help you build a better future for that beautiful girl of yours. And it's free! Mr. Farley will pay your tuition because he has taken such a liking to you. He said you are like the son he wished he had."

Harvey sighed again and slumped on his elbows over his coffee. "How long is this college program? And where is it?"

"It's in Alabama."

Harvey shook his head and closed his eyes.

"There are two different ways you can do the program. You can finish in two semesters of September through the first of June, coming home for the summer, which would be eighteen months of school. Or you could stay there through the summer and do a continuous fifteen-month program and be finished next December."

"I was hoping to be married by then," Harvey mumbled. "I need to think about this and do some praying. But worst of all, I need to tell Eva about this and start our relationship with a big problem."

"Harvey, you are looking at it all wrong. Look at it as a wonderful opportunity. I'm sure Eva will see it as such. Time away from each other now will provide so much hope and security for your future together."

****

Harvey broke the news to Eva that evening as they strolled toward the diner. Trying to explain as apologetically as possible, he also attempted to be practical, assuring himself as well as her, this was the right thing to do.

"Harvey, I think that's wonderful news. It's an opportunity you can't pass up."

Instantly he was flooded with disappointment at her joyful reaction. He thought she would share his feelings of being torn. Stopping and turning to her in shock, his heart instantly melted. Her misty eyes and slightly quivering chin defied the words she was saying. She quickly pasted on a smile, tugged on his arm, and continued walking.

He kept his hand on hers as they walked for several minutes in silence.

Finally, she cleared her throat and drew in a deep breath. "I have a bit of news also, which is much easier now that you have shared yours."

He nodded for her to continue.

"The school has had a problem keeping a teacher. Not many people around here are qualified to teach, and my parents have been trying to fill the position for the upcoming school year." She sighed. "There haven't been very many responses yet.

"Last night we had a family discussion of sorts, and they feel like I need to go to college for a year and get a teaching certificate. Ma says she will fill in at the school if necessary until I can start teaching the following year.

"I must admit," she giggled a bit, "I didn't take the news so well and almost got sent to my room."

"You?" Harvey mocked. "You mean you aren't sweet and kind all the time?"

She squeezed his arm. "Of course, I am, and don't believe anyone who tells you otherwise."

They laughed for a moment.

After another sigh, Eva continued. "They ended up convincing me that it would be good for my future, and..." she paused, clearing her throat.

"And what?"

"And for our future," she spoke so softly, he could barely hear her words.

"Our future," he beamed while repeating the words. "I like the sound of that."

****

August was upon them before they knew it, bringing happiness to some and bittersweet to others.

Olivia was turning sixteen and Asa couldn't wait to talk to the preacher about starting to visit her. He, along with Harvey, had been invited to her birthday celebration.

Harvey teased Asa from the time he finished his bath until they arrived at Olivia's. "You smell so sweet, Asa. None of us will have to worry about mosquitoes tonight because you will be drawing them all to you.

"Oh, hold on a minute," Harvey looked serious as he stopped Asa on the top step of the porch.

"What Harvey? Is something wrong?"

After a long moment of looking at his brother, he smiled and patted his shoulder. "No, it's alright. I just thought you had a hair out of place."

Asa breathed a sigh of relief. "That's not funny, Harvey."

"I thought it was. Now, just take a deep breath and relax. Olivia is still the same as she was yesterday when we had lunch together."

"I'm not so worried about Olivia," Asa tugged at his shirt collar. "I'm afraid of being clumsy or foolish around her parents."

Harvey chuckled as he knocked on the door. "I understand. I was in your shoes six weeks ago, very uncomfortable shoes, I might add. But it gets better after the initial talk with the folks."

Asa nodded and smiled as Olivia opened the door. What a beauty she was, and he intended to have that beautiful young lady in his heart and arms for the rest of his life.

****

Mr. Farley called out to Harvey as they were leaving church on Sunday. Harvey stopped with Eva on his arm, waiting for the older man who was waving his arm and smiling, walking as fast as he could towards them.

"I'm so glad I caught you!" Mr. Farley paused to catch his breath. "I don't want to take a moment of time from you and your beautiful young lady, so let me just give you this."

He reached in his coat pocket and pulled out a thick envelope. "You can look at this when you get to school. I have written down several of my friend's addresses. They have all received a letter from me, telling them about you. If you find yourself in need of anything while at college, feel free to contact them."

Harvey smiled at the kind man. "Thank you, Mr. Farley. I could never begin to repay all the kindness you have shown towards me and my family."

"Won't you join us at the diner for lunch?" Eva asked sweetly.

"Thank you, Missy. That is a kind and tempting offer, but I must refuse. I would be upset with anyone that intruded on the time you two have left together." He shook Harvey's hand, then walked away.

"That is one of the nicest men in the world." Harvey looked down at Eva and smiled. "Don't know why he took such a liking to me, but I'm sure blessed that he did. I intend to do my best to make him proud for taking a chance on me."

"I'm sure you will make all of us proud," Eva smiled admiringly at him and squeezed his arm.

****

The morning of Harvey's departure was a sad affair. Eva had tried to be so brave for the days leading up to it, only to fall apart in Harvey's arms at the last moment. Her pa had to gently scold her for making such a spectacle of herself as he physically pulled her from Harvey's arms, guiding her back to their buggy.

Harvey wished with all his being that he could change his mind and stay, then looked at his pa, Asa, and Mr. Farley, knowing this was the right thing to do. He quickly hugged his pa and Asa. Holding his hand out to Mr. Farley, he was shocked when the man embraced him.

The wheels of the train were already in slow motion when he jumped on the step, turning to wave and shouting, "I love you, Eva!"

She stood up in the buggy, waving until he could no longer see her.

****

Asa and Olivia comforted each other's misery of missing their siblings and the pleasure of another couple's company, as much as they could. But Preacher and Mrs. Upton had made it very clear that Olivia was too young to be with a young man unaccompanied, and he was only allowed to visit her on weekends. That only added to their misery.

He worked all week on the ranch and even picked up a few extra shifts to ease his loneliness. When he went to see his pa on Sunday night, after leaving Olivia, he found he wasn't the only miserable person on the farm.

Abe decided quickly that something needed to change. "There's no sense in us walking around like sad sacks. It makes the time drag by slower and takes too much energy."

"What do you suggest, Pa?" Asa sulked over a cup of coffee. "I've already been filling every hour with working."

"Well, let's see. Why don't you move back home instead of staying at the bunkhouse? We would at least have each other's company in the evenings."

"Umm, that sounds good except for one thing. At least there is a cook at the bunkhouse. I won't starve to death there," Asa tried to lighten the conversation.

"How is the food there?"

"It's not bad, but it's the same thing most of the time. We have a few different men that take turns cooking when it's their day off."

"Well then, it looks like we have three choices. Either I come to eat with the men at the bunkhouse, we learn to cook, or we head for the diner." Abe grinned at him. "So why don't you consider moving back in and we will look out for each other?"

"Sounds good to me. But don't be making any plans for me from Saturday afternoon until Sunday night," Asa teased. "It wouldn't be safe for anyone to be in my path to Olivia's."

Chapter 4

"Pa, there hasn't been a social or anything lately. There is absolutely nothing to do other than work. I know most people are busy with their families, getting ready for the holidays, but I was talking with some of the men today, and all of them are loners. Some are getting cabin fever."

Abe thought for a moment. "You know, son, I have said several times that our workers are treated like family. Maybe I should act more like that. Let me see if I can figure out a celebration of sorts for us to share Thanksgiving together."

"That would be great, Pa! Several of the men play instruments and could liven things up."

"Alright. Now let's take this idea and run with it, see where it leads." He got a piece of paper and sat down at the table, motioning for Asa to join him.

Within days, the ideas had spread to include the entire community, on Thanksgiving evening, with ladies bringing leftovers and desserts, while men provided music. Abe instructed his men to set up makeshift tables and benches ahead of time and have plenty of wood for a bonfire. He would order a big Thanksgiving lunch ahead of time for all the ranch hands, from the diner. It was turning into a major event everyone was looking forward to.

Abe and Asa were invited to the Upton's for Thanksgiving dinner to which Abe graciously turned down to stay with his men. He insisted on Asa going without him, declaring that he could and would take care of everything for the event.

It was finally time for some fun!

****

On Thanksgiving, people started arriving in the early afternoon. Everyone was in great spirits, and everything was going as planned. Abe had a hog and a deer roasting on the spit to add to the supper table.

Welcoming each family as they arrived gave him another opportunity to get to know the men that didn't work for him. The Upton's arrived early for the preacher to do the same while inviting everyone to the church services. His wife, always at his side, talked with the ladies as they arrived, not only inviting the women to church but making sure they all knew the school was available for every child of school age.

Asa and Olivia made themselves busy hanging lanterns to be lit later, along with a few decorations that Olivia and Amy had made for the festive occasion.

When the music started, Asa and Olivia were the first to step on the dance floor. Several young couples followed quickly, soon joined by some older couples.

The cowpokes took turns dancing with some of the widows and older women. One younger, new man at the farm, got his nerve up to tap Asa on the shoulder as he was dancing with Olivia.

"Mind if I cut in, Asa?"

Asa looked shocked and disturbed but didn't want any trouble. "Umm, I guess you can finish this song with MY girl if she is agreeable?" He looked at Olivia apologetically.

Her smile had faded but she courteously nodded in agreement.

Asa backed away, feeling something inside himself that he had never felt before. His eyes never left Olivia. Being tall enough to see over most of the crowd, he kept a good eye on the situation.

Abe walked up behind him. "Son, there is steam coming out of your ears. That's one of our new men, isn't it?"

Asa nodded without taking his eyes off Olivia. He could tell she was engaged in conversation, but she certainly wasn't smiling. "Yes, and apparently he doesn't know she's MY girl."

"Take a breath son. The song will be over soon. I don't want any trouble if it can be avoided."

"Yes sir. I won't start any trouble, but I sure won't run from it either," he growled.

"That's all I ask." Abe walked away, but not far. This was something he needed to keep an eye on. He could remember a time long ago, when he felt the same way Asa did right now, and that night hadn't ended well; at least not for the other man.

Asa was on the floor, ready to take Olivia from the other man's arms before the last few notes of the music died.

Olivia smiled as he approached, then turned to the young man. "Thank you for the dance, Tobias." She curtsied graciously before Asa put himself between the two and wrapped his arms around her.

"Yes, Toby, I will see you later." Asa smiled as kindly as he could, then danced Olivia out of reach before anything else could be said.

"I'm sorry, Olivia. I didn't know what else to do. Did he make you too uncomfortable? I am so sorry."

"It's fine, Asa. I could have refused, I suppose, but I didn't know what to do either. Let me reassure you, I will never be comfortable in any other man's arms."

Asa looked down into her eyes, took in every detail of her beautiful face, and melted. He gave her a quick squeeze, while he swallowed past the lump in his throat. His heart pounded.

"Olivia, talk like that will lead to trouble. Your parents have already made it known we have a long time in front of us before we can get serious."

Her smile faded. "Yes, they are even talking about sending me to the same college as Eva next year so I can become a teacher."

Asa looked at her sadly. "Why would we need two teachers? When did all of this come about?"

"They are hoping all the residents will eventually send their children to school. If they do, there will be a need for four or five teachers, and they want us to be prepared."

He looked at her tenderly. "I don't think I could live a day without you in it."

"Oh Asa, that's so sweet!"

"It's truth," he swallowed hard then checked his emotions as he looked around, anywhere except in her eyes. If he didn't, he feared he would say too much, and he had planned to save that for a very special time and place when they were alone.

When the song was over, they walked to the punch bowl where her parents and Abe were standing. Asa poured her a glass, then surprised everyone when he asked her ma to dance. Mrs. Upton stammered for a moment in surprise before graciously accepting.

As he whisked her across the floor, they engaged in conversation.

"I saw another young man dancing with Olivia. I was ever so surprised."

"Yes ma'am. We were too. His name is Toby, and he works here."

"Hmm, yes, well, I was hoping it wouldn't cause trouble. It didn't, I hope."

"No ma'am. Not yet. I will be sure Toby knows my inten..." he stopped short, falling silent.

"I see," she chuckled. "So, you were upset but still conducted yourself as a gentleman? How did that make you feel?"

"Yes ma'am. I may have gritted my teeth the entire time, but yes." He looked at her seriously. "May I ask how you felt when you saw them? Were you upset or did you find it amusing? Please tell me the truth. Would you like for Olivia to see other suitors?"

She almost looked insulted. "Asa, I'm sorry if I struck a nerve. I was only intending to praise you for keeping calm during an awkward situation. The truth is, Olivia is very young with her whole life ahead of her. We hope our prayers and guidance will keep her on the right path. So many things can happen in the next few years that it almost makes me wish you had met when she was a bit older."

"I'm afraid I don't understand, ma'am."

"Asa, you are a good man, and I would be proud, even overjoyed to see you and Olivia have a life together. It's just a long time before she is old enough to think in that direction. I'm afraid you may grow weary with waiting, perhaps someone else will catch your eye and you will leave my girl heartbroken."

"Oh, Mrs. Upton," Asa smiled and shook his head. "Meaning no disrespect, of course, you couldn't be more wrong. I haven't said anything yet because I want to abide by your wishes, but I am completely in love with her." He felt her tense.

"Ma'am, please don't tell her. I'm letting the Lord lead. If it's His will for us to be together, He will guide us. And don't fret yourself about propriety; I will always treat her with ultimate respect."

She relaxed and smiled at him. "Asa, you just won my heart. No wonder she lo…, umm, thinks a lot of you."

When they rejoined Olivia, the preacher, and Abe, Asa refilled Mrs. Upton's glass and poured one for himself. Asa was smiling at Olivia when Toby approached and asked Olivia to dance again.

"Young man," Mrs. Upton reprimanded. "I will have you know that it is proper etiquette for a young man to ask the young lady's parents for permission. Since you have already broken that rule once tonight already, the answer is no. Now, run along and enjoy the rest of your evening."

The preacher and Abe looked at her when Toby walked away, shocked at her abruptness. She looked at her husband. "What? She's Asa's girl. I don't want anyone else dancing with her."

Olivia choked on her punch as Asa spewed his on the ground, bursting into laughter.

"Thank you, Mrs. Upton."

****

Harvey and Eva had written to each other at least three times a week. They both anticipated the upcoming Christmas break. Harvey had decided to leave his school a day early, taking the train to Eva's school, surprise her, then ride home with her for Christmas.

He had thoroughly enjoyed his classes and would always be grateful to Mr. Farley for it. He was also grateful for what he found in the envelope Mr. Farley had given him. Not only was there valuable information and resources, but there was also quite a bit of money with a note:

Harvey,

I hope you find your college days to be as wonderful, interesting, and memorable as mine were to me. Please use this money to help with anything you may need or want. Anything you have left at Christmas, you may want to spend on something special for your beautiful young lady.

Please try to enjoy every minute. All too soon your life will be filled with responsibilities.

Your Friend,
Samuel Farley

Mr. Farley had said it right; he was a real friend, and Harvey felt honored. Several of the men on the list he had been given had contacted him to make sure he was settled in at school without any problems. One had even taken him to supper at an exquisite restaurant one evening, telling him about the area and how much it was growing. The man, Mr. Landon, was one of Mr. Farley's associates in the railroad business, and there were plenty of major railroads in this area. His business was booming.

For now, Harvey had his mind set on a nice little jewelry store he had seen right off campus. As badly as he wanted to put a ring on Eva's finger, he opted to wait for now, selecting a beautiful Ruby pendant, which was her birthstone. The stone was small but brilliant. As tiny as Eva was, anything too large would look outlandish. He smiled to himself as he thought, *"She is so beautiful, anything I buy would pale in comparison."*

After making his selection, he browsed for a few moments looking at the rings. He saw the one he was sure of.

The salesman explained that in fashionable trends, a birthstone set in gold was common practice as an engagement ring or even a wedding band. "Celtic designs are the most popular at this time." He pulled out a Celtic ring with two gold hands holding a heart-shaped ruby stone.

"That's it. I would like to purchase that, sir, but I will have to pay over time. I don't need it for a few months, if you would be willing to work out some kind of arrangement with me?"

The man gladly made arrangements that were acceptable with Harvey. Of course, he would have to see about finding a job on weekends to pay for it, but Eva had to have that ring. The man was kind enough to remind Harvey that he needed an exact size so the ring would be ready when he was.

"Thank you, sir, and Merry Christmas!" He walked out of the store feeling better than he had in months. He was within three days of seeing the woman who held his heart, and he had a plan for their future. Nothing else mattered.

****

"Eva," her roommate teased, "We are all looking forward to going home, but I swear you are glowing! This Harvey of yours must really be something special."

Eva just smiled. "Oh, he is. He is kind, gentle, handsome, and tall."

Several girls giggled as one burst out in laughter. "Eva, anyone would be tall for you! You are such a tiny thing. He could be five foot four inches and you would think he was tall. You will have to be more specific to convince us."

"Alright then," Eva was glowing yet adamant. "Miss smarty pants, he is six foot three! I would call that tall."

"Are you serious? That should almost scare you! He is a giant compared to you."

Eva looked dreamy eyed as she swooned. "Yes, and it makes me feel so safe and totally surrounded by love."

The girls giggled again.

She gathered her thoughts and came back to reality. "Girls, it's getting late. We have our finals tomorrow and then one last day of instruction for the holidays. We need to get in bed."

They all said their goodnights and headed off to their own beds.

****

When Harvey stepped out of the store, he ran into Mr. Farley's friend, Mr. Landon, who had taken him out for supper.

"Harvey, how are you?"

"Fine sir, and I hope you are?"

"Yes, yes." The man noticed the store Harvey had exited from. "Oh my, looks like you are pretty serious over this young lady of yours."

Harvey smiled. "Yes sir, I am. I will be leaving in two days to surprise her. I will get to escort her home for Christmas. She doesn't plan to see me until she gets home."

"I see," he nodded. "That will be a wonderful surprise."

The man looked toward the store again. "Do you mind stepping back in here with me? My son is getting ready to ask a certain young lady for her hand in marriage and I would like to see what kind of money rings are costing these days."

"Certainly sir."

During their conversation, Mr. Landon found out that Harvey hadn't purchased his train ticket yet and offered him a free ride home.

"I appreciate that sir, but I can't accept."

"I insist, Harvey. You mean a lot to Samuel, and I certainly respect the man. In fact, my son that is about to get engaged is marrying Agnes Farley's niece. I help you with a kindness now that may be looked on kindly by Samuel in the future if my boy needs a helping hand.

"How would you feel about leaving tomorrow afternoon instead of the next morning? You could be with your girl by early afternoon the next day."

Harvey glowed with excitement.

****

It was Thursday, December 13th. Eva walked into her last classroom for the day, feeling good about the tests she had behind her, with one more to go. A half-day of instruction on Friday and then she was on her way home for three whole weeks. She relished in the thoughts of Harvey holding her. She had missed him so.

She cleared her mind and settled at her desk to quickly go over her notes one last time. The instructor came in as the bell rang for class to start.

"Girls, I want to say Merry Christmas to all of you. As a present of sorts, I have made the test very simple. There are no essay questions. Simple answers will do because I'm sure your minds are on other things. Don't be deceived, it is still a serious grade. Take your time and do your best. You may leave quietly when you finish."

Within twenty minutes, Eva was walking with a group of girls, talking about getting their packing done. When they were approaching the main office building, Eva noticed a tall man step out with another man pointing towards the dormitories as if giving directions. No one paid much attention as they continued with their chatter of plans. Then Eva looked again and froze. She blinked her eyes and gasped as the others turned to her in alarm.

"Harvey!" She yelled, scattering her books on the ground as she took off running.

He looked in the direction of her voice to see her sprinting across the lawn. Smiling, he thanked the man quickly and closed the distance between them, catching her in his arms and twirling her around. He was kissing her before her feet touched the ground.

"Oh, my darling Eva," he held her close. "I have missed you so!"

He looked down at her seeing tears of joy running down her face.

"Oh, Harvey!" was all the words she formed before he was kissing her again.

The girls had picked up all her discarded books and papers, slowly making their way toward her. They wanted to get a closer look at this man that Eva had gone on about endlessly.

One of the girls cleared her throat loudly, bringing Eva and Harvey out of their cloud. "We brought your books, Eva."

Eva turned around, blushing, wiping her eyes. "Thank you. Harvey, let me introduce you to my friends."

After introductions were made, Harvey walked with them as far as he was allowed, then made a plan to take Eva to supper. All was right in their world, now that they were together.

Chapter 5

During the weeks following Thanksgiving, Mrs. Upton made sure to make Asa feel more welcome than ever. She was convinced that he was a true gentleman and that he loved her daughter. She even convinced her husband to allow Asa to take Olivia to the diner one evening, but on a time limit; straight there and straight back.

Christmas was approaching fast, with the families excited about Harvey and Eva coming home, as well as all the special Christmas programs Mrs. Upton and Mrs. Farley had put together.

Getting help from several ladies in the community, Mrs. Farley orchestrated a Christmas collection. They had made up a basket of goodies for each of the families that were in need, and the elderly that couldn't get out much.

Mrs. Farley had also visited the Darnells when her husband went. She had asked a favor of Abe and Asa, of course having a way of making them feel they were obligated to her husband, which embarrassed Mr. Farley.

She gave them a list of people who needed help with firewood and gave them explicit instructions on where and how to stack it.

"I think these men know how to do that without you telling them, dear." Mr. Farley rolled his eyes and then apologized. "Please forgive my wife. She is very excited about finding a role to play within the community."

Abe chuckled. "Nothing to forgive, Samuel. We are more than glad to help, now that we have been made aware of the need. Thank you, Mrs. Farley, for being concerned enough to bring it to our attention."

Those words brought a sincere smile to Mrs. Farley as she puffed up like a proud peacock, yet saying nothing for a change, except, "You are most welcome. I do appreciate you doing this."

Asa gave a report to Mrs. Upton about the firewood every time he visited Olivia, in hopes that perhaps Olivia could ride with him and his pa to deliver it occasionally.

"Well, young man, I don't suppose it would hurt, as long as it doesn't interfere with her schoolwork. Your pa will be with you?"

"Yes ma'am, every minute."

"It's so cold, I just can't understand..." she stopped, momentarily feeling foolish. "Yes, I do understand. Just bundle up good. Don't any of you be getting sick before Christmas."

"We will pick you up tomorrow afternoon," Asa flashed a winning smile to Olivia, giving her hand a quick squeeze. "Thank you, Mrs. Upton. We will take good care of her."

The next afternoon, Mrs. Upton followed them out to the wagon full of wood to find Asa taking better care of Olivia than she had ever dreamed. He had heated a brick to keep her feet warm, brought an extra blanket that he tucked around her, and had her hold a jug of hot coffee wrapped in several layers of cloth.

"Asa, you never cease to amaze me." She shook her head and quickly went back into the house, escaping the cold.

When they were out of sight of the town, Asa stole his arm around her as his pa drove. Abe pretended not to notice, keeping his eyes on the road and his thoughts to himself. He sure hoped neither of his boys got their hearts broken.

****

"I'm sorry, Olivia, but you need to stay home tomorrow afternoon and help me get the house prepared for your sister's arrival."

"I understand, Ma," she conceded with disappointment.

"It's alright, Olivia," Asa consoled. "Just think, Eva and Harvey will be home for three weeks. We are going to have some fun times together."

Mrs. Upton pulled a cake out of the oven and set it to cool. "Eva will be on the train arriving around midnight, tomorrow. When will Harvey be arriving? Are you making special preparations for him?"

"Uh, well, no, I don't think so. He will be home sometime Saturday. We will be leaving his horse at Henderson's store Saturday morning so he will have it whenever he arrives. I'm sure you will see him before we will. You know he's gonna stop here to see Eva first thing."

She shook her head. "The difference between men and women. Tsk. I'm set on having everything spotless, decorated, big meal planned with special desserts, all because my daughter is coming home. Men, on the other hand, just drop off a horse and go about your daily business."

"Well, if it helps any at all," Asa teased, "We just figured we would both spend all our time over here and not wear ourselves out too much fussing with preparations. Pa can take care of himself."

Olivia slapped his arm playfully. "Asa, you shouldn't tease so much. Tell Ma the truth."

He snickered. "Yes ma'am, we are making some preparation and we are very excited, but truthfully, he will probably be coming here before he comes home.

"Pa happened to tell Mr. Farley the house sure could use a good cleaning and a woman's touch before Harvey comes home. He, in turn, mentioned it to his wife, and she got two widow women to come work on the house all week. We have stayed out of the house every day from breakfast until after supper at the bunkhouse. The place looks about as good as it did before Ma died."

"Oh Asa," Olivia sighed as she put her hand on his arm. "I'm so sorry. This wasn't supposed to be a sad conversation."

"It's not. The house looks good, my brother is coming home, and I'm ready to sample that cake!"

Mrs. Upton playfully slapped his hand as he reached toward it.

****

Harvey kept his arm around Eva as she slept with her head against his chest. He leaned down and kissed the top of her head, imagining how life would be with her by his side forever.

He thought back to how his ma and pa were always so close, so kind. That's the kind of marriage he wanted and felt sure he would have that with Eva.

It had been a long day and he felt blessed to have spent almost all of it with her. From the time she finished her last class, they had been together. The train had pulled out of the station at two and should have them home by midnight.

It was already dark outside, and he was getting drowsy. He repositioned himself carefully, scooting down in his seat and stretching his long legs out. He laid his head forward against hers, kissed it again, and then drifted off, thinking of waking up beside her every morning.

The train stopped, waking them both. The conductor came through telling everyone they would be there for nearly an hour if anyone wanted to stretch their legs or go to the diner.

"Sweetheart, let's go get some supper. It's nearly eight o'clock."

She nodded her head and swiped at her hair. "I'm sure I look a fright. Consider yourself warned."

"If this is as bad as it gets, I am one very lucky man." He kissed her quickly and stood to help her to her feet.

Over supper, they couldn't keep their eyes off each other as their conversation flowed with plans for the next few weeks.

"Eva, let's talk a little farther into the future. What do you see for us?"

"Oh my," she blushed. "I can't be telling you all that. You will be running for the hills!"

He chuckled. "As long as you see us together in the future, there's nothing you could say that would scare me away."

She squinted her eyes at him. "You are one brave man to make such a statement." She set her fork down, took a sip of water, and continued.

"Alright, I see myself teaching until I have a family of my own. After that, I see myself working by my husband's side on a big farm." She winked with a playful grin. "In the afternoon, I will take the children in the house, cook supper while I get them all washed up, and be setting supper on the table as my husband comes in the door."

He nodded as a grin passed over his face. "Hmm, this husband of yours, I suppose he would be tall, strong, and handsome, with a winning personality? He would be a hero to his wife and children with never a cross word?"

"Well of course! And as soon as I finish school, I'm going to run an advertisement in the newspaper to try to find him."

Harvey roared in laughter. "You are really something, Eva. You are beautiful, intelligent, and witty. What in the world are you doing with an old backwoods, farm boy like me?"

She reached across the table and took his hand. "I happened to fall in love with you. I knew you were someone special way back when you came to Raleigh. God was just giving me a glimpse of good things to come if I would just wait on Him."

He got a lump in his throat. He couldn't get over how much of a hold this tiny woman had over him. "I guess it's pretty plain that I want to spend the rest of my life with you?"

"I feel the same way, Harvey."

"Let's just go get married."

"Harvey! Have you lost your mind?" She spoke quietly with her eyes wide. "We are taking very practical steps toward building a wonderful future. We aren't ready for marriage. We don't even have a place to live."

"If we did, would you marry me?"

"Harvey, please don't tease about something so serious. I'm already teetering on the edge of giving in to you. I would live in the back of a wagon with you. I want to start our life together as much as you do, but to do it right, it takes time."

Harvey sighed loudly. "You're right, I just hate to wait. I hope that you're always practical and sensible, where we can pray and talk everything through together."

****

Preacher Upton was uncomfortably shocked when he saw Harvey arriving with his daughter. The first thought that crossed his mind was they had secretly married.

He hugged Eva, then looked sternly at Harvey as he shook his hand. "Young man, do you have anything to tell me?"

Harvey stammered for a moment, looking at Eva in confusion. "Umm, Merry Christmas, and it's good to be home, sir."

"No, Harvey. I would like an explanation of why you are arriving together."

"Oh, umm, I just wanted to surprise Eva and accompany her during her travel. I left school a day early to do so."

The preacher exhaled with relief. He turned to Eva. "It's good to know you are both sticking with your plans. You had me concerned for a moment."

Eva hugged her pa. "Pa, you should know that if something *important* happened, you would be there, in fact, you would be playing an active part." She kissed him on the cheek.

Harvey loaded the two satchels they had brought with them, then helped Eva in the buggy. "Sir, I find myself in need of a horse to get home. Could I borrow one of yours until morning?"

"Certainly, son," he chuckled. "I have no question of you returning to my house first thing tomorrow, probably with your brother leading the way."

"Yes sir," Harvey beamed. "From what I hear, you should be getting used to the Darnell family by now."

Arriving at the house, Harvey said a quick goodbye to Eva, sending her in from the cold, while he and the preacher walked to the barn.

"Sir, I appreciate this. I will be back in the morning." He started saddling the horse the preacher pointed out.

"So, Harvey, in case I didn't already know, tell me your intentions with my Eva."

He turned to squarely face the man. "I love your daughter with all my heart, and I want to spend the rest of my life with her. I want to give her the best life possible and the sacrifices we are making now, hopefully, prove to you how serious we are."

Preacher Upton nodded and slapped Harvey on the back. "Get on home to your folk. I will see you tomorrow. Welcome home, son."

Harvey picked his way slowly down the road toward the farm. It was almost pitch black in most spots along the way. He couldn't wait to see his pa and Asa. Then it hit him; he couldn't go to the house tonight…he would get shot for sure, with them thinking he was someone breaking in. Suddenly, feeling extremely tired, he wished he had asked to sleep on the preacher's couch, floor, or even in the barn.

He quickly decided to head on over the foothill and sleep in one of the bunkhouses. The way the ranch was running, there was always at least one bunkhouse active at all times. Maybe he would find an empty bunk or enough room on the floor. He felt sure he could sleep on a rock right now if he had to.

The next morning, he arrived bright and early to find Asa doing a fairly good job burning breakfast, while his pa was setting out some plates and pouring coffee.

He quietly entered the house and spoke, "Mind setting another plate?"

Both men quickly set aside what they were doing and hugged Harvey.

"Welcome home, son! We weren't expecting you until later. We haven't even taken your horse to town yet! How…?"

"I came a day early so I could join Eva during the travels."

He walked toward the stove. "Mind if I join you for some black bacon and crispy eggs?"

Asa slapped him on the back. "If you can do a better job, have at it."

****

Breakfast was interrupted by a visit from a very excited Mr. Farley. He entered the house with his excitement reaching full height as he saw Harvey. "Welcome home, son!" he embraced him quickly.

"I wasn't expecting you until this afternoon, but I sure am glad to have you here to be a part of this exciting news for your brother." He rambled on while he sat down, joining them for coffee.

"Asa, there have been times that I feel like you may have felt slighted by me. Seems that all my attention has been focused on Harvey. I want you to know, you mean just as much to me. You boys are the kind of young men I would have hoped for in sons of my own."

"Mr. Farley, I..." Asa was interrupted by Mr. Farley putting his hand up.

"Let me finish. The opportunities that have been on the forefront over the last few years were of more interest to Harvey. But now," he paused as his eyes twinkled.

"Last night I received a telegram that may present an opportunity for you. It seems as though the iron and steel business is booming up in Virginia. I know you have an interest in such. There is an apprenticeship opening up for several young men, and I was wondering if you would like to advance your education in that direction and join?"

Asa looked perplexed. "Mr. Farley, this sounds great, but I'm not as keen on book learning as Harvey. I do appreciate..."

Mr. Farley interrupted him. "But you see, an apprenticeship is much more hands-on than book learning. You will be learning the different methods and ratios of mixing ore and such, but for the most part, you will be working side by side with professionals in the business of shaping the metals into, well, everything they are used for."

Asa smiled at Harvey and his pa. "Alright, tell me all the details and give me a little time to think and pray about it."

Mr. Farley slapped the table in excitement. "The program lasts a year and is in the mountainous region of Virginia. It starts January 14th."

For the next half hour, Mr. Farley filled in all the details and sparked a high interest in Asa. This was just the kind of thing he had always been intrigued with.

Mr. Farley stood to leave, turning back, with less of a smile. "Asa, there are some class studies and I know you aren't thrilled about that, but we need intelligent young men like yourself to keep these businesses running in the future. Just think of the bright future you will be building for yourself and your future family."

"Thank you, Mr. Farley. I will let you know." Asa shook the man's hand.

"Yes, well, do let me know before this upcoming weekend. I will need to reserve you a spot."

When Mr. Farley was gone, Abe turned to his boys and chuckled. "Is there nothing that man can't do? He has a great mind for business and runs several, doesn't mind getting his hands dirty, has built a town, yet still stays mindful of individual people. That's a good man, boys, and don't ever forget it. There will never be another like him."

****

Harvey, Eva, Asa, and Olivia went to the diner for lunch, picking up where they left off months earlier. It was so good to be together again, with everyone talking as quickly as possible, trying to catch up on all they had experienced the last few months.

One subject caused a lull in the conversation, the other caused it to stop abruptly.

Asa told Harvey about Toby cutting in to dance with Olivia. Eva had already heard some about it through Olivia's letters. Harvey was surprised at the nerve of the man.

"Has he caused any trouble since?"

"Umm, no, not really. But the reason I'm bringing this to your attention, dear brother, is because he just left the diner a few minutes ago and he was getting an eyeful of Eva while he was here."

Eva blushed as Harvey got agitated. "Why didn't you tell me, Asa? I could have taken care of any doubts he may have had about OUR girls."

Asa chuckled. "That's why I didn't tell you. I shot him some warning looks, but I didn't want any trouble started. We can talk to him later, back at the farm." He winked at Harvey. "I will be glad to introduce you."

A few minutes later, Mr. Farley was mentioned, and Asa knew he couldn't keep putting off telling Olivia about the offer. She didn't take the news near as well as Eva had taken Harvey's a few months earlier.

"You're going to leave me?" she shrieked. Tears welled in her eyes. "I can't believe you would leave me!"

She pushed her chair back and started to stand as Asa stammered and reached for her hand. "Olivia, it's a great opportunity for us. Besides, you already said your parents were going to send you to teacher college."

Olivia jerked her hand away, turning, half running to the door, sobbing loudly before she got outside.

Eva stood. "I will talk to her Asa. Perhaps you and Harvey should visit with each other back at your farm, until supper at our house tonight?"

By this time, they were all standing. Harvey gave Eva a quick kiss and squeezed her hand, then watched her walk quickly to find Olivia.

Asa slumped down into his chair, putting his face in his hands, elbows propped on the table. "That didn't go nearly as well as I had hoped. I can't stand to see her cry."

Harvey sat back down. "Let Eva talk to her before you make any decisions. Olivia is so young, she can't be fully reasonable yet."

"Yes, and that concerns me, a lot. She thinks she loves me; she thinks life is easy to plan out and just make everything fall into its right place. I don't think she sees anything going on behind the building of a future."

Harvey nodded. "That's because she is just becoming a woman. Up until recently, she was a child, having most everything taken care of for her, not being worried with finding her own way and how to go about getting there. She's just finding out that there's much more to life than walking through the meadow picking pretty flowers.

"Don't despair and don't give up; not if you truly love her."

Asa nodded. "I guess now I understand more about what Mrs. Upton has been warning, saying Olivia had a long way to go before she is capable of getting in a serious relationship."

****

Supper at the Upton's was unusually quiet, with Amy being the one to keep the chatter going about the excitement of having Eva home and Christmas drawing near.

Asa caught himself thinking about what Harvey had said and some of the conversations with Mrs. Upton, as he half listened to Amy. He was paying more attention to her zeal for life and seeing everything from a child's excited perspective. Nothing so devastating in life had yet tainted her view of a perfect world. That's how it should be for a child.

Less than two years earlier, Olivia had been that same child. Maybe he was expecting too much of her, too soon. He was five years older than her, which wouldn't make a lot of difference in years to come, but right now, it was huge. He had to face the fact that he was an adult, and she was still mostly a child, then decide how he should and could deal with it.

But she had his heart, plain and simple. One of the things he loved about her was her innocence and zeal for life. He wanted to be the man to keep her from any hurt or harm in life. He wanted to protect her from everything and provide her with anything her heart desired.

He wiped his mouth and folded his napkin. "Mrs. Upton, thank you for another delicious meal, but if you would please excuse me? I have picked up a shift tonight for one of the men that is feeling poorly."

"Of course, Asa, but we hate to lose you so early in the evening."

"Thank you, ma'am." He glanced at Olivia and nodded, noticing her eyes were still red and swollen from recent floods of tears.

"Asa, if you have a few minutes, we would like to talk to you." The preacher nodded toward his wife. "We will be brief."

"Yes sir, ma'am." He knew he was getting ready to get his hide scalded for making their daughter cry.

"Girls," Mrs. Upton instructed. "Clear the table and clean the kitchen, please. Harvey, I'm sure they can find an apron to fit you if you care to join them."

"Oh, ma!" Eva giggled. "That's my dream come true! To see Harvey Darnell in an apron! How did you know?"

Harvey smirked. "Funny girl!" They all stood, gathering dishes and disappearing into the kitchen.

Asa was sweating as he entered the parlor with the Upton's right behind him. He waited until Mrs. Upton was seated and she motioned for him to sit.

"Mrs. Upton, Preacher," Asa nodded as he swallowed hard. "I promise you I never meant to make Olivia cry. I had no idea she would get so upset. Besides, it's just a suggestion. I haven't given an answer yet. I intended to discuss it with her first and come to an agreement."

"Calm yourself, Asa," Mrs. Upton soothed. "We feel this may be exactly what the two of you need. Olivia is struggling to grow into an adult. She sees the freedoms and advantages of being an adult, yet she lacks the knowledge and patience for it.

"This is a very crucial time in a young lady's life. So many changes between the ages of fourteen and eighteen. It's the difference between Amy and Eva. Some adapt quicker and more easily to responsibility than others. Of course, no two are the same, but there is hope. This could be an awakening for Olivia. She could begin to see that everything won't always go her way or the way she thought it should, and she may start to think about solutions instead of just ideals."

Asa nodded. "It rips my heart out, ma'am, to think that I've upset her."

"Well, Asa, I appreciate you saying so, but the fact of the matter is that you can't tiptoe around someone's feelings in this life. Relationships take work, with both people willing to give for the other one's sake. Otherwise, it's a one-sided relationship with someone being miserable."

"Asa," Preacher Upton began. "Son, we think a lot of you and couldn't imagine a better man for our Olivia. We think this opportunity you have been offered may be a good idea. It will help build a future for you and meanwhile, it will give Olivia time to mature."

Asa's face went pale. "Are you saying I can't see her anymore?"

"I'm not saying that at all. I'm just saying that some time apart between your visits home, will give you both time to mature and think things through more clearly. Hopefully, put some plans in place for your future together.

"We will talk to Olivia some more about it. She will eventually come around if the Lord is in it."

"Do you think she will talk to me for a minute before I leave? I will feel much better if I know she still wants to see me."

Mrs. Upton stood as both men did the same. "I will ask her, Asa." She put her hand on his arm. "Just keep praying about your future. God will see you through."

A few moments later, Olivia walked into the parlor, humbly with eyes downcast. "You wanted to see me?"

"Umm, yes, uhh, would you mind stepping out on the porch with me for a moment?"

She walked toward the door and took her coat off the peg. He helped her with it, then quickly shrugged into his own.

Once outside, he gently turned her to face him, tipping her chin up to look at him. "Olivia, this is not how I planned to do this. I have thought of a million ways, but not over a broken heart. I can't hold back any longer."

His eyes grew tender as he swallowed past the knot in his throat. He looked deep into her eyes. "Olivia," he spoke barely above a whisper. "I love you, with all my heart. I will love you for the rest of my life."

Tears rolled down her cheeks. "I love you, Asa."

He bent down and kissed her as she tenderly wrapped her arms around his neck while standing on her tiptoes. In the few seconds their lips were touching, their hearts pounded, their insides felt on fire, and jolts of energy coursed through them as if hundreds of fireworks were going off.

He wrapped his arms around her and held her close, quietly for a few moments. He finally broke the spell. "You need to get back inside. I will see you tomorrow?"

She nodded as her face flushed.

He mounted his horse with his mind in a whirl. If there was ever a moment of doubt about loving Olivia, it was totally erased now. She had his heart and always would.

Chapter 6

At the end of the first week in January, the two families were bustling about, making preparations for the Darnell boys and Eva to leave for school. They had all planned to ride to the next town the day before the three boarded their separate trains. Mr. Farley rode along with them, discreetly slipping each boy an envelope before they left.

Harvey opted for taking an extra day of travel to be able to ride with Eva. Asa would be heading in the opposite direction. Even Olivia attempted to keep her spirits up and join the excitement. But when her and Asa's eyes would meet, sudden sadness and longing would overcome both.

Asa pulled his pa to the side, moments before he stepped on the train. "Pa, keep an eye on Toby. I just don't trust him."

"I will, Asa. But just remember, you trust your girl, right?"

Asa nodded. "Thanks, Pa. I will write as soon as I get settled." They embraced quickly before Asa rejoined Olivia for one last, brief moment.

"I miss you already, Asa," she choked back a tear.

He gave in to a brief hug as her parents looked on. "I will miss you, my darling. I love you, and don't forget that." He looked down at the beautiful, silver cuff bracelet he had given her for Christmas. He ran his fingers over the two entwined hearts engraved in it. With one last kiss on her cheek, he squeezed her hand, then turned to leave.

Just as his hand touched the railing at the steps of the train, Olivia called to him. He turned to see her running toward him, in time to catch her in his arms. She threw her arms around his neck and kissed him like crazy. When they stopped, they both smiled.

"I love you, Asa. Don't you worry about anything here, you just do what you have to and hurry back to me."

He nodded as the preacher came and took her by the arm, scolding her for her outburst. She wasn't hearing a word.

Abe and Mr. Farley stood back and chuckled to each other quietly.

Within an hour, Harvey and Eva were boarding their train, waving their last goodbyes until June. They had eight hours together on the train, then would have supper together and go their separate ways for another agonizing five months. At that time Eva would return home for good, but Harvey would only have two weeks before he would have to be gone for another six months. When they thought of it that way, they both got discouraged, so they decided to make the best use of the time apart to focus on things to be done.

"If we make a list of things, we can check them off and maybe it will make us feel better," she suggested.

He shrugged. "We can try if you like, but what I'm thinking can't really be done until later."

She looked at him in confusion. "Like what?"

"Okay, umm, for example, how many children do you want?"

She looked at him and blushed. "Six or so would do. Why? Do you want me to put that on the list?"

"Sure," he grinned as he put his arm around her. "We can get started on that."

"Harvey Darnell!" she chided quietly as she glanced around. "You are incorrigible!"

"Look, you are the one who wanted to put it on the list. I was just trying to figure out how big of a house we will need. There's a lot to think about just with that, like where we want it, what we can afford, do we build just enough for us and then add on as needed? You know, all kinds of decisions."

"Well, even though we need to think about those things, I was thinking of more practical, things that can be accomplished along the way. Like, I need to start the paperwork to be hired at the school, I need to see about a wedding dress, even though I've not been asked properly yet, and things like that."

"Ahh, you know we're going to get married. Isn't that good enough? All that fancy proposal and stuff is overrated."

She elbowed his ribs.

"Oww! Alright!" he laughed and pointed to her paper. "Put it on the list. I will see about getting around to it."

Harvey noticed that it seemed every few minutes, Eva would put her hand to her necklace, fingering the stone. "Is your necklace bothering you? I noticed you keep messing with it."

"Oh, no, not at all. I just love it so much and can't believe you would give me something so beautiful. You may be a keeper after all.

"You have such a tough exterior, but I see a big softie. Lord help if we ever do have a daughter, she will have you twisted every way but loose."

"You may be right, especially if she's anything like her ma. Just don't tell anyone I'm a nice guy. Don't want my reputation tarnished."

"Your secret's safe with me."

****

Asa hadn't been gone two weeks before Toby, all dressed up and smelling good, was knocking on the preacher's door. He was there under the guise of being interested in becoming a member of the church.

The preacher, not being fooled easily, talked to the young man as patiently as possible. "First of all, Toby, it would be nice if you joined us for services and found out how we believe and what we stand for. Church membership is a serious commitment."

"Well sir, I thought I may be able to volunteer for some work on my days off."

"That would be fine and greatly appreciated. Abe Darnell may need some help with cutting and delivering firewood to the needy now that Asa's gone."

"I kinda wanted to get off the farm on my days off, sir. I was hoping you may need help here or across the street at the church."

Olivia walked into the parlor to let her pa know supper was ready. "I'm sorry, Pa. I didn't know you had company."

Toby stood and smiled at her. "Good evening, Miss Olivia."

She nodded before leaving the room without a word.

"Toby, thank you for stopping by. I look forward to seeing you in church sometime. Meanwhile, if you want to help Mr. Darnell, that's about the only thing I know of right now."

"Thank you, sir. Don't hesitate to let me know if you need anything. Goodnight."

Olivia didn't dare mention Toby in her letters to Asa. There was nothing he could do, and it would only worry him. She was trying her best to grow up and be a responsible adult, not a chattering, moody child anymore.

She wanted to marry Asa with all her being, and her parents wouldn't allow it until they were convinced she was mature and responsible. She was working on it.

****

Asa was able to come home for a weekend about every six weeks. He was allowed to escort Olivia to the diner every

Saturday he was home and was invited to Sunday dinner with them before he caught the train back to school.

He and her parents were impressed with the way Olivia seemed more mature each time he came home.

Little did they seem to take notice, but Amy, who had turned fifteen in January, was listening and learning as Olivia was, and also beginning to attract quite a bit of attention from the boys in town.

Asa was the first to notice when he took the two of them to the diner one evening. There was a young man, sitting with his family, at a table nearby. He could see them shyly glancing at each other throughout the meal.

He couldn't help but tease her about it after the boy left. "So, what's his name Amy?"

"Who?" she blushed.

Olivia looked around. "Who, Asa?"

"Amy knows."

Olivia looked at her sister and gasped. "Oh my, you are red as a beet!"

Amy took a sip of water. "We call him Perky. His name is Theodore Perkins. He's just a friend from school."

"Uh huh. Looked like a pretty special friend to me."

"Asa, please don't tell ma or pa! They won't ever let me out of their sight again if you do. I promise we are just friends, and we are never alone, always in a group." She finished with her eyes misty.

"Don't worry, Amy. I won't say a word as long as you don't cause me to. You know how to behave."

"Yes sir. Thank you."

"Sir?" He turned to Olivia. "Did she just call me sir?"

"Well, you are old, Asa," Amy teased. "I mean older."

Asa's mouth fell open, feigning hurt, putting his hand on his heart, as they all burst into laughter.

****

Harvey was missing Eva more than ever. His studies this semester, until late March, would be all about business instead of agriculture. It was important and tough but didn't hold his interest. He was keeping his grades up, even through his distraction.

He had secured a job on the weekends with Mr. Landon and was making regular payments on Eva's ring. He had sworn Olivia to secrecy and found out what size ring Eva wore.

By the time he went home for two weeks in June, he would have the ring in his pocket. She would get her formal proposal, then they could talk more freely about their future plans.

He was saving every dime he could to put towards a house, but of course, with working only weekends and buying the ring, there wasn't much left each week. He certainly didn't want Eva to feel like she had to use her teacher's pay to build their house, but knowing her, she would want to. He would figure something out because he wasn't going to let that happen.

****

Eva's graduation was coming up quickly with much enthusiasm throughout the campus. All her friends had been submitting applications to schools for teaching positions, with each one having more than one school in mind. Eva didn't say too much about her employment situation. She knew no one else was applying for the position, yet that was the only school she was interested in. Her concern was if the town council would even see the need to pay a teacher full-time with no more students than they had.

The college had taught them how to let people know about the importance of education for their children and she knew back home that would be a big task. She set her mind that she could improve attendance and was capable of convincing the town council of the importance of keeping a school open, with a regular teacher.

Then she wondered how long she would actually be a regular teacher. Her mind drifted to Harvey. She hoped that within her first year of teaching her name would change to Darnell and then hopefully by the next year she would have their baby to keep her at home. By then, Olivia would be certified to teach, and surely she could take over.

Eva was suddenly so homesick, especially for Harvey. He wouldn't even be attending her graduation because he would be in the middle of final exams. She understood, even though it didn't make her feel any better. He would be arriving home a few days after her, with so little time to spend together. Before she knew it, she had dwelled on it long enough to work herself into a frenzy.

She shook herself out of it and decided to take a nice, long walk. The flowers and trees were gorgeous, the breeze was gentle, and the sun was warm and inviting. On the way out the door, she asked if anyone wanted to join her and within seconds, they had a chatty group together.

Parents and families would be arriving the next week and the campus was buzzing with activity. *"Next Friday, seven more days, and I will be checking that off the list,"* she thought to herself. She smiled when she thought back to the conversation she and Harvey had on the train about her list.

Harvey...that seemed to be all she lived for, and that, in her mind, was enough.

****

"Sir," Harvey spoke with confidence. "My fiancé is graduating on June 7th, which is the last day of our exams. I was wondering if I could take the exams early and be excused to join in the celebration of her hard work?"

The dean looked at him seriously. "Please have a seat, Mr. Darnell." The man walked out of his office for a moment, returning with Harvey's file. "I see that you have opted for the fifteen-month accelerated program. Hmm," he rubbed his chin, never looking up from the file.

"It looks as though you have had perfect attendance with no tardiness, no reprimands, no problems reported, and high recommendations from your professors."

He flipped the page. "We usually run a very strict program and frown upon these types of requests. Not that it is unreasonable, mind you, we just don't want to be over-run with requests and excuses."

"I understand sir, and I didn't mean to put you in a bad position. My fiancé will understand."

He flipped to the last page and looked up at Harvey with a smile on his face. "You know Samuel Farley, personally?"

"Uh, yes sir. He's the reason I was able to attend school. He's a very good man."

"Yes, indeed he is. You came highly recommended by him, in fact, he says you are the son he wished he had been blessed with. Do you realize what a high honor that is?"

"Sir, I am honored, but don't know what to say."

"Let me ask you this. Do you really think you will be prepared to take your exams early and still make a good grade? Lots of students wait to cram at the last minute."

"Yes sir, I'm ready."

"Well then, if you don't spread the word of this, I will grant your request. I will send a note to your professors today and see to it they have your exams ready on Monday. You will take them in the library under a proctor. Take them at your own pace and you will be excused as soon as you have completed them."

Harvey jumped up. "Thank you, sir. I don't know how to thank you!"

"Just tell Mr. Farley that I said hello."

"Yes sir!"

Harvey wasn't able to get to Eva's school until late on the night before graduation. He wouldn't see her until she walked across the platform. He was so proud of her.

He stopped at a little shop on the way to her graduation and bought a bouquet of flowers. He never imagined himself as one to do something seemingly so silly, but something about being in love had changed his way of thinking.

Her parents saw him when he walked into the garden where the ceremony was being held, sending Amy to let him know where they were.

He did a double-take, not believing his eyes when he saw her. "Amy? My goodness, you have grown up in the last few months."

She blushed and curtsied. "Why thank you, kind sir. My folks sent me to show you where we are sitting." Hooking her arm around his, she walked gracefully, like a real lady, leading him through the crowd.

After a round of hugs from Mrs. Upton and Olivia, he sat down with them as the music began. With only thirty-two in her graduating class, the ceremony didn't take long. When Eva's name was called, she looked out at the audience and saw Harvey. Her smile brightened and her heart raced. Her Harvey. One step at a time, checking off the things on her list, she finally felt like they were making progress. Soon, very soon, he would really be her Harvey, forever.

****

Asa came home for a three-day weekend while Harvey was in town. He wasn't only excited to see his brother, but he also wanted to show them some of the iron and steel things he had made. He came riding up in a buckboard with light weight, durable steel sides, that would be great for hauling some of the produce at the farm. In the back of his wagon was a heavy, ornate wrought iron door with intricate detail.

"I'm going to put some screen in this and use it on the front door of my home one day." He flashed a smile at Olivia. "Do you like it, sweetheart?"

"I think it's quite wonderful." She ran her hands over it. "I think it will fit on *our* front door perfectly."

He put his arm around her and gave her a quick squeeze.

"Pa, this wagon is for you. It was an old wagon that we took on as a class project. We refurbished the wheels, reinforced the floor, and added the sides and tailgate. One of my friends and I got extra credit for how good it turned out."

"Thank you, son! It's wonderful and will be put to good use. I will let you and your brother go on out and fill it up right now, starting with some squash."

Harvey and Asa looked at each other and immediately started making excuses for why they had to leave, quickly.

Abe laughed and waved his hand. "I'm serious, son. This is really nice, and I appreciate it."

****

Harvey and Eva walked along the edge of the creek, hand in hand, enjoying their time together, alone, quietly.

"Eva, let's go get married. I can take you with me back to school. We can get a place off campus until Christmas when my schooling is over. Then we can come back here."

"Harvey, are you serious?" She stopped and looked at him. "You know we can't do that. I'm taking over the teaching position in September. Besides, I've already told you what I expect, and you are doing a poor job of it."

They walked to the swimming hole and he had her sit on the big flat rock that he always sat and played on as a child while he let himself dry from swimming.

"This is one of my favorite spots in this entire area. I would love to own it, but the government has it tied up in some kind of treaty or something. Maybe one day."

She smiled as he sat down beside her and wrapped his arm around her. "So, I can't talk you into running off and marrying me, huh?"

"Nope. It's not on my list. It doesn't fit with the plan. And I'm still waiting."

"Alright," he sighed. "Thought I would try to see if you would waver and lose some of that practicality of yours."

"So, this was a test?"

"In a way, I suppose, because there is a right or wrong answer." He slipped off the rock and fell to one knee. "Eva Upton, will you marry me, making me the happiest man in the world, allowing me to love you for the rest of my life?"

He opened the ring box as she gasped, clutched her throat, then threw her arms around his neck, knocking him off balance. He held on to the ring as they fell to the ground. Holding her in his arms like this seemed the most natural and beautiful thing in the world.

She lay in his arms looking at him. "Yes! I would be honored beyond measure to be your wife." Their lips touched and for long moments they delighted in the pleasure they drew from each other.

Finally, Harvey pushed her back gently. "Eva, unless you will change your mind and marry me now, I suggest we head back towards the house."

Breathless and speechless, she nodded, allowing him to help her to her feet.

He cleared his throat. "You didn't even get a good look at your ring. Here, let's put it on your finger." He slid it on her.

"Oh, Harvey! It's beautiful! I will cherish it forever." She reached up and kissed him again. "It's a perfect fit. How did you know what size to get?"

"Well, I picked it out myself, with lots of meaning in it, but I had help from Olivia to know what size."

"Olivia knows? She never said a word. She must not have known for long because that girl isn't good with secrets."

"Then you will be surprised and proud. She's known since Christmas."

"Harvey Darnell! You have let me nag you all these months over something you already had planned?"

He just smiled as he wrapped his arm around her and started her back toward the house. He had to guide her because she wouldn't take her eyes off that ring. He was one happy man.

Chapter 7

Abe was glad to welcome all three Upton girls to work at the farm for the summer. They were a delight and a real bright spot in his life with his boys being gone.

Harvey and Asa had been back to school for a couple of weeks; Harvey leaving Abe with a lot to think about.

Harvey and Eva had sat down with him and discussed that they would like to build a house on the farm. He had hoped the day would come when both his boys would want to do so. He had even set most of their earnings aside for years so they could build without debt.

The couple had decided on an April 19th wedding. Harvey would be home in December, but the house really needed to be started before then. They hadn't had time to choose where to build before Harvey had to leave. He had left it up to Eva. Abe knew she shouldn't have to make all the decisions by herself, although she was plenty capable, and he attempted to be helpful.

Eva refused to pick a spot without Harvey. She wrote to him and they finally decided to wait until he came home in December. Abe gladly offered to let them stay with him if their house wasn't finished by the wedding day.

That wasn't the only problem Abe was faced with. Toby kept coming around to the fields on his days off, under the pretense of helping the ladies, when he was only a nuisance. He wasn't really doing anything to be fired for, and he was a good worker, but Abe was having to keep a closer eye on his boy's girls and Amy.

Gerald Henderson told Abe that Toby flirted with all the ladies and seemed to be getting cozy with a couple of them.

"Well good! Maybe one of my problems will solve itself."

The girls refused to tell Harvey or Asa about Toby because they didn't want trouble, plus he hadn't actually done anything but be a nuisance. He just made them uncomfortable.

****

In August, Asa came home, this time bringing a friend. He rode to the Upton's first thing, to see Olivia. She met him on the porch with a big hug and kiss.

"My heavens! You do get sweeter all the time, my dear!"

"Why, thank you, sir."

"Sweetheart, let me introduce you to my friend, Vincent Grayson. He is a genius and is the youngest man in our class."

Vincent blushed a bit as he reached for Olivia's hand. "Nice to meet you, but don't be believing everything this jokester says."

"It's nice to meet you, Vincent. Please, come in the house and let me fix you both something cold to drink."

Asa had to pick around with Mrs. Upton for a few minutes while he made introductions to her and her husband.

"So, is it true, Vincent?" Olivia asked. "Are you the youngest and brightest in the class?"

"Youngest, yes. Brightest, absolutely not. Your man here is the one who excels beyond all of us. And please, if all of you would call me Vince? Every time I hear Vincent, I feel like I'm about to be scolded."

The door slammed as Amy entered hurriedly. "Sorry Ma, but..." she stopped in mid-sentence when she saw Vince. She blushed. "Oh! I'm sorry, I didn't know we had company. Hello, Asa, welcome home."

"Amy, this is my friend, Vince."

She curtsied. "It's nice to meet you, sir."

"Amy, did you get the eggs I needed?" Mrs. Upton asked.

"I did," she set the basket on the table, continuing to steal glances at Vince. "But I had an accident with the basket and had to go back for more. That nuisance, Toby, made me drop the basket and..." She stopped mid-sentence again when she saw Olivia's face crinkle.

"Anyway, here are your eggs. I will clean the basket out for you."

Asa saw the look on Olivia's face and on Amy's. "Toby? Is he still bothering you, Olivia? Is he bothering Amy now?"

"Well, Asa, not really," she gulped. "He just likes to make himself known and make himself *helpful* if possible. He hasn't really done anything, and he is like that with all the young ladies in town. It's really nothing to concern yourself with."

"You feeling the need to say that causes me concern. Maybe I should talk to him, again."

"No, Asa, please don't. Your pa..." she cringed. "Now I've really stepped in it."

"Maybe you better tell me everything, Olivia, Amy, Preacher, Mrs. Upton. If my pa already knows, then he has been quite a nuisance, or worse."

The front door slammed again as Eva shouted. "I swear I'm going to start carrying a gun! That To..." she stopped as she rounded the corner to the kitchen, seeing Asa.

"Hello, Asa," she blushed. "Who do you have with you?"

"Hello, Eva. This is Vince, but don't let us disturb you. What were you saying? What did Toby do to you?"

"Oh, nothing. I'm just having a bit of a day."

Asa looked around. "Alright, if no one will tell me, I will go beat the truth out of him." He stood.

Everyone started chattering at once until Preacher Upton raised his voice. "Everyone calm down. Asa, sit down, please. Don't you think if the man had done something wrong, your pa, Mr. Henderson, or someone including myself would have taken care of it by now? Truly, the man is just a nuisance. He just happens to be everywhere the girls, or any girls are. He hasn't put his hands on any of them or been ungentlemanly, at least not that I've heard."

The girls shook their heads.

"We knew you or Harvey would get upset over nothing, so we chose to stay quiet and put up with the gnat. That's exactly what he reminds me of, just a little nuisance, like a gnat."

Asa calmed down as Mrs. Upton set glasses of tea in front of him and Vince. "Alright, I certainly don't like it, but I will be home for good soon enough, and I will see for myself what's going on. I will protect my own." He reached for Olivia's hand.

"Vince," Mrs. Upton spoke. "I'm sorry for the upheaval. We are usually much more jovial."

There was a knock on the door, and Eva went to answer. A moment later she returned. "Pa, Ma, Mrs. Farley says it's important to speak with you. She's in the parlor."

When they left the room, Olivia and Amy took over with supper preparations. Eva sat down to join the men.

Asa wouldn't leave it alone. "Eva, when you came in, you were mad, talking about carrying a gun. Please tell me why. I've never heard you mad before."

"Asa," she looked at him and sighed. She knew he wouldn't stop. "Alright. Toby came into the school this afternoon, just for a few minutes, right before I came home. I was dusting all the books and getting things ready for my students. Did you know I will actually have twenty-three students? Isn't that wonderful?"

He smiled. "Nice try, Eva. Don't change the subject."

She huffed and started again. "He came in and looked around at everything, touching my books and sitting down at a few desks. That's all."

"He didn't say a word? Just looked around?"

"Asa, you just won't stop, will you? Yes, he said a few things. He said he wished he had a teacher as pretty as me. If he had, he would have stayed in school. And he said," her words were so mumbled, no one could understand her.

"I'm sorry, could you repeat that? This time where we can understand you?"

Olivia and Amy had turned their complete attention to Eva, knowing whatever was coming, wouldn't be good.

"He said that if Harvey was really serious about marrying me, he certainly wouldn't leave me alone, and the same for you leaving Olivia."

Asa's face got red with anger.

"Then I asked him to leave, and he started walking toward me. I ran out the side door and came home."

Mrs. Upton came back in the kitchen.

"Where's pa? Is Mrs. Farley alright?" Olivia asked.

"Mrs. Farley is in a lather about some propriety issues. She and your pa have gone to talk to the sheriff."

"Does it concern Toby?" Asa asked.

"Asa, you know I can't betray a confidence as a preacher's wife. I really can't say."

The rest of the evening went well. On the surface, Asa seemed calm, just like his normal self. But in reality, he continued to think about the situation with Toby. *"What if Eva couldn't have escaped through the side door? How far would Toby dare to go?"*

The conversation turned to much better things, and the real fun began when Mrs. Upton brought out the checkerboard. There was much bantering going on over challenges at checkers, between Eva's chatter of school starting and wedding plans.

The only time she was half quiet was when she was seriously challenging Asa. Near the end of the game, she saw her winning move and quickly drew Asa's eyes from the board with a challenge.

"If I win, you have to build a bookshelf for the school tomorrow." She gave him a winning smile as her eyes twinkled in mischief.

Asa didn't mind building the bookshelf and was tickled at her sudden confidence. He chuckled. "Alright, and if I win," he thought for a moment as he tapped his chin. "You have to clean my saddle."

"Deal!" Eva reached across and shook his hand. She quickly made her move and wiped out his checkers, jumped up, and danced around, gloating.

"Who wants to play the winner?" Mrs. Upton laughed.

Eva graciously replied, "Someone can take my place. I have a catalog to look at for wedding things."

Amy noticed that it was Vince's turn to play the winner, and she quickly volunteered to play in Eva's place. As of that moment, no one had noticed all the glances and smiles going on between the two.

"Oh Eva, do you mind if I look with you?" Olivia blushed slightly as she felt Asa's eyes on her.

"That would be fun, Olivia. Let's sit in the dining room." Eva ran to her room, reentering with the catalog and a glowing smile.

After Asa watched Vince willingly lose to Amy, he joined Olivia and Eva at the table. Soon, everyone else had joined and Mrs. Upton brought in a plate of cookies and a pot of coffee.

"Ma, look at this dress!" Eva swooned as she held the book up. "Isn't it the most beautiful thing you've ever seen?"

"Oh my, it certainly is. But Eva, sweetheart, that is awfully expensive. That money would be much better spent on items you will need for your house."

"But what if it only cost ME half that price? Would you think any differently?"

"Well, yes. It would be affordable then, but I don't understand. How could you get it for half the cost?" She looked at the catalog closer, then back to Eva. She noticed Olivia with a glowing smile and figured out their scheme.

"I like it too, Ma." Olivia glanced at Asa. "Hopefully I won't be waiting too terribly long to need a dress myself. I could go in half with Eva."

"Hey! What about me? You aren't a full two years older than me, Olivia," Amy spoke up, not wanting to be forgotten. "I've been working at the farm earning my own money this summer, and I have saved every penny."

Eva looked at Olivia, then back to her ma and shrugged.

Mrs. Upton sat down and took a sip of her coffee. "I must say it sounds practical enough, not that I want it to make either of you other girls get any wild ideas."

Eva took her ma's hand. "We can get a special box to keep it in. It says so right here in the book. It will keep it clean and away from harm for years. We may even be able to pass it on to our daughters!"

Preacher Upton interrupted. "Ladies, I think that's enough of this talk while we have company. Save the catalog for later? Besides I cannot fathom the thought of losing all three of you. I don't want to think about it until I must."

"Yes sir," Eva grinned at her pa, closing the catalog. "But you shouldn't think of it as losing us, you should think of gaining good, strong sons-in-law." By mistake, she pointed to Vince instead of Asa.

He blushed.

"I'm sorry, Vince," she laughed. "I meant to point to my soon-to-be brother-in-law."

****

Asa and Vince worked on the bookshelves as Eva instructed, Olivia handed them nails, and Amy helped any way she saw a chance.

As the day wore on, Asa and Olivia became a bit melancholy. This was the last time they would see each other until Christmas. Olivia would be leaving the next week for college.

By now, they had gotten used to saying goodbye, though it was never easy. This time it would be for a little longer, but Asa was very encouraging.

That evening, they were allowed to take a walk to town and through the park, alone, but were to be back in the house by dark.

Asa squeezed her hand. "Well, my dear, we are finally getting to our last hurdle apart. Nine months from now, we won't have to say goodbye again, at least not for days and weeks at a time."

"I am so looking forward to that. I'm a bit excited when I think about school, though. Eva has made it sound wonderful except for her missing Harvey. She says the time will pass quickly as I make friends and get into a regular schedule."

She stopped and looked at Asa seriously. "At least that's what I keep telling myself." Her eyes filled with tears. "Asa, I am going to miss you so much, and to tell the truth, I'm scared!"

Tears rolled down her cheeks as he put his arm around her.

"Hey now, what are you scared of?"

"Everything! I've never been away from my family, I keep getting torn away from you, and..." she sobbed as she put her face against his chest.

He wrapped his arms around her, kissed the top of her head, and tried to console her while letting her cry.

After a few moments, she wiped her face on the hem of her dress. "The worst thing is that I'm afraid of losing you."

"What? Why would you say such a thing? You know I only have eyes for you and that you have my heart. I love you, Olivia. How could you doubt that?"

"I know you do Asa, at least for now."

He put his hands on her shoulders and made her look in his eyes. "What are you going on about? Where is this kind of talk coming from?"

She sighed. "Now you make me feel like I'm being silly and childish again."

"Olivia, if something is bothering you, I would like to know what it is. You can tell me anything."

She looked sheepish. "I just overheard some ladies talking in Henderson's store the other day. I don't suppose they saw me, because I'm so short."

She took his hand and started walking slowly. "Anyway, the two of them were saying how glad they would be for you to be back home, and what a shame it was that Harvey was engaged. The one sounded distressed about the wedding, almost spitting hatred toward Eva, calling her the new school marm, not even using her name."

"Sue and Emma?"

She stopped and turned to him, putting her tiny fists on her hips, attempting to look stern, as her lip quivered and her eyes misted again. "Yes! How did you know? Asa? Did one of them use to be your girl? Were you in love with one of them?"

"Absolutely not," he chuckled as he reached and pulled her to him. "You are the only girl I have ever loved. No one else has ever come close."

"Then why...?"

"Emma and Sue have always lived here. Harvey and I have known them all our lives. We never were especially close, but there weren't very many people around here back then. I guess they kinda set their caps for us and are having trouble moving on with their own lives."

He shrugged. "We can't help we are so good-looking, you know."

She punched him in the stomach. "This is serious, Asa!"

"Alright, alright. They are just annoying, but you don't have anything to worry about. Maybe I can set Sue up with Toby. Sounds like they may suit each other well."

He tipped her face up. "I love you, Olivia, with all my heart. I always will." He embraced her in a passionate kiss.

****

Asa told Olivia goodbye right after lunch at the Upton's. As he and Vince approached the farm, he asked Vince to wait at the house with his pa. "I need to take care of something at the bunkhouse. I won't be long. Then we can be on our way."

Vince nodded, having a good idea what, or who, Asa needed to take care of.

Asa quickly found Toby near the corral. The look on Asa's face as he approached the group of men, must have been enough warning to cause the men to scatter, quickly.

Toby stood with a look of defiance. He was a decent looking young man, strong and stout, but was certainly no match for Asa. Toby stood his full five-foot ten inches, looking straight in Asa's eyes as his six-foot two-inch form towered over him.

"Toby, I'm telling you one last time to stay away from the Upton girls. Even if they weren't spoken for, they are too good for the likes of you."

"Well, spoken for." Toby looked and felt cocky. "Only one of them has a ring on her finger and her man won't even stay around long enough to claim her."

Asa's blood boiled.

"Looks as though no one has a claim on the other two." He shook his head mockingly as he looked down. "It would be such a waste for someone not to take care of them."

Asa's head felt as if it would explode as he punched Toby in the face with all his anger and strength behind it. Toby fell to the ground, but to Asa's surprise, didn't stay down.

He got to his feet, wiped his face on his sleeve, then rammed his body into Asa, full force, with both landing on the ground. Both continued punching each other until the men jumped in and broke it up.

They looked at each other as the men held them back, both winded. Asa had a few scratches and probably would have a few bruises, especially across his knuckles. He could tell he had hurt Toby more than the stubborn man would admit to. There was blood all over his face, streaming from his nose and mouth.

Asa shook himself from the men, pointing to Toby. "Stay away from the Upton girls." He picked up his hat, dusted it off, and walked away.

Vince was sitting on the porch with Abe when Asa rode up. Asa just motioned for him and waved bye to his pa. They rode quietly for a long way before Vince broke the silence.

"What happened to your knuckles, Asa?" he grinned teasingly.

Asa looked down at his hand, stretching and clenching his fingers several times. "I fell."

****

Vince enjoyed his weekend so much, that was all Asa heard about for weeks to come. It was plain to see that his friend had been smitten by Amy. Good thing he was three years younger than Asa, much more suitable for her age.

They were approached by their instructor. "Have either of you given thought to your job prospects after you finish your training?"

Looking at each other, they shrugged before Asa answered. "Not much, sir."

"Have you at least thought of where you will be located? Are you going back to your hometowns and attempt to find employment there? Or are you willing to go elsewhere?"

"Yes sir, I plan to go back home and work close by, if possible." Asa looked at Vince.

"Umm, I don't really have anything or any family to go back to, sir. I had been thinking of perhaps sticking close with Asa, but haven't talked to him about it yet."

"I see. Why don't both of you come by my office this afternoon? It's time to start figuring out a plan for your future employment. We can go over the jobs available in that area and I can start the application process with my recommendations."

"Thank you, sir. We will see you this afternoon."

Asa turned to Vince, mischief dancing in his eyes. "Has Amy gotten to you that much?"

"Well, I am certainly intrigued by her, Asa, but it's not just her. I really think a lot of you, and when I saw how you interacted with your pa and even the workers at the farm, well, I've never been a part of something like that before.

"I was raised in an orphanage and never had a family. This apprenticeship was because I had excelled in my studies. I never had anything to concentrate on except studying and surviving. I didn't even know for sure what family life was like. Now, since I went home with you, it's all I think of."

"Well Vince," Asa slapped him on the back. "Welcome to the family."

****

94

By the time Harvey graduated and got settled back into the arms of the love of his life, it was time to get busy. Through their recent correspondence, he and Eva had settled on building a very small house for now, with plans to add on as needed. Neither wanted to start out their marriage living with someone, although they appreciated his pa offering.

"I understand, Harvey, but I sure was looking forward to having some home-cooked meals for a change." Abe teasingly winked at Eva.

She reached across the table and squeezed his hand. "You will have the best of both worlds, I assure you. We will be just across the meadow with supper waiting for you every night."

He licked his lips. "Can't pass up an offer like that!"

Harvey squeezed Eva's shoulder. "We need to get you home. It's windy and getting colder by the minute. Asa and Vince are waiting for me at your house. Of course, they wouldn't mind how late we get there, as long as they get to stay and visit while waiting."

Satisfied with their decisions about their house, they talked quietly as they rode.

"I will talk to a few men tomorrow about getting our house started. Are you sure about having it so small? I can afford quite a bit more if you just say the word."

"Thank you, Harvey. Money isn't the issue. I'm tired of waiting; time is the issue."

He smiled at her lovingly. "I understand and feel the same. But I'm thinking we could at least make the rooms bigger so we can have our families over and not be cramped."

She thought for a moment. "That would be nice, but not necessary. Why don't you discuss it with the builders? If it's going to take one day more, then I say no."

He looked at her. "You're really serious about this, aren't you?"

"I'm serious about being your wife, Mr. Darnell. I feel as if I will die if we have to wait any longer."

"Well, I certainly don't want that to happen! Let me see what I can do."

Chapter 8

Pulling his collar snug to his neck, Asa rode closer to Harvey. "I hate to bring this up, with you just getting home and all, but has Eva told you anything about Toby?"

"No," he glanced at his brother. "What's to tell?" Asa's tone had already put Harvey in defensive mode.

Asa told Harvey everything he knew. "But I have a feeling something is being planned by him, Sue, and Emma. The three of them have been seen together a lot and I'm sure he isn't courting both."

"What are you thinking, Asa?"

"I'm thinking we need to stick together and watch our backs. Never be alone and that goes for the girls too. I already spoke to Olivia and Amy. Mrs. Upton said she is praying about the situation."

****

The next week, the ladies of the town were meeting to get Christmas baskets done for the needy in the community. Mrs. Farley, although bossy, excelled at organizing people and events.

When the ladies started dispersing, Mrs. Upton and Mrs. Farley were able to sit and visit for a few minutes over a cup of coffee. Since Mrs. Farley was so strict on matters of propriety and had brought several things to the preacher's attention, the conversation eased toward Mrs. Upton's suspicions of Toby, Sue, and Emma.

Mrs. Farley listened intently, taking in every word. This was just the kind of thing she lived for; someone needing her help and with something she passionate about. She promised to discreetly keep the matter under a watchful eye, as she patted Mrs. Upton's hand. "Don't you fret about your girls, dear. They are good girls and I will help any way I can."

****

Harvey was leaving the livery around dusk, heading to the Upton's for supper. Turning the corner, he thought he heard someone crying, and soon found the source.

"Emma? What happened? Are you alright?" He approached slowly, cautiously, suspiciously, seeing her sitting on the ground, crying as she rubbed her ankle. Her dress was smudged with dirt and ripped in a few places. He looked around to see who may be close. This was exactly what he and Asa had been cautious about.

"Oh, Harvey. I need help. Please help me. I have hurt myself."

He reached his hand to help her to her feet.

"Oww!" she screeched as she began to put weight on her foot, sinking back to the ground quickly.

"Let me go get help," he suggested.

"No, please just help me on my horse and I will be on my way. Pa can help me when I get home and Ma can doctor me."

Harvey looked around, thinking that was a simple enough request. "How did this happen and where is Sue? She's always with you."

He continued looking around for her horse as she explained. "Sue and I had been shopping at Henderson's. We had just said goodnight and we left each other. I guess I was walking too close to the ravine and I slipped and fell. I've spent the last twenty minutes or so dragging myself back up."

"Emma, I don't see your horse anywhere."

"Dern thing probably headed for home without me." She started whimpering again. "Harvey, could you just take me home?"

"Uh, no, I can't, but I will find some help for you."

"Harvey! I can't believe you won't help me!"

Toby and Sue were watching from the other side of the road, behind the brush. They had planned to get the sheriff after Harvey put Emma on his horse, but now they had to hurry and change the plan. Their hope was for them to lead the sheriff to them after Harvey had supposedly gotten rough with her, with Emma swearing to it.

Toby whispered to Sue. "Go get the sheriff quickly. Tell him someone sounds like they are being attacked. Hurry before Harvey leaves for help!"

"Emma, I would like to help you, but I don't know how, so let me get someone that does."

"No, no! Don't leave me. I'm hurting so bad, I feel as if I will faint."

"Well then, I really need to get you some help. I will be back soon."

He turned to leave while she continued to whimper loudly, suddenly yelling for help. He turned to her in shock, knowing he had fallen into her plan, just as the sheriff and Sue came around the side of the building.

"What's going on here?" the sheriff demanded.

"Sheriff! Oh, thank goodness you've come! I've been attacked!"

"Harvey," the sheriff greeted. "Go on and eat your supper but stop by my office on the way home. Let me see if I can get to the bottom of this."

Harvey stood in confusion with his mouth gaping open. "Umm, yes sir. I will see you in a bit."

He shook his head as he passed Sue, hearing Emma beginning to protest loudly. "He attacked me and you're going to let him go?"

Harvey walked quickly to the Upton's.

An hour later, as everyone sat in the parlor, Mr. Farley knocked on the door asking to speak with Harvey in private.

"That was a close one, my boy." He slapped Harvey on the back. "Mrs. Upton had told my Agnes about Asa's suspicions. I happened to mention it to the sheriff so he could keep an eye on the situation.

"I just left the sheriff and he said you could go on home. Apparently, when he told Emma he could arrest her for filing a false report, she decided it wasn't worth her time and effort."

Harvey blew out a sigh of relief. "For once, I am thankful for gossip." He laughed and shook Mr. Farley's hand. "Thank you, sir."

"Well, son, I wouldn't call this one gossip. Mrs. Upton was very prayerful about this situation. Perhaps the Lord was leading the conversation she had with my Agnes. And then, of course, a man and wife can share anything. I'm hoping that my Agnes will see this as an opportunity to let God lead her more often, instead of taking matters into her own hands."

"Yes sir, thank you sir, and please tell Mrs. Farley how grateful I am."

The next day, Abe gave Harvey permission to fire Toby. Maybe things would get easier now.

****

Toby wasn't to be distracted from the pretty Upton girls. He got a job in town where he could make himself readily available for them, catching glimpses of them as they walked through the town.

He acquired a job at the small printing press, that had a big front window, with his machine sitting right in front of it. Every time he saw them, especially Eva, he would tell his boss he was going in search of new business to print for. News, bulletins, menus, any kind of print job he could scrounge up would be acceptable to his boss.

The printing press was also the office for the telegraph. He loved being the first to know any news coming across the wire, making himself feel more important.

Harvey, Asa, Abe, Preacher Upton, Mr. Henderson, the sheriff, and Mr. Farley had all talked to him about leaving the girls alone, some even came close to threatening. He always stood by his innocence, saying that it was just a coincidence that he ran into them.

Asa's temper was about to boil. "Yes, and one of these days my fist is going to coincidentally collide with your face again!"

Harvey pulled him back. "That's enough Asa. He's been warned."

When it came to tempers, although it took a lot to get the Darnell men riled, Asa had the shortest fuse. Harvey could get plenty riled if necessary, but he was very calm and quiet all the way up to the explosion.

****

Spring had finally arrived, with the meadows full of wildflowers and the fields full of workers. The Uptons and Darnells were filled with excitement, looking forward to the wedding.

Harvey hadn't allowed Eva near their house ever since the walls and floors started being built. "It's a wedding surprise for you."

She would always jump up and down in excitement when he would tell her of the progress. He loved seeing her excited. Then she would throw herself around his neck; he loved that too.

Asa was impatiently waiting for Olivia to come home. She had received permission to leave school for her sister's wedding and would be arriving three days ahead of time.

Meanwhile, Vince had spoken with the Upton's about courting Amy. He didn't waste time asking just to visit her, he wanted to get serious and have what he saw Harvey and Asa had.

He was mesmerized by everything she said or did. When he looked into her eyes, saw her smile, or heard her voice, his heart would flip. There was nothing he wouldn't give or do for her.

With this being Amy's last year of school, she knew her parents would soon be talking to her about going to teacher's college. She and Vince had already discussed it.

Even though he left it totally up to her, he made sure she knew that he had a great job, made good money, and would like for her to stay at home, letting him provide for her every want and need. Anytime he said things like that, she would melt in his arms. He made sure to remind her often.

Asa and Vince had started jobs at the refinery seven miles away, in January. Both were saving almost every penny they earned for something very special. The two of them had recently made an overnight trip to Raleigh, knowing they could find exactly what they were looking for in a big city like that.

****

The day of the wedding was warm and sunny. The entire community was excited, planning a huge reception and dance afterward. The preacher had invited the congregation,

Abe had invited all his workers, Harvey and Eva invited the rest of the community.

That morning, Eva rushed to the church, which also housed the school, to make sure all her papers were in the cabinet, and orderly, for her ma to teach in her place for the next week.

The church was decorated for her wedding, and she took a moment to look around and soak it all in. "My wedding," she whispered. "Today I will become Mrs. Harvey Darnell, marrying the best man in the world!"

She heard someone enter and turned to look.

Toby stood there smiling. "That's what I came to talk to you about, Eva. I could love you better than Harvey can even imagine. I just wanted to give you one last chance to ditch him and marry me."

At first, she was shocked and intimidated. Then she got mad. Her face turned red, and instead of running from him as she had before, when he started walking toward her, she walked toward him.

"How dare you!" she spat as she slowly reached into her pocket. "I am sick of you following along behind me and my sisters. How dare you come to me on the most wonderful day of my life and try to ruin it with foolishness and childish dreams filled with lies! I will give you one chance to walk out that door and never speak to me again. Now leave!"

"Or what?" he laughed. "Exactly what do you think you can do to a big, strong man like me? I am here to protect you because you can't protect yourself."

She straightened and bristled even more. "Oh really?" Quickly she pulled a sock half full of rocks from her pocket, smashing the side of his face with it.

The first blow knocked him silly. The second blow knocked him down. She was just raising her arm to hit him again when Olivia walked in.

"Eva! Stop!" she screamed when she saw blood running from Toby's nose and mouth. "Leave him be. We have to get you ready."

She bent close to Toby. "I suggest you get out of here. Consider this your lucky day because it looked like she was really going to kill you."

She took Eva's hand and started leading her out when Eva stopped long enough to kick Toby right in the face. "Now I feel better! This is going to be a wonderful day! Come, Olivia, I am ready to become Mrs. Harvey Darnell."

The girls couldn't believe how calm Eva was. She felt proud of herself and was sure thankful that their ma had suggested they always keep a sock full of pennies or rocks in their pocket for protection.

They secretly told Amy about what had happened and asked her to check the floor of the church for blood. She happily agreed and headed over to the church with a bucket of soapy water and a scrub brush. She laughed to herself when she saw the puddle Toby had left behind, along with a trail. "Good for you, Eva!" she exclaimed to herself.

****

A few hours later, Abe, Asa, and Vince sat on the front pew, heckling Harvey as he wrung his hands and paced. People started arriving, congratulating the groom before finding their seats.

Preacher Upton arrived with his wife, helping her get situated on the opposite front pew, before going to speak with Harvey.

He put his arm around Harvey's shoulder. "I'm so proud to be giving my daughter to such a fine man. You take good care of my girl." He finished speaking with a tremor in his voice.

"I will, sir. I will always put her before myself."

The preacher swiped at his eyes. "I know you will, son. Are you ready? I have an anxious young lady waiting on the other side of that door."

"Yes sir," Harvey gulped.

"Take your places then." He motioned for the pianist to start playing, then hurried down the aisle and out the door.

Amy appeared, looking absolutely stunning, which took Vince's breath away. He couldn't tear his eyes from her.

Next, Olivia made her way up the aisle, keeping her eyes fixed on Asa. My, her heart ached for this man. He felt the same as he swallowed past the lump in his throat. He wished with all his heart this was their day, their wedding. *"Soon,"* he thought. *"Real soon, I hope."*

The doors swung open as everyone stood and turned to watch the bride walk up the aisle on her pa's arm.

Harvey felt faint when he first took in her beauty, then his emotions changed from thankful to blessed, proud to humbled. "She loves me, Lord, and only me. How did you ever think to bless me with such a wonderful, beautiful woman? But I thank you, Lord, and I will thank you every day for the rest of my life." Harvey finished his silent prayer, with tears in his eyes as the preacher put Eva's tiny hand in his giant one.

They gazed into each other's eyes as they repeated their vows, promising to love each other and care for each other, as long as they lived.

When the preacher pronounced them husband and wife, Harvey kissed her gently, caressing her face and whispering, "I love you, Eva Darnell."

She quickly put her arms around his neck, pulling him into another kiss. "I love you, Harvey, and I always will."

He picked her up in front of everyone, twirled around with her, then instead of setting her back down, he walked out of the church, carrying her in his arms as she clung to his neck with her head on his shoulder.

There were laughs, gasps, clapping hands, and general merriment all around as they walked out of the church, Asa following Harvey with Olivia on his arm, then Vince with Amy on his. This was truly one wonderful day.

The afternoon wore on pleasantly with the couple being swarmed with well wishes and gifts. Mrs. Farley was even more pleasant than usual. She was caught up in nostalgia, remembering her own wedding.

Approaching Eva, she hugged her warmly. "Eva, my dear girl. I am so proud of you and so happy for you. What a beautiful young woman you are, and such a lady. What a good example you are for the young ladies of this community."

"Thank you, Mrs. Farley. It really humbles me that you would say such."

"It's true, dear." She touched Eva's face. "Every word is truth."

She turned to Harvey. "And you are quite an exceptional young man. I'm sure you will take good care of this special young woman of yours."

"Yes ma'am," he looked at Eva as he beamed. "I look forward to spending the rest of my life with her, taking care of her every need."

The music began and the bride and groom started the first dance, inviting the wedding party to join them. The rest of the guests soon joined, filling the atmosphere with lively chatter. After a big meal that was brought by all and shared with all, the bride disappeared into the house to change from her gown, with the help of Olivia and Amy.

Soon afterward, Harvey and Eva stepped into their decorated buggy. Harvey held on to Eva as she stood to throw her bouquet over her shoulder.

Although the sisters were wishing for Olivia to catch it, instead, a girl that was fairly new to the community did. Olivia didn't care, she knew it wouldn't be much longer.

In just a short while, Harvey pulled the buggy up to their house, making Eva promise to keep her eyes closed until he said to open them. He tied the horse, knowing Asa or his pa would come by later and take care of it. Then he reached for Eva and set her on the ground.

He stood beside her, watching her face as he told her to open her eyes. He wasn't disappointed.

She gasped, with her hand flying to her gaping mouth. "Oh, Harvey! This is wonderful! The house is much bigger than I had anticipated. So charming and inviting! When…? Who…?"

She couldn't even form her questions for being so overwhelmed. Tears came to her eyes as she hugged him tight then looked back at the house, noticing shutters, porch furniture and a swing, curtains fluttering in the windows, and a beautiful, ornate wrought iron door from Asa and Vince.

"I got the stove you saw in that catalog, along with a few other surprises, Mrs. Darnell." He put her hand around his arm and walked her up the cobblestone walkway.

Approaching the door, he took her in his arms and kissed her passionately, then picked her up in his arms and carried her in their house, their home.

Chapter 9

Asa and Olivia danced a bit more before escaping the crowd. He led her across the street into the park, where they walked quietly, hand in hand, down to the pond.

"One day, soon I hope, it will be our turn." Asa stopped and pulled her close. "It may sound a bit selfish, but that's all I could think of during the wedding. I could almost imagine it being us. That is what you want, isn't it, Olivia?"

"You know it is, Asa. I love you with all my heart. I always will. I can't wait to be your wife, with you coming home to me every evening."

"Never being separated again," he turned sad for a moment. "Tomorrow when you head back to school, it will be the last time we have to say goodbye like that."

She nodded against his chest. "I do so look forward to graduation day. Then I feel like I can come home and start building a future."

"With me, I hope." Asa teased.

"Well," she nudged him as she pulled back and took his hand, beginning to stroll again. "I suppose so, but of course, I haven't exactly heard you be specific."

"Hmm, just how specific do I have to be? I already gave you my heart, told you that I will love you the rest of my life, what more do I have to do?"

She looked momentarily disappointed.

"I even know how many days until your graduation. That's how specific I'm being. Forty-one days until I can hold you in my arms every day, for at least a moment."

"I'm impressed! You actually know how many days until graduation?"

"Sure I do. That has to count for something."

"It's alright, Asa. You will figure it out. You will know when we can get serious about planning our future." She smiled and squeezed his arm.

He led her over to the bench she had sat on at their first social. "Remember sitting here with Eva beside you, Harvey and me sitting right in front of you?"

"Of course," she nodded. "I knew there was something special about you that very night.

He motioned for her to sit. "Yes, sweetheart, I did too. I fell in love with you right then and there."

He bent down on one knee and opened a ring box. Olivia's eyes went wide. "Will you marry me, Olivia? I will cherish you for the rest of my life, giving you everything I have to give, loving you until my dying breath."

"Oh! Asa! Yes, I will marry you. I love you with my entire being. I can't wait to be the kind of wife you deserve. You are the most wonderful, compassionate, kind man I know. I feel blessed and honored that you would want me for your wife."

He slipped the ring on her finger. She wrapped herself around his neck and kissed him until she felt her insides tingle. She wanted this man badly, and soon.

Asa felt like melting one moment and shouting the next. This tiny woman would be his to love freely for the rest of his life and he knew it would be wonderful.

She gazed at her ring. "It's beautiful, Asa. It looks somewhat like Eva's except with a pearl."

"The salesman and Harvey told us all about the latest trends and what you girls would like best, we hoped."

"It's beautiful. I love it! Does Pa know?"

"Of course. I know a bit about etiquette and propriety."

"Wait, a minute. You said the salesman and Harvey told 'us' about it. Who is 'us'?"

"Ahh, that was just a slip of the tongue."

"Asa? What are you not telling me?"

He looked sheepish. "Don't you tell a soul, but Vince has a ring for Amy. He's going to hold on to it for a while though. They've only known each other since August and have only been seeing each other since December."

"Sometimes it doesn't take so long. You know as well as I, Eva and Harvey, you and I, probably wouldn't have waited this long had it not been for each of us going to school."

"Very true. I wish them the best."

****

Harvey and Eva weren't seen for a week. Harvey had enlisted the help of Mrs. Upton, Olivia, and Amy, prior to the wedding, to help get the house ready and the kitchen stocked. He was so glad he had. They spent every moment together, exploring their house and each other, planning out their future.

On Saturday morning, they went to town and invited her family to supper that evening along with Abe, Asa, and Vince.

The house was plenty big enough for all of them, along with a huge table that would seat ten. Harvey had expanded the house plans to include a big kitchen that would hold a nice size table with six chairs, a big dining room next to that with the big table, a China hutch, and a buffet table.

The parlor was a nice size but sparsely furnished. Harvey wanted Eva to pick out some of her own furnishings. There was only one bedroom, which was all they needed for now. It was a nice big room, with a dresser, chest of drawers, a vanity, a cedar chest at the foot of the big bed, and an armoire. Two small tables were on each side of the bed holding beautiful lamps.

There was another small room next to the bedroom with a hall between. "This, he explained is for everything we need after we expand, but don't need right now. Or it can be used as a baby's room."

Eva blushed. "I like the thought of that. Let's try not to clutter it with anything but a baby."

His smile broadened and he pulled her close, distracted by her once again, momentarily.

He had a pantry built off from the kitchen, a nice porch on the back and front, and a root cellar under the pantry floor, with a second access to the back yard.

That night, they had everybody looking all over their house, exclaiming how nice it was. They were so proud.

Two days later, Eva had to leave her beautiful house and loving husband to start back teaching. They pulled away from each other reluctantly.

****

Olivia's graduation was a glorious affair. The entire crowd was there to cheer her on. When she stepped off the platform, she ran to Asa's waiting arms, taking the bouquet of flowers from him quickly before wrapping herself around his neck.

"You did it, sweetheart," he whispered against her hair. "I'm so very proud of you."

"Thank you, Asa." She pulled back from him and grinned. "Now let's go get married!"

"W...what?" Asa stammered, completely caught off guard. "Umm, well, I, umm..."

Olivia cackled out laughing. "I'm teasing you, but now we can at least set a date and talk about it?"

Asa blew out a breath as he joined her laughter. "Don't misunderstand, I would marry you this minute if I thought that was what you really wanted. We may have to live in the barn for now, but I would do it."

Mrs. Upton joined them as the others started to surround Olivia with congratulations being said. "Yes, dear, I think we can come up with a much better plan than living in a barn."

"I know, Ma. I was just teasing. But," she turned very serious, "I am ready to start making plans."

****

Life started settling back into a normal routine. School was out for the summer, with Eva returning to work on the farm, alongside her sisters. Amy had finished school and was delighted to have both of her sisters with her every day, like it used to be.

"I've missed you both, more than I thought was possible," she admitted. She looked down shyly. "I need to talk to you both and get advice on relationships.

"I'm not sure I could be away from Vince for months at a time, and I've already talked to him about not wanting to go to college. He's in agreement with whatever I decide on, but the time is drawing near. Every night at supper, I hold my breath, knowing this may be the night Ma and Pa talk to me about going."

She stopped working, standing straight to stretch her back. Her sisters did the same, noticing there were tears in her eyes.

"I know I love Vince enough and I'm sure he feels the same. It's just the thought of leaving that literally makes my chest hurt."

"Oh sweetie, it's the hardest thing I've ever had to do." Eva reached out and touched her arm. "Of course, I'm glad now that I did it, and have it behind me, but I'm not sure I would be able to do it again."

Olivia agreed with a nod.

"I don't want to hurt our parents, but I just don't want to go. I've made a few mentions of it to Ma, so I'm sure she knows, but I'm not sure that I could actually bring myself to go against their wishes."

"Have you prayed about it? Have you prayed together with Vince about it?" Olivia wiped her forehead as she squinted against the sun.

Amy shook her head slowly. "No, in fact, Vince and I don't talk very much about God. He grew up in that orphanage, not experiencing things like love and compassion, and seems to think that God has dealt him a bad hand in life, until now."

"Oh, sweetie! That's not good." Eva put down her hoe and stepped up to Amy, putting her arm around her shoulder. "You know you can't marry someone that isn't a Christian. Life is already hard enough. You would be setting yourself up for more trouble that you wouldn't be able to pray together about. The Bible says we aren't to be unequally yoked."

Olivia joined in the hug. "But this is something you must pray about. You can't force him into it."

Amy nodded silently as tears ran down her face. Wiping her face with the hem of her dress, she agreed. "I know, and I am praying. Now that you know, you can help me pray."

****

The Uptons were used to having Asa and Vince at their supper table, but on this night, they had invited Harvey and Eva also. After a delicious meal and good conversation, Preacher Upton stood, motioning for everyone else to stay seated.

"I usually save these kinds of conversations for my family only, but since you all seem to be a part of the family, I will make all of you listen." He smiled playfully, taking in the looks on each face.

He blew out a breath and became serious. "After weeks of fervent prayer, I feel that the Lord is leading us elsewhere."

There were gasps from all around the table as the girls began to get teary eyed.

He took his wife's hand. "We will be starting a new church farther west, but we won't be leaving until early spring."

"But, Pa! We can't just leave!" Amy was almost hysterical. "I mean, we have our lives here. Eva and Olivia will be staying here. I can't bear the thought of leaving them. And I have Vince. I can't leave him either. I can't bear the thought of not having my whole family here, together! Please reconsider, I beg you!" By the time she finished, she was in a full frenzy of tears.

Mrs. Upton went to Amy, putting her arm around her. "Darling, please don't get so upset."

"Baby girl," Preacher Upton said sadly. "I'm sorry if this hurts you, but the Lord has already made the path very clear for me. I have to obey Him and so do you."

Vince sat in silent dismay. *"How can this be happening?"* he thought. He couldn't believe that once again, God was turning His back on him, taking yet another person from him that he truly loved. He wanted to strike out, scream, hit something, but he certainly couldn't strike out at Amy's parents, knowing how much she loved them, even though he felt as if they had just stabbed him right through the heart.

He slid his chair back, stood quietly, leaving the room. They heard the front screen slam as he left.

"Vince!" Amy screamed. "Please don't leave me! Vince, please!" She doubled over in fits of agony.

Her sisters went to her as Harvey and Asa went out the door to find Vince. They didn't have to go far. He sat on the porch steps slumped over with tears streaming down his face.

They sat on either side of him, not knowing what to say.

"Looks like this wonderful God of yours is taking the love of my life away from me, again." He sniffled and wiped his face with his sleeve. "First, my parents, now Amy. I guess I should just get used to it. I am on the outside, looking in, as always."

"Vince," Harvey consoled. "Instead of blaming God, why don't you cry out to Him for help? He is all-knowing. He has a plan for each of us, even though we don't understand the way He works sometimes. If it's His will for you and Amy to be together, no one or no circumstance can stand in the way, if you both stay in His will."

"His plan, His way, His will," Vince raised his voice a bit as he stood. He threw his hands up in exasperation, walking down the steps before turning back to them. "I don't understand how a God, who is supposed to be so loving and caring, can put people through such heartache. Please enlighten me. My Amy is so sweet, good, and innocent, yet she's in there crying her eyes out about something she has no control over. My heart has been ripped from my chest. Please tell me why."

Asa stood, walking towards him. "It may be just what Harvey said. Maybe God is trying to put you in a situation where you have to ask help from someone much bigger than yourself. He uses situations to show people their need for Him, but He gives all of us free will to choose for ourselves.

"I admit, I have been concerned about you not being a believer for a long time now. I have tried a few times to talk to you, and you even asked a few questions recently, about keeping yourself out of hell. I've prayed about it a lot. I have specifically asked for God to show you your need for salvation. I want you to go to Heaven one day, but I am also concerned about your and Amy's future together. God doesn't smile on a believer and a non-believer being united"

"Wait!" Vince shook his head. "I'm not understanding all of this. I have been very concerned lately about going to hell.

I have been listening closely as the preacher preaches and have started understanding what he says. The last few weeks I have had several fitful dreams about dying and falling into that dark pit of flames, full of torments."

He got quiet for a moment. "I wanted to talk to you about it, Asa, but this week, it just seems like everything got in the way of us having a serious conversation. So, I thought about talking to the preacher one evening while Amy and Mrs. Upton were busy in the kitchen.

"But now, everyone will believe it's just because of Amy, that it isn't for real. I can't do it now, not after this."

He turned to leave when Mr. Upton stepped out on the porch. "It doesn't matter who believes you, Vince, as long as God knows your heart."

Vince turned back towards the house.

"I'm truly sorry about upsetting everyone tonight. I'm afraid I wasn't allowed to tell the entire story. But if that's what it took to bring you to your senses about your need for God now, instead of putting it off, then it was worth it." He motioned for Vince to come back and have a seat on the porch. "Let's have that talk, Vince. Let's get serious about God, then see if everything else will fall into place through praying for His will to be done in all of our lives."

Harvey and Asa sat quietly and prayed as Preacher Upton and Vince talked.

"Do you believe you are a sinner?"

"Oh, yes sir. I mean, I'm a good person but yes, I have sinned."

"The Bible says:

Romans 3:10 – As it is written, There is none righteous, no, not one.
Romans 3:23 – For all have sinned, and come short of the glory of God.

"Do you know where sin came from and why everyone is a sinner?"

"Not exactly, sir."

"Well, God made a perfect world for Adam and Eve. He intended for it to stay perfect, but He gave them free will because He wanted them to choose to love Him, not force them.

"Then Satan came along and tempted Eve, deceived her into thinking that she could be as smart as God and that He wouldn't hold it against her. He had her eat the fruit of the tree that God had forbidden them to eat of. God had given them everything, except that one tree. She was overcome by temptation. Adam, on the other hand, wasn't deceived by Satan. Even though God had told them that if they ate of that tree, they would surely die, he willfully disobeyed.

"As soon as they did, they realized the world was no longer perfect and tried to hide from God. They were suddenly sinners and had lost that sweet fellowship with God, instead, they were fearful of Him.

"When God confronted them, he pronounced his sentence, even though He still loved them, just as parents love their children.."

Romans 5:12 – Wherefore, as by one man sin entered into the world, and death by sin; and so death passed upon all men, for that all have sinned.

"Though death didn't come immediately to them, from that day they started to have all the sickness, hurt, and began to age and eventually die. The sentence was passed to all mankind.

"But God had a plan of escape, of forgiveness, if they chose to take it, just as he still has for every one of us today.

Romans 6:23 – For the wages of sin is death: but the gift of God is eternal life through Jesus Christ our Lord.
Romans 5:8 – But God commendeth His love toward us, in that, while we were yet sinners, Christ died for us.

"No sin can enter Heaven. God cannot look on sin, so there had to be an ultimate sacrifice to cleanse away sin. God sent His only, perfect son, and allowed Him to be the sacrifice for all of our sins. He died a cruel death to allow our sins to be forgiven, washed away from the Father's sight by his shed blood because He loved us so much and didn't want any of us to go to hell.

"All we have to do is believe it and accept this free gift from God. We have to sincerely ask Him to forgive us from our sins and come into our heart."

Romans 10:13 – For whosoever shall call upon the name of the Lord shall be saved.

"Do you understand, son?"

"Yes sir, I believe I do."

"Would you like to receive God's free gift of salvation and never again have to worry about going to hell?"

"Oh, yes sir. Would you help me pray?"

"I would be honored to." Preacher Upton kept his arm around Vince's shoulder as the young man poured his heart out to God, asking for forgiveness for his sins, to come into his heart and save him from a sinner's hell.

When they finished praying, the preacher patted him on the back. "One last thing, Vince. Now that you are a Christian, you need to try to live your best life for Him by being an example to other sinners, leading them to the saving knowledge of the Lord Jesus Christ."

Romans 10:9-11 – That if thou shalt confess with thy mouth the Lord Jesus, and shalt believe in thine heart that God hath raised Him from the dead, thou shalt be saved. For with the heart man believeth unto righteousness; and with the mouth confession is made unto salvation. For the scripture saith, Whosoever believeth on Him shall not be ashamed.

A moment later, the door flew open and Amy ran to Vince, hugging his neck while tears continued to run down her face.

As he hugged her, he asked, "You heard?"

"Yes. We were right inside the door praying for you. Eva was stepping out to find Harvey when she heard, then came to get the rest of us to pray quietly. Oh, Vince, I am so happy!"

They smiled at each other for a moment, then reality came back into focus. Vince looked at the preacher while still having his arm around Amy.

"Sir, I respectfully ask that you not take my Amy away from me. It breaks my heart to think of her leaving."

The preacher motioned toward the house. "If everyone would come back in, we have a few things to chat about."

They all congratulated Vince on becoming a Christian as they gathered around the table once more, in much better spirits than when they had left. Mrs. Upton and her girls made quick work of pouring coffee and setting out dessert.

Finally, the preacher spoke. "Amy, my darling, baby girl. The last thing I ever want to do is cause you distress. You are still too young to be making your own decisions, even though you have proven to be responsible and mature for your age.

"You created a bit of a problem by letting your ma know that you don't want to attend college. That would have given us an extra nine months to try to decide on the path we felt you should take and would have brought you within six months of your eighteenth birthday. But as it is now, you are finished school and only sixteen.

"Your ma and I have discussed some options about your future and are praying about it. I suggest you and Vince, and everyone at this table do the same.

"As I said, I don't ever want to cause you distress. I am trying to be mindful of your feelings and do what is best for you. Just trust God to lead us all in the right direction. Fair enough, for now?"

****

The Darnells had a big July 4th celebration planned. They included the entire community, and it was greatly anticipated by all. There would be games and events starting at three, supper at six, then dancing and socializing until dark when they ended the evening with a firework display.

Abe and Harvey threw in with the other men at the farm and ranch in preparation for the event.

Harvey was absolutely worn out by the time he headed towards his house. He had done all his regular work and then helped with the extras for the celebration.

He saw a man riding away from his house as he entered the clearing. He was going the opposite direction, but Harvey was sure it was Toby. Suddenly he was filled with two emotions; rage toward Toby and concern for Eva. He kicked his horse into a run, jumped off as he got to their yard, rushing into the house.

As he pushed the door open, he immediately put his hands in the air, yelling, "Don't shoot! It's me!"

Eva was standing a few feet from the door with the shotgun in her hands. She went limp as she lowered the gun, "Oh Harvey! I thought you were Toby coming back!"

He took the gun from her and wrapped her in his arms. "Tell me what happened, Eva. I will see to it he doesn't bother you again."

"When I heard someone come up in the yard, I thought it was you. I heard footsteps on the porch by the time I reached the door, but when I opened it, expecting to see you there, it was him.

"I asked what he was doing here and started closing the door. He held it open and said I was being rude. I told him that was the last thing he needed to worry about if you came home and saw him here."

She paused and fought back tears. "He said that if you saw him leaving the house, you would think I had been unfaithful and cast me aside.

"Then he said he had only come to check and see if you were being as good to me as he would have been, and that if I reconsidered, he would be waiting for me."

She looked up at Harvey as he still held her close. "Harvey, I swear to you, I have never given him any reason to think I would have anything to do with him. I despise him and told him so, right before I slammed the door on him."

Harvey rubbed her back. "I believe you, sweetheart. Don't you worry about any of it."

He kissed her and wiped her tears away. "Come on with me. I don't dare leave you here alone."

She nodded without asking any questions.

Moments later, they pulled up in front of the sheriff's office. He had her tell the sheriff what had happened and asked what could be done.

"Well, Harvey, not much, I'm afraid. Once again, he didn't actually do anything illegal, except for trespass, but your farm is pretty well open to everyone. He didn't make threats, didn't destroy property, or anything."

122

"Sheriff, if something isn't done, I will be the one behind bars in your jail. We fired the man and told him not to come back, so isn't that trespassing?"

"Yes, I suppose it is. It will look petty on the record books, but it may be a deterrent for him to come back out there again. The best I can do is lock him up for seventy-two hours and make him pay a fine. If he gets a lawyer, which is highly unlikely seeing we don't have one close by, he will probably go free."

"Alright, do it, before I take matters into my own hands."

Toby was arrested an hour later, at the diner while flirting with another young lady. He was still sitting in jail during the July 4th celebration.

Chapter 10

Amidst the pie eating contest, the three-legged race, and all the other activities, the word was circulating that Asa and Olivia had set a date for their wedding; Sunday, December 14th.

Mr. and Mrs. Farley congratulated the young couple, then Mrs. Farley prodded her husband to tell them some more news.

A wide grin passed over his face. "Miss Olivia, it seems that if all the children are enrolled as their parents promised, there will be a need for an additional schoolteacher. I was given the honor to ask if you would be interested."

Olivia gasped, jumped up and down, and clapped her hands. She grabbed Mr. Farley and hugged him, then went on to Mrs. Farley, landing back in Asa's arms.

"Oh yes! I would love that!"

"Come by Henderson's and fill out your application, then the job will be yours, mind you, if enough students actually enroll."

"I understand, sir. Thank you so much!"

Asa held her tight. "Congratulations, sweetheart. I'm so proud of you. And your ma will be here to fill in while we get used to married life." He wiggled his eyebrows at her.

She blushed, quickly changing the subject. "I need to tell Eva. Do you see her anywhere?"

Asa led her in the right direction, being able to see over most people, especially when it came to searching for Harvey.

The girls clung to each other excitedly, starting to make lesson plans.

"Umm, ladies," Harvey teased. "Can we perhaps save that for later? We don't want to upset the children by making them think of school."

****

Asa and Olivia sat down with Abe one evening after taking him to the diner for supper. "Pa, we need to get started on a house, and I would like to build here at the farm if you don't mind."

"Son, I don't mind at all, but there is no need for you to go through the expense and aggravation of building.

"Just hear me out before you say anything. I don't need this house and I intend to move to a smaller place. I want you and Olivia to move in here. I know it's not much, but it is home. You can add on to it and change it as you see fit, but I just don't need this much room."

"That is quite an offer, but I can't kick you out of your own house. What would you do?"

"I'm not here other than to sleep. I can do that anywhere. Eva has me over for supper almost every night, and I eat breakfast and lunch at the bunkhouse.

"I was thinking that I could build a place about like the bunkhouse for myself, between here and Harvey's house, and in the future when I am dead and gone, you could use it as a smokehouse or cold storage."

"Have you talked to Harvey about it? I don't want to explain that I'm putting you out."

"Yes, I have. He wasn't too keen on it at first but couldn't give any good enough reason for me not to."

Asa looked at Olivia. She didn't give an indication either way, just shrugged.

"The house isn't much, that's why I said you could do what you wanted to change it. Just two bedrooms, an upstairs

126

loft, a nice sized kitchen, and parlor. I only need one room and a heat stove. You've seen the bunkhouses. That would be plenty for me."

"Thanks, Pa, but if you could give us time to discuss it?"

"Sure thing, son. Wouldn't have it any other way."

* *

"Asa, if I had known we wouldn't have to build a house, I could have planned the wedding sooner."

"So, does this mean you would be agreeable to moving in there?"

"Yes, I certainly would, if we could at least be responsible for building a place for your pa. If you think he is serious...he seemed serious to me."

"If he's already talked to Harvey about it, then I think he's really thought it through. So? Think we've found a house?"

She squeezed his arm and nodded.

* *

July was hot, and August hotter yet. There was no rain for weeks at a time. If not for Harvey's irrigation system flowing from the river and creek, the crops would have been burnt to a crisp.

Abe wanted all the women and children out of the fields as early as possible every afternoon. Several of them had been reporting heat stroke symptoms; nausea, dizziness, and fatigue.

One day near noon, Eva complained of not feeling so well right before she fell to the ground. She held her head and began to be sick. "My head hurts and I'm so dizzy."

Amy ran to the water barrel and wet her kerchief, bringing it back to bathe Eva's face with the cool, wet cloth.

"Thank you, Amy. I feel some better now." As she began to stand, another wave of nausea and dizziness hit her.

Olivia instructed Amy to get Eva's horse. "We've got to get her home. It was about time to quit for the day anyway."

Abe came up about then, helping to get Eva home. "I've had several women like this. We're going to cut the hours back a little more until the heat passes."

Olivia and Amy stayed with Eva until Harvey got home. She had gotten sick several times. They took over with fixing supper, ordering her to stay in bed or on the couch, continuously bringing her more cool water to drink and bathe her face and neck. She finally gave in to them, feeling weak as a kitten.

Harvey fussed over her the rest of the evening, not letting her lift a finger. He sat down on the couch, holding her in his arms while she rested against him.

"Feeling better?"

"Much, thank you. All I needed was to cool down. I will be just fine now. I will be sure to get out of the field before it gets hot tomorrow, and from now on."

"Umm, I think you should stay home tomorrow. I've been hearing about some people getting seriously ill with heatstroke."

"Harvey, I promise you, I am fine."

"Eva, you don't need to push yourself. In fact, you don't even have to work."

She sat up and looked at him sternly. "Harvey Darnell, I promised to work beside you and that's what I intend to do. I refuse to back down from my word after only four months."

"Eva, I promised to take care of you, and especially when you are sick, I intend to do so. Otherwise, I wouldn't be keeping my word."

She squinted her eyes, "Are you forbidding me to go to work tomorrow?"

"Whoa! Eva, what has gotten into you? Are you mad at me for trying to take care of you? This isn't like you at all. No, I'm not forbidding you. But I am asking you to be smart about things. If you're sick and you push yourself too much, you will only get sicker. Then it will take longer for you to get well."

"Now you say I'm not smart?" She stood quickly and stormed toward their bedroom.

He put out the lamp and followed her. She was quickly dressing for bed, not saying a word. He shrugged and began to get ready for bed also.

By the time he was climbing into the bed, Eva was already in bed, covered up to her neck as if it was winter, with her back turned toward him.

He slid in and put his arm around her. "Eva, sweetheart."

He tugged at her. "Look at me. I love you more than life itself. If I didn't, it wouldn't matter to me if you worked all day in the blistering heat."

She slowly turned toward him. "I know, and I'm sorry I snapped at you." Tears ran down her face. "I don't know what came over me. I'm so sorry."

He wrapped his arms around her as she cried against his chest. "It's alright, sweetheart. You've had a rough day."

****

The next morning Harvey answered a knock on the door, finding Mrs. Upton, holding a basket.

"Good morning, Mrs., umm, I mean, Ma."

She hugged him as she walked in. "The girls dropped me here on their way to the field so I could spend the day with Eva."

"I'm glad you're here." He spoke quietly. "She was getting ready for another day in the field when she started feeling poorly again. But boy, she is stubborn!"

Mrs. Upton chuckled, "Yes, I know, and she isn't even the worst of the three sisters. I figured she would be wanting to get back to work and perhaps you may need my help."

He put his arm around her. "You are a wise woman, brave too if you are going to face her." He laughed half-heartedly.

Pointing toward the kitchen, he grabbed his hat. "She's in there eating a piece of toast to settle her stomach and drinking some tea. I've already said goodbye, and I'd rather be on my way.

"Oh, and she is fully intending on working today, just as soon as she finishes breakfast." With a quick kiss on her cheek, he turned and left.

Mrs. Upton squared her shoulders and entered the kitchen.

"Ma! What are you doing here?"

"When the girls told me you were sick, I decided to come over here and spend the morning with you. Perhaps I can help you." She set her basket down on the table and started pulling things out.

"I have fresh lemonade, and chicken broth, and..."

"Ma, thank you, but I'm fine. I just got too hot yesterday, but I'm fine now. I'm sorry you came over so early, and I do appreciate it, but I need to get to work."

She stood, hugging her ma for a moment. "You are welcome to stay. Make yourself at home, but I need to..."

Suddenly another wave of nausea hit her, causing her to run out the kitchen door. Barely making it off the porch, she bent over and got sick again.

Mrs. Upton grabbed a cloth and wet it quickly before going to her. "There now, dear. Let's get you in the house. Let me enjoy taking care of you for a while." She kissed Eva's cheek. "I miss you needing me."

Eva finally conceded and followed her ma's instruction. They sat and talked for a long time, enjoying each other's company while Eva stayed propped and comfortable on the couch.

With a little prompting and some slightly piercing questions, Mrs. Upton got the information she needed to make her diagnosis.

"Eva, sweetheart," she reached and took her hand. "I can't be for certain, but you will know for sure before long. I think I know the reason for your emotional flips and also your physical ones."

Eva looked at the twinkle in her ma's eyes and knew immediately what she was thinking. "Ma? Am I ... Do you think I...?"

Her face was shining as she nodded to her daughter. "Yes, I think you may be in the family way. But," she held her hand up, "Please don't get too excited yet. We don't know for sure."

She gave Eva some advice on what to do and not to do, what symptoms to look for, and then one final piece of advice. "Eva, as much as you want to share this with Harvey, I advise you not to, until you are sure."

"But why not, Ma? He will be beside himself!"

"And that's why. When a man finds out he's going to be a Pa, especially for the first time, he loses his mind, walking around on a cloud for at least days if not weeks. He can't stay focused on things and is very easily drifting into daydreams. I'm not saying Harvey would be careless, but I know your pa was!"

She started laughing. "Your Pa was so excited, he accidentally took someone else's wagon and was almost arrested for being a horse thief!"

Eva covered her mouth as she joined her ma in laughter.

"I would hate for Harvey to go through that if it wasn't really happening. Plus," her voice became more serious. "Men don't take that kind of disappointment as well as women. I have seen men become downright despondent with that kind of disappointment.

"So, my advice to you, unless a doctor happens to appear out of nowhere within the next week or so, that can tell you for sure, just take care of yourself, rest when you can, and watch for the signs. And please be kind to that man of yours. He does love you so."

Harvey was immediately concerned when he stopped by the house at lunchtime, being greeted on the porch by Mrs. Upton telling him Eva was napping.

"She's a lot worse than she was letting on then," he slapped his hat against his knee. "What can I do? We need a doctor. I'm going to talk to Mr. Farley and see if he can get one."

"Harvey," she reached out and took his hand, smiling calmly. "She's going to be fine. She just needs to rest. The heat affected her more than she thought, but she will be fine. You have no need to worry.

"Eva doesn't need a doctor, but you could still talk to Mr. Farley about it. This town needs one badly. I know he's a busy man, but he is all for helping this town and I think a doctor should be the highest of priorities. Perhaps I will talk to Mrs. Farley. She knows how to light a fire under that man."

"Yes ma'am," Harvey chuckled. "She sure does. You're sure Eva's fine?"

"Yes, son. It may take her a little while to get to feeling herself, but she has agreed to take care of herself and not worry about working until she is completely well."

"Thank you," Harvey hugged her. "Oh, the girls should be here anytime to pick you up. Pa is closing the fields at noon until it cools off some."

"Good. You will find your lunch on the table, and I will see you soon."

****

A week later, Eva was feeling much better. She only felt sick in the mornings, carefully hiding it from Harvey so his concern wouldn't grow. She was careful not to get overly hot or to stand or turn too quickly.

She soon found out exactly what her ma was talking about. She fixed a wonderful supper, took her bath early, fixed her hair, and put on her best dress. One last glance in the mirror, she placed her hand on her belly and smiled. "It's time to tell your pa."

Harvey was so dirty and sweaty, he didn't want to get her dirty but couldn't help himself when he saw her. He took her in his arms, kissing her passionately. "My, you are a vision. Let me get washed up a bit before I make you look and smell as bad as I do."

"I have a bath ready for you. I figured you would appreciate it on a day like today."

When he returned, he was completely clean, shaved, smelling and looking good.

It was her turn to be aggressive. She set the last of the food on the table and rushed to him, wrapping her arms around his neck and kissing him for a long time.

He pulled back from her. "I sure am glad you're feeling better. I was getting worried about you."

"I'm more than better, Harvey. I'm," she paused and placed his hand on her belly. "You're going to be a Pa!"

His mouth dropped open, taking a moment to register what she just said. "I'm going to be a pa? You're...?" His smile went wider than she had ever seen as she nodded.

"Oh my! I'm going to be a pa!" he exclaimed loudly as he picked her up and twirled her around. Kissing her again, he held her for a moment.

"I've got to go! Hold supper for me, I will be back soon."

He almost ran out the door with Eva following down behind him. "Harvey, whe...?"

Her sentence was interrupted as he ran into the yard, threw his hat up in the air and shouted, "Yahoo! I'm going to be a pa!" He jumped on his horse and took off toward town.

Eva stood in amusement, watching him return a moment later. He ran up on the porch, grabbed her and twirled her around again. "You have made me the happiest man alive!" Then he was running toward his horse again and disappeared down the road.

"Well, Ma was right!" she laughed as she went back toward the kitchen.

****

Harvey rode straight to Mr. Farley's house. When he invited Harvey in, he got right to the point.

"I hope I'm not interrupting your supper, sir, but I really need to talk to you."

"No, not at all, son. Have a seat, supper won't be ready for a while yet. Whatever is on your mind must be good. I don't believe I've ever seen you look this happy."

"Yes sir, I am very happy, and that's why I'm here. I want to help you any way I can to get a doctor, lawyer, banker, and everything else we need to make this a real town. I especially want to get a doctor here. I'm going to be a pa!"

"Well, congratulations, son! I am thrilled for you and Eva." He shook Harvey's hand then got a serious look on his face.

"So, this has inspired you to make a better place for your family, I see. I can use your help in a few areas to try again getting some professional people here, like a doctor.

"The main problem is that most of the people around here still aren't convinced we need such. They trust their home remedies and wouldn't trust a doctor if he was available. Which means, he wouldn't stay here long, not making any money.

"I have offered several doctors a year's salary in advance, from my own pocket, if they would come here. I even had a few visit, but they all concluded that they didn't want to make such a move for only a year. They didn't feel like the people were interested enough to support their practice.

"Now, if you could help convince the people around here to agree using a doctor, perhaps have them sign a petition showing potential doctors they are serious, maybe we can move forward and get one."

"I could do that, sir. I know all the old timers and the ones who grew up here. We could talk to our workers and start getting the word out. I really would feel better if there was one here by the time my Eva needs him."

"I understand completely. You have a whole different outlook on life when you have that kind of responsibility."

"Yes sir." Harvey stood. "Thank you for your time, sir, and if I may ask one more favor?"

Mr. Farley nodded.

"Please don't tell anyone, not even your wife about Eva being in the family way. In my excitement, I came straight here and haven't even told our families yet."

Mr. Farley laughed. "You are such a delight! Your secret is safe with me."

Chapter 11

The family gathered at Harvey and Eva's house to celebrate the new arrival due in February. There was joyous chattering in every corner of the house. The conversation took many turns throughout the evening, with everyone excited about one thing or another. They all agreed that God had been so good to them.

The ladies sat in the dining room discussing Olivia's wedding plans, Eva's baby, and the new school year about to start with both of them being teachers. Then they would circle back around and cover all the subjects again.

The men sat out on the porch talking about crops, yields, Asa and Vince's jobs at the refinery, Harvey's baby, and then almost by accident, gold was mentioned.

Abe puffed on his pipe. "Mr. Farley says we need to get our hands on as much gold as possible. He says the country is getting so divided that the only thing that may hold value is gold.

"He suggested that maybe we start getting some shipped in here and use that as our money to pay wages and make purchases. That way, if things ever do get bad, we still have something of value."

"Mr. Farley is certainly intelligent, and I would have to listen to his advice. What would be the harm of us paying in gold coins instead of paper currency?" Asa was in total agreement.

"Sounds like something we need to consider," Harvey added, "but we have some other pressing issues to discuss." He went on to tell them about his discussion with Mr. Farley, and the need for people to agree on using a doctor.

Abe shook his head. "That's not going to be easy, son. Most of the old timers wouldn't walk across the street to pay a doctor to look at them, let alone come down out of the hills to see one."

"The younger people may be easier to convince, Harvey." Asa stood in thought. "What about the town council offering a free house and office to the doctor? You know, like we do for the preacher."

Harvey nodded, "That sounds like a good idea, Asa. It would sweeten Mr. Farley's offer. The doc wouldn't have many expenses to worry about."

"You know, boys," Abe shook out his pipe, "We have a lot of cause for a doctor's services here on the farm. Perhaps if we signed a contract promising to send our wounded or sick workers to him, that would help. May be expensive, but it would help get him here."

Harvey smiled. "It's nice to know I come from a family of creative brains."

Asa playfully punched him in the shoulder. "Yeah, it's a shame your cornbread didn't get quite done in the middle."

"Funny man." Harvey laughed along with everyone.

"I think I will take these ideas to Mr. Farley tomorrow."

"Uh, Harvey," Preacher Upton interrupted. "Seems as though Mr. Farley and myself will be busy talking with a new preacher for the next few days. We are going to be showing him around, hoping the Lord will lead him here, but only if he's the man the Lord sees fit. His train doesn't arrive until two, perhaps you can see Mr. Farley in the morning?"

Harvey nodded.

Vince's eyes dimmed when the preacher spoke about leaving. He and Amy hadn't heard anymore about what kind of preparations they were trying to make for her. He had certainly been praying about it.

"Preacher, sir? Would it be agreeable with you if I asked Amy to take a walk with me?"

"That's fine, son. Just stay close."

"Yes sir," Vince quickly responded as his face lit up and he went in the house.

Moments later he returned with Amy on his arm. "We won't be too long, sir." They bounded happily off the porch and down the road.

"Have your parents given you any idea about what they are thinking or planning?" Vince asked cautiously as he squeezed her hand tighter on his arm.

"No, nothing. I've even tuned my ears to hear them talking in another room. Still nothing," she sighed. "But they have promised to take our feelings about each other into consideration, and I trust them. My parents love me, and I know they would never intentionally hurt me. Besides, even if I did have to move away, who's to say you couldn't find a job close to where we are going? Or as soon as I get old enough, I could come back here."

Vince sighed sadly. "Everyone keeps saying that God will find a way if we are meant to be together. I keep praying and thinking. That's all I know to do."

She leaned her head on his shoulder. "I'm so glad you aren't as tall as Harvey and Asa. I can actually reach your shoulder, well," she looked up at him," Almost."

He looked down at her beautiful face, taking in every feature. They stopped and he turned to face her, taking both her hands in his. "Amy, I love you. I can't stand the thought of being away from you even for a few hours. I think about you every minute. My heart aches when you aren't with me." He kissed her hand tenderly.

She put her hand on his face. "I love you, Vince. It rips my heart out with all of this indecision surrounding us. But I truly believe there is hope. Everything is going to turn out right."

She wrapped her arms around his neck as he pulled her close, touching his lips to hers. Their first real kiss, and it was more wonderful than either of them had dreamed. The rest of the world with all of its troubles melted away. They both knew there was no turning back for either of them, not now, not ever.

****

Preacher Smith and his wife were very pleasant people. Mr. Farley would spend his days with both preachers and their wives, then in the evenings, he would stay busy formulating plans and contracts, writing to everyone he knew, hoping someone would respond with a candidate for a doctor...soon.

On Saturday afternoon, the preachers, their wives, and Mr. and Mrs. Farley were invited to Harvey and Eva's for supper to meet the Darnell family.

They enjoyed a delightful afternoon and evening together, getting to know and like each other. Preacher Smith was intrigued by the Darnell's knowledge of the Bible. He also enjoyed hearing about their enthusiasm for life, the upcoming wedding and the new baby.

"Excuse me for asking," Harvey cleared his throat, "I must be missing something. Are we going to have two preachers?"

Preacher Smith chuckled. "No, son. There are a couple of us circuit preachers looking to settle down and have one flock. Over the next few months, until Preacher Upton leaves, we will be coming through here often, taking turns preaching. The congregation will be able to vote on who to take on as their full-time preacher by that time.

"If they don't find any of us suitable, we continue to ride the circuit with new candidates being asked to come until they find the one God has intended for here."

After a lengthy visit, he announced that he must be calling it a night. "I will be preaching tomorrow, and I see now that I better be studying extra hard to be able to impress men with such knowledge of the scripture." He laughed jovially.

After saying goodbye, Mr. Farley drove them back to the Upton's house, where the Smiths were staying. He had just said goodnight when Mr. Peters from the telegraph office rounded the corner.

"Mr. Farley! You have an important telegram!" the man shouted.

Mr. Farley reached out as he thanked the man, putting a coin in his hand for being so good to find him quickly. He opened it and read while the two preachers stood close by.

"Is everything alright, Mr. Farley? Do you need any help with anything?" Preacher Upton asked.

Mr. Farley smiled kindly. "Everything is quite wonderful, preacher. At least it looks as if it will be. This may be an answer to prayer."

He took his wife home and then rode back to Harvey's where the men were still congregated outside.

They walked out to meet him. "Is something wrong, Mr. Farley?" Harvey asked.

"No, my goodness, no!" He handed Harvey the telegram.

A moment later, Harvey shouted with enthusiasm, "A doctor is coming on Wednesday's train. It's one that has already visited here and he has reconsidered and wants to take a closer look! This is wonderful news!"

"Yes, indeed it is," Mr. Farley beamed. "To make it better, this is the one I liked best, and he doesn't know about the incentives that we are willing to offer. Surely when he finds out, our town will have a doctor with a contract to stay here for at least five years. I had to let you know immediately. I know all of you have been praying. Now, I shall say goodnight again. See you all in the morning."

****

"Mr. Farley, I have to be completely honest with you," Doctor Powell confided. The two men had just approached the Farley's house from taking a walk around town. They stopped before stepping on the porch.

"I have no idea why I'm even considering this move. I have a good practice back home, my wife is a schoolteacher, and our children are very content.

"Having said that, I am a man of faith, and I prayed about this, even before I came to visit months ago. It seems like the Lord has burdened me for this place and won't let me put it to rest."

"I understand, doctor." Mr. Farley looked at him with kindness and concern. "I hope that with the extra incentives we are offering, you may be able to make your decision."

Doctor Powell smiled. "The offers are very generous indeed, but I think God had already made the decision for me before I even sent that telegram. He's just making sure I know He is providing for me."

Mr. Farley chuckled. "Yes, God does have a way, doesn't He? So, you will take the position then?"

"Yes sir," he reached out and shook Mr. Farley's hand. "It may take a month or two to get my affairs in order, but it looks as though you have yourself a doctor."

"Wonderful! You just let me know when you will be arriving, and I will have the house freshly cleaned and waiting for you."

"That sounds good, sir, but there is something I promised to do while I'm here. My wife wants me to check on the school and the credentials of the teachers. She, umm," he paused and colored slightly. "She would also like for me to check on the possibility of her obtaining a teaching position, perhaps for next year."

Mr. Farley got tickled and patted the doctor on the back. "God does work in mysterious ways, son. Seems as though we just may have a teaching position opening up, maybe even before the end of this year!"

By the time the men had talked through supper, they were both convinced the Lord was in this.

Mr. Farley offered to take the doctor to meet both the teachers, finding that they didn't even have to leave town to meet them. They were just riding past the diner when he saw Harvey and Eva step out of the diner, followed closely by Asa and Olivia. They agreed to meet at the Upton's house, with great anticipation.

When they all settled in the parlor, the doctor was pleased to find himself at ease with these people. He had felt a bit intimidated by Mrs. Farley, almost as if he was indebted to her, being under a microscope the entire time.

He shook Harvey's hand, "I hear that your wife will be one of my first patients."

Harvey glowed. "Yes sir, and let me say what a pleasure and relief it is to meet you."

During the evening they enjoyed getting to know each other, filling every moment with plans for the future. They discussed the school, the farm, the growing community, and the new preacher.

"Depending on how many children we have enrolled in school this year," Mr. Farley added, "I may need to speak with the town council about building an actual schoolhouse.

"This town is growing fast and we want to be able to offer everything in our power to help keep it growing in the right direction."

****

School started with Eva and Olivia thrilled to see thirty-six students enrolled. Finding that some of the older students had yet to learn to read, they couldn't separate the classes by age. It was soon decided that they would teach together, both giving one on one time to the students when needed.

There were a couple of older boys who felt like they didn't need to be there, and that school was a waste of time. Eva quickly formed a small group including these boys and headed outside for a hands-on teaching experience.

She was able to show them the importance of being able to read by the different signs and notices posted in town. She taught them the importance of math by making a purchase in Henderson's having him purposely give her back the wrong amount of change.

History and government was on everyone's minds these days, with the upheaval in the nation. She went over how important it was to know the facts, not just the rumors, so they could form their own opinions on what was right.

By the time she finished her field trip, it was lunch time, and her group wasn't only hungry for food, they were suddenly hungry for knowledge. This group was excited about school and never once uttered another word about school being a waste of time.

****

Asa and Olivia's wedding was just two weeks away when the new doctor arrived with his family. It seemed as though everyone was excited about something, the new doctor, the wedding, the new baby, the new school that was in planning or the new preacher. So many exciting things seemed to be happening at once.

Eva and Olivia spoke with Mrs. Powell about teaching in Olivia's place during the last week before Christmas, then take Eva's place when school resumed after the New Year. She was overjoyed.

Harvey and Asa worked every evening on the small cabin for their pa. They kept wanting to make it larger, but he kept everything to a minimum, declaring he didn't want a lot of wasted space to have to keep warm or clean.

While the men worked on the cabin, Eva and Olivia worked on the larger house, getting it cleaned and ready for Asa and Olivia to live in.

Occasionally, Vince and Amy would join them. He had finally been granted permission to visit Amy unchaperoned, for short periods of time. They still had no idea what her parents were working out on their behalf. Other than when he was working, they clung to each other every minute, as if it may be their last.

Olivia had planned the wedding for a Sunday. Knowing it may be freezing on that day, she planned it for right after the church service so people wouldn't have to make an extra trip in the possible bad weather. They would have a brief gathering in the church afterward, then the family would have a private celebratory meal together.

The Friday before the wedding, Olivia seemed very distracted. Eva knew she had the jitters, but it seemed more than that. When the children left that afternoon, Eva noticed tears in Olivia's eyes.

"Sweetie, what's wrong?" She put her arm around her sister.

Olivia shrugged. "I don't know, Eva. I should be bubbling over, but instead, I just feel, I don't know, scared. Having the children leave, knowing by the time I see them again, so much will have changed, I just get nervous knots in my stomach."

"But Olivia, you are marrying the man of your dreams, aren't you? Are you having doubts about that?"

She shook her head as tears fell from her eyes. "I love Asa with all my heart. I can't imagine life without him. I just hope he won't be disappointed in me."

"Oh sweetie, how can you think such a thing? The man worships the ground you walk on. To him, you could do no wrong." Eva coaxed a smile out of her.

"I suppose I'm just nervous and being silly."

Eva hugged her. "You are being normal. Marriage is a big step, not to be taken lightly. But if you are sure about each other, there is nothing better."

As they embraced, Olivia could feel the baby move. "Oh, Eva!" She put her hand on her sister's belly. "What a wonderful miracle that is!"

Eva smiled. "It certainly is. You should see the thrill on Harvey's face every time it moves. The man is silly over this baby. Soon, I hope you will find out for yourself."

"Yes, I hope so. Now, if you don't mind, you get on home. I want to spend a few minutes alone here. I will see you later."

Eva squeezed her one last time before leaving.

Olivia went around tidying up, then found herself engrossed in a book she was putting away. Lost in thought as she read the pages, she didn't realize someone had entered the building until he put his arms around her from behind.

She turned quickly to find herself face to face with Toby.

"Olivia, I have loved you since the first dance at the social. I could never understand why you never gave me the chance to show you."

146

She struggled against his embrace. "Toby, you need to get your hands off me and leave!"

Seemingly not hearing a word she was saying, he continued. "I have tried to fall in love with other women, even your sister, but no one can take your place in my heart."

He held her tightly with her not being able to move her arms. Bending down, he began to kiss her as she twisted her head away to no avail. She stomped his foot, yet it never seemed to phase him. She tried to scream out, but only muffled cries escaped because his mouth was pressed against hers so tightly.

Suddenly, she bit him, hard, right on his mouth. His grip loosened and she quickly hit him in the head with the book she still clutched.

He wiped his lip. "I will forgive you, darling, because I know you are just nervous." He reached for her as she backed away.

He attempted to kiss her again, but this time she sunk her fingernails into his face. He grabbed her hands. She spit in his face and began to scream, loudly.

Almost as if he had been in a trance, her screams brought him back to reality and he fled.

Mrs. Farley saw a man running from the church as she left the Upton's house. Thinking it was curious, she went toward the church, saw the door open, and entered.

Hearing someone crying, she went toward the front, seeing Olivia crumpled in a heap on the floor. "Olivia!" she gasped as she hurried to the girl, wrapping her arms around her.

"Dear girl, are you hurt? Who was that? What happened?"

After a moment, she was able to respond. "Thank you, Mrs. Farley. I'm not hurt, I just need to go home."

"Come dear, I will walk you home."

****

Eva was starting to get concerned when Olivia hadn't shown up to help with the finishing touches on the house. It was almost sunset. She could hear the men across the meadow at their pa's cabin when she stepped out on the porch.

She was walking in that direction to ask Asa if he knew where Olivia was when she saw someone riding up. It was the sheriff and he arrived at the cabin right before she got there.

"Asa," the sheriff greeted sternly. "I need you and Mrs. Darnell to come with me."

"What's going on, Sheriff?" Harvey asked as he walked up beside Eva and put his arm around her.

"It seems as though Miss Olivia was attacked..."

"What?" Asa yelled, interrupting the sheriff.

"She's not hurt, as far as we know. But she has locked herself in her room and won't speak to anyone. I need to get details from her, and Mrs. Upton said to come get you and her sister."

Asa ran for his horse, while Harvey asked the sheriff, "If you don't know if she's hurt, and she isn't talking, how do you know she was attacked?"

"Mrs. Farley saw a man running from the church, then found Olivia inside, on the floor crying. She helped her home, but then she locked herself in her room."

Asa heard the conversation but didn't say a word as he rode off quickly.

"Sheriff, you get my wife to her buggy. I've got to keep my brother out of jail." Harvey turned to Eva, apologizing, then ran for his horse, taking off to catch Asa.

By the time Eva got to her parent's house, Asa had Olivia in his arms. He had broken her bedroom window and climbed through when she wouldn't open her door.

Mrs. Farley was there fussing about propriety. "Something needs to be done about that young man, sheriff! He is a menace, not to mention an absolute disgrace! He has caused trouble numerous times with several young ladies. I've told you about several times I've seen him carrying on."

"Yes, Mrs. Farley, but when the young lady is a willing party, my hands are tied."

"And what about this time, sheriff?" Asa barked. "Olivia wasn't willing."

"I will go arrest him, Asa. It was a type of assault, I suppose."

"You suppose?" Asa bristled.

Preacher Upton grabbed Asa's arm. "Asa, he has already explained that everything Toby does seems to be petty, not really a crime. He isn't saying he doesn't believe Olivia."

"The safest place for Toby right now is in jail," Asa stated firmly. "He has gone too far this time."

****

Toby was nowhere to be found. The sheriff inquired about him at the printing press, being told by his boss, "Toby took some time off. Said he had some urgent family matters to attend."

All he could do was keep watching for his return, hoping he saw him before the Darnell boys did.

Chapter 12

Olivia's wedding day dawned bright and sunny, although windy and cold. She had asked Asa not to join them at the morning church service because he wasn't supposed to see the bride before the wedding.

She was a bundle of nerves. The night before, Asa had thought she was upset because of Toby. She quickly let him know that wasn't the case, in fact, she told him she was proud of herself for fighting back.

The nervousness she was experiencing was coming from nothing other than the thoughts of marriage. She was sure of her and Asa's love for each other, knew that she could handle the upkeep of a house and cooking, and even felt confident about her teaching job. Her problem was with the unknown between a husband and wife, and that scared her to death. She didn't even know how to approach the subject with her ma or Eva.

She heard people start arriving for church and quickly finished getting dressed. It wouldn't be long until she and her sisters would excuse themselves from church early and start getting dressed for the wedding.

For a long moment, she caught herself daydreaming of Asa, wrapped in his arms, feeling safe and loved. She did love that man. Then the nervousness began to creep into her thoughts again. She shook herself, put her coat on, picked up her Bible, and walked across the street to the church.

Not taking in a word that her pa was preaching, Eva nudged her. "It's time for us to go."

It seemed as if she was in a dream, not able to fully function for all the emotions running through her. Suddenly she found herself weepy.

"Sweetheart," Eva hugged her. "What's wrong?"

"Oh, Eva, I'm just nervous, happy, sad, excited, and scared all at once! I've never felt this way before."

Eva cupped her sister's face in her hands. "Olivia, every bit of what you just described is natural. It's your wedding day, the most wonderful day of your life. It's filled with hopes and dreams, promises and happiness. But it is also frightening to think of the responsibilities that come with it. Try not to think so far ahead, at least not today. Enjoy your beautiful wedding day, cherishing every moment."

She motioned for Olivia to sit down so they could continue talking while they fixed her hair. "Today, you transition from a girl to a woman and that, in itself, is enough to make you nervous." Eva smiled in the mirror at her. "But, Olivia, let me tell you, there is nothing more magical than to be wrapped in so much love. Asa does love you so. Don't be nervous, just allow yourself to be loved by that man."

Olivia dabbed at the tears in her eyes as she nodded. "Thank you, Eva."

Mrs. Upton came into the room. "Are we about ready? Your pa just finished his sermon. Oh, Olivia! You look gorgeous!"

Olivia stood and turned a full circle. "Do I look ready? I feel so giddy, I need someone to pinch me!"

Eva and Amy giggled as they each took one of her arms and led her to the parlor to wait for her pa.

Within minutes, she was standing on the church step watching her sisters start down the aisle as the music grew louder. Her heart beat so loudly, she could barely hear the music as she followed on her pa's arm. Then she saw Asa. Instantly her world was perfect. This was the love of her life standing in front of her, with moist eyes as he looked at her so tenderly.

When their eyes met, it took her breath away. They couldn't pull themselves away from each other. The rest of the room faded. There was no one else in their world at that moment. When her pa placed her hand in Asa's, it was as if her heart would burst with the love she had for him. She had never been so sure of anything, or so happy, any other time in her life.

She heard Asa promise to love her, take care of her, and cherish her for the rest of his life. Then she heard herself pledging her life and unwavering love to him. Still, as if in a haze, she felt him gather her in his arms and kiss her tenderly. Finally, she was able to shake out of the dream and kissed him back, passionately, while wrapping her arms up around his neck.

Everyone stood and cheered as he led her down the aisle and across the street to her parent's house. They spent a few minutes there alone, loving on each other, then went back to the church to mingle with their guests.

Within an hour, the wedding party had changed their clothes and were sitting at the table together, enjoying a special lunch, celebrating the joyous occasion.

Everything seemed normal, with everyone teasing and chattering, until Asa turned to her and quietly asked if she was about ready to go home.

She felt herself blush as he took her hand and helped her stand. Suddenly she was filled with panic but was determined not to let it show.

"Thank you, everyone, for helping make this the most wonderful day of my life." She went around hugging everyone goodbye, smiling.

Through her nervousness, she started chattering on the ride home. "Mrs. Asa Darnell, or is it Mrs. Olivia Darnell?"

Asa chuckled, "I like the sound of both. I am absolutely the happiest man alive, and it's all because you love me." He tightened his arm around her.

When they arrived at the house, he went around and lifted her out of the buggy, never letting her feet touch the ground until they were in the house.

"Welcome home, my darling." He held her close and kissed her. "Here, let me help you with your coat, and then I will get this fire going better."

She smiled at him. "What would you like for me to do? How can I help you?"

He kissed her again. "You just make yourself comfortable on the couch and I will join you in a minute."

She nervously plumped the pillows before sitting down. He joined her a moment later and held her close, starting a comfortable, quiet conversation. He could tell she was nervous, and he tried to calm her without bringing it to her attention.

They talked for nearly an hour, with her beginning to act like her normal self. She was propped back against him feeling the calmest she had all day.

"Asa, I feel so loved and so safe when I'm in your arms."

"That's because you are, my darling." He kissed the top of her head. Clearing his throat, he continued cautiously. "It's been a right busy day. You about ready to turn in?"

He felt her tense. "You know, I feel a bit hungry."

"Hungry?" His voice was filled with disappointment. "We just ate a big meal."

"Well, maybe it was all the excitement, but I really didn't eat much." She stood and started toward the kitchen. "Would you like something?"

He stood to follow her. "Umm, no, but I will help you."

After thirty minutes of watching her push food around on her plate, listening to her ramble on about anything that came to mind, he stood and took her hand. Suddenly she grew silent as he pulled her gently to her feet and wrapped his arms around her.

He felt her tremble as he held her. "Olivia, I love you with all my being. But I must confess something to you."

She looked up in his eyes, seeing the tenderness and love shining through.

"I'm just as nervous as you are, sweetheart. We will get through this together, you'll see."

She nodded as he bent and blew out the lamp, keeping his arm wrapped around her.

****

Vince had moved to the boarding house in town, and other than missing his friends at the farm, this suited him perfectly for now. He was much closer to Amy.

He needed to speak with the preacher about starting to make plans for his and Amy's future, but with everyone preparing for Olivia and Asa's wedding, then Christmas less than two weeks after, he couldn't find an opportunity.

Finally, when the girls were busy cleaning up from Christmas dinner, he spoke to the preacher quietly. "Sir, I really need a chance to sit down and talk with you."

Preacher Upton excused himself from the group of men gathered in Harvey and Eva's parlor. "Harvey, would you mind if Vince and I talk in your spare room?"

"Go right ahead, Preacher, and while you're in there, feel free to hang curtains or assemble the crib." Harvey teased as he waved them on.

The preacher led the way, then closed the door behind Vince. Vince began to sweat and pace the small room.

"Preacher, sir, I was wondering if you have made any preparations for Amy? We have prayed about it but haven't heard you or your wife speak of it."

"Ahh, yes." He sat down in Eva's rocking chair. "Everything has been so unsettled, here, across our nation, everywhere we look. Seems as though our travel plans change daily. That's why I haven't said anything. I don't know what to say."

Vince got his hopes up. "You mean, there's a chance you may be staying?"

"No, Vince, the Lord keeps prodding me forward. I'm sure we will go, I'm just not sure where or when at this moment."

Vince paced some more. "Preacher Upton, sir, I certainly mean no disrespect, but Amy and I are trying to make plans for our future. Until you know your plan, it's almost impossible to make our own."

"I understand, son." He nodded his head, leaning forward to rest his elbows on his knees. "My wife and I have talked extensively about your situation and we both know how you feel. We can see the love for each other in your eyes and in your actions. I must say, we are very pleased with the way you and Amy conduct yourselves."

"Thank you, sir. But we would like to move forward in our relationship. I realize she is young, only seventeen next month, but sir, I assure you, I want nothing more than to love and provide for her the rest of my life.

"I have an excellent job, make good money, have saved quite a bit..." he paused, not knowing what more to say.

He finally broke the momentary silence. "Sir, I want to ask her to marry me. I want to be ready to marry her before you leave. I can't fathom the thought of life without her in it."

The preacher nodded, sighing as he rested back in the chair. "I see. Vince, you are a good boy and we are thankful the Lord sent you to our Amy. We couldn't be happier.

"Amy is mature for her age, has a good head on her shoulders, is practical, respectful, and a hard worker." He sighed.

Vince noticed tears fill the preacher's eyes. He wiped his eyes, cleared his throat and stood. "I don't have a problem with you marrying our Amy. I think both of you are mature enough to handle it, although marriage is never easy.

"Because my plans to leave keep changing, I will allow you and Amy to begin planning your future, and I will pray that the Lord sees fit to work things around them."

"Thank you, sir," Vince gushed, filled with relief. He extended his hand toward the preacher.

He reached past Vince's outstretched hand, embracing the young man. "I know you will be good to my baby girl."

****

Early afternoon on New Year's Eve, Vince and Amy stepped out into the falling snow, making their way to the diner. They hurried, yet still took time to enjoy watching the snowflakes. Amy remarked how beautiful it was as she attempted to catch one on her tongue.

Vince laughed at her, putting his arm around her tighter. "Look at that, Amy!" He pointed to a horse and buggy tied outside of the diner.

"That is one magnificent horse! And look at that buggy, it's fancy and looks brand new."

Amy reached out and petted the horse as they approached. "Yes, it's one fine looking horse and buggy. I don't believe I've seen it in town before. Maybe we have visitors."

She glanced in the buggy, not wanting to seem nosey. "Look at those beautiful, padded seats, Vince, and the canopy to keep the rain and snow off the passengers. Yes, that is one fine outfit."

"Yes, it is." He nudged her forward. "Let's get out of this weather and get something good to eat." He smiled and nodded to the proprietor as they entered, then guided her to a table in the corner.

The conversation flowed easily throughout their meal, with both enjoying every moment. "Has your pa mentioned anything to you about their plans?"

"Yes, it seems as though everyone is having trouble getting through Indian territory right now. They are still waiting for God to lead them. He did say something about perhaps settling in the Oklahoma Territory.

"Ma says it will probably be June before they leave if things don't change again before then." She winked at him. "Looks as though the Lord is answering our prayers by putting things off a little while."

"It sure does," he grinned as he spoke softly. "Amy, do you know that I love you more than anything? That I will always put your needs and wants ahead of my own?"

She took his hand across the table. "Yes, Vince, I do. And I feel the same about you. I dream of the day I…umm, never mind." She blushed as he continued to hold her hand.

He rose from his seat, reached in his pocket, and fell to one knee. "Amy, will you marry me and let me show you how much I love you for the rest of my life?"

Her hands cupped his face while tears filled her eyes. Her heart raced as she forced herself to stay calm, especially while in public. "Yes, Vince, I would be honored to be your wife."

He kissed her softly, opened the ring box, slid the ring on her finger, then kissed her again, sweetly. As he stood, she could contain her excitement and sit still no longer. She quickly stood and threw her arms around his neck.

"I love you so much, Vince." She kissed him again before turning him loose.

Returning to his chair, he continued to hold her hand and gaze in her eyes. "I love you so much, Amy. I can hardly wait for us to start our future together.

"I was sure hoping you loved me enough to say yes, and I took much pleasure in buying you an early wedding present."

She looked at her ring. "Vince, you don't have to spoil me with things. All I want is to start a life with you."

He squeezed her hand. "I want the same, but I couldn't resist. Come on, I want to show you the surprise."

He helped her with her coat, then offered his arm.

"Even though I don't want anything, you sure have got me excited. Just the proposal was enough to put my head in the clouds, then the ring, and now another surprise? Vince, you really didn't need to…"

She stopped short as they stepped outside and he waved his hand toward the horse and buggy. "It's yours, sweetheart."

Her hand went to her mouth as she gasped, then squealed in delight while she threw herself around his neck. "Oh, Vince! This is wonderful!"

He kissed her quickly before assisting her up in her new buggy. "I'm so glad you like it, Amy. I hope to see you happy every day. It's the biggest thrill for me to see your smile."

She insisted that he drive while she cuddled in close to him.

"Amy, if you feel up to taking a short drive, I would like to show you something."

"Vince, you are really something today! Sure, let me see what else you've been up to."

They started out of town, toward the farm. About a half mile outside of town he pulled in front of a house. "This house is going to be available for rent come April. I wanted to see if it meets your approval before I rent it."

Her eyes went wide. "You mean, we could start planning a wedding?"

He nodded with a smile.

"I would love to Vince, but I'm not sure my parents would…"

He put his finger on her lips. "I've already talked to them. Your ma seems to think a spring or June wedding would be beautiful."

She squealed again, almost jumping in his lap while hugging him. "Oh, Vince! I am so happy! Are you happy? Please tell me I'm not dreaming, and you are happy too!"

"Oh, my darling. I can't begin to tell you how happy you've made me."

Arriving back at the Upton's, the happy couple was greeted with a surprise, family celebration. Apparently, everyone knew about everything Vince had planned, except for Amy.

She looked at him lovingly and teased, "My, you have had a busy week!"

****

Harvey and Eva were blissfully happy. They were glowing more than the newlyweds or the newly engaged couple as they all gathered around the table. He couldn't keep his hands off her, constantly massaging her shoulders, putting his arm around her, or resting his hand on her bulging belly. Every time he touched her belly, he was quickly rewarded with movement.

Eva took it all in stride, relishing in the love they shared with each other. He was so caring and attentive. When she started to join the women to clear the table, he scolded her gently.

"You sit, sweetheart. I will help them."

"Oh no you won't," Mrs. Upton rebuked. "You two just sit there and enjoy the company. Eva needs to stay off her feet, and I don't need a big man like you plundering around in my kitchen."

He smiled and nodded. "Thanks, Ma."

When school began again in January, Harvey was afraid Eva would be sad about not being able to return. Instead, she seemed overjoyed to stay home, making preparations for the new baby. She never complained and always seemed happy, even though she had really blossomed over the last few weeks and seemed to tire easily.

Harvey made arrangements for Amy and Mrs. Upton to take turns staying with her during the day while he worked. They were more than happy to do so. He also took some time off from work and accompanied her to the doctor, barraging the man with all kinds of questions. The doctor teased that if Harvey didn't soon settle down, he was going to prescribe him some tonic.

Every evening, as soon as he walked in the door, he went to her and held her, as if he was starving for her touch. Amy would watch them, thinking it was quite wonderful, hoping that was what her future held with Vince.

"I sure will be glad to meet this little one," he spoke softly, as they cuddled on the couch together, filled with emotion knowing Eva was truly happy. She was a wonderful woman, and he was honored she was his.

He sat her upright, carefully. "Sweetheart, I need to go check on Pa. He was feeling kinda poorly today." He started pulling on his boots. "I won't be gone long."

****

Harvey knocked on Asa's door with urgency. Asa pulled the door open in a flurry. "Eva?" he asked.

"No, Asa. Something isn't right with Pa."

Asa quickly put his boots on, grabbed his coat, while yelling to Olivia. "Something's wrong with Pa. I'll be back as soon as I can."

"Olivia, I hate to ask, but would you..."

"Harvey, you and Asa go take care of your Pa. I will go over and stay with Eva."

He quickly thanked her and kissed her cheek.

Asa and Harvey entered their pa's cabin, seeing him shivering. He was running a fever and talking nonsense. He kept refusing their help, insisting that his wife could take care of him.

They knew they needed to get him some help, and he wasn't going to go easily. Looking at each other, not knowing what to do, Harvey suddenly came up with an idea.

"Asa, go get the buggy ready, quickly," he whispered.

He turned to his pa. "Eva needs you, Pa. I've got to get back to the men, they have a problem out there. It's already dark and she needs a ride home. I don't want her to have to walk home. She needs you, pa. Will you please go get her?"

"Eva? She is such a sweet soul. I love that girl, you know." Abe started to smile. "Yes, get out of my way, Harvey, Eva needs me." He sat up and pulled on his boots. Harvey helped him get his coat on and wrapped a blanket around his shoulders.

Harvey helped him out the door just as Asa pulled around in the buggy. "About time you got here with the buggy!" Abe scolded. "Don't you know Eva is waiting for me! My lands! It's already dark, she will be scared out there all by herself."

They helped him in the buggy and drove as quickly as possible to town. By the time they got halfway there, Abe fell asleep or lost consciousness, they weren't sure which.

The doctor was just finishing a late supper when they arrived. He asked questions as the two men carried their pa in and put him on the bed he led them to.

After several minutes of examining him, he mixed some medicine and coaxed it down Abe's throat as he started waking up a bit.

"Abe? How long have you been feeling poorly?"

He mumbled incoherently.

The doctor turned to the boys and asked more questions. He checked Abe's body from head to toe, probing and poking until Abe moaned in pain.

"I think he has a stomach problem. Let me get this fever under control so he can answer some questions. You boys go on home and let me tend to him. You can come back in the morning and check on him."

Harvey seemed almost panicked. "Is it serious doc?"

He shook his head. "Boys, I can't say for sure. It could be as simple as something he ate, or perhaps the flu. But I won't lie to you, it could be something serious. Hopefully, by tomorrow I will know more. Go home and pray for him."

Chapter 13

After three days, Abe's fever broke. He was talking more sensibly, finally able to answer the doctor's questions. He was sitting up on his own and taking his medicine without help, even though he was still weak as a kitten.

Since Harvey and Asa were spending every waking hour at the doctor's house, they moved Eva and Olivia back to their parents for now. There was no way they were going to leave them out at the farm at night by themselves.

The fifth day at the doctor's, Abe was getting tired of being confined, adamant about going home and getting back to work. The doctor gave him some more medicine and told him they needed to talk.

"Abe, I have done every test I know to do for you. I've asked probing questions and made my own observations. I'm afraid to say that my conclusion is not favorable. I need you to listen carefully and do as I say."

Abe became somber as he nodded. "Alright doc, tell me."

"Your kidneys are failing. I can give you medicine that will help, but I'm afraid there is no cure." He shook his head sadly.

"I see." Abe sighed. "Well, give it to me straight. What can I expect to happen and how long do I have?"

"You could have a few years ahead of you with following my instructions, but I advise you to get your affairs in order as soon as possible. This ailment can cause confusion that will hinder you from making legal decisions. I suggest you get everything in writing, the way you want it, making it all legal, while you are in your right mind."

For the next half hour, the doctor explained everything in detail. Abe listened carefully, asking questions along the way.

"I can keep you comfortable all the way to the end, but if you have any fever or any other symptoms, you get to me as soon as possible. If you try to be a tough man, it could turn into peritonitis, and it could be fatal before you get help. I need you to take it very seriously."

"I understand." Abe turned away for a moment. "I've had a good life, a very blessed life, except for when my wife was sick. I finally got to see my boys marry fine young ladies and have a grandchild on the way. I have no right to be bitter."

He turned back to the doctor. "I take you very seriously, doctor. I will do everything you said. I would like to live long enough to see a few more grandchildren, perhaps be around long enough for a few of them to remember me.

"But for now, if you would just let me rest a while, I have some thinking to do."

"I will check on you after a while, then." He stood and started to leave the room.

"Doc? Please don't let my boys know anything is wrong. They need to hear it from me."

****

Harvey and Eva wouldn't take no for an answer.

"Pa!" Eva stood with her hands on her hips. "We will have the baby in our room for a long time. You are staying with us and that's that!" She stomped her foot and almost fell sideways.

Harvey chuckled as he steadied her. "Well, you heard the boss! I would suggest you not cross her when she gets like this, Pa."

Abe smiled and reached out to Eva's face. "I do appreciate the offer, really, I do, but I don't want to be a bur..."

"Don't you dare say it! I don't want to hear it again. All that nonsense!" Eva huffed as she turned toward the kitchen speaking over her shoulder. "Your bed is ready, and supper will be too if you will stop arguing long enough to let me finish it!"

Harvey and Abe laughed quietly after the kitchen door closed.

"We already moved your things in. Come on and let me show you." Harvey put his hand on Abe's shoulder.

"Son, I do appreciate this, but this isn't how it's supposed to be."

"Pa, please just give in for now. You certainly aren't a burden and at least until you fully recuperate, we really want you here."

****

"Eva, aren't you ever going to have that baby? I'm wanting to see my grandbaby." Abe teased while they sat together one afternoon. He had been there a week and was feeling much better, even though he had the constant burden of telling his boys the truth, bearing on his mind almost every minute.

Eva sighed. "Doc says I have a few more weeks. I'm getting anxious myself. I suppose he feels safe, warm, and content right where he is though."

"He? You think it's going to be a boy?"

"Well, I don't know, of course, but I don't like calling this precious little one 'it'. Sometimes we say she, other times we say he. It doesn't matter to us which, but we sure are looking forward to his or her arrival." She shifted to get more comfortable in her chair while she continued to knit.

"It's time for my medicine." Abe stood. "Can I get you anything while I'm up?"

"No, thank you. You must think I asked you to stay here so I could have you wait on me. You are as bad as Harvey!"

"Yeah," he teased. "You are quite the taskmaster!"

They laughed together before he disappeared into the kitchen. Every moment he was alone, his countenance would fall, almost bringing him to tears. Maybe it was good to be around the family, otherwise, the depression may be overwhelming, and the doctor had warned him about that.

The only way he could get relieved of the biggest burden was just to force himself to tell the boys. Then they could work everything out together. He made up his mind that he would do it tonight.

He approached Harvey over supper. "I was wanting to throw out a few ideas to you and Asa. Care to walk over there with me after supper? Maybe Olivia would come over and sit with Eva?"

"Anything wrong, Pa?"

"Nah, just had too much time on my hands and been doing some thinking."

Harvey looked at Eva.

"I'll be fine Harvey. You don't have to send Olivia over here. Even if the baby decided to come, it does usually take quite a while from start to finish."

"Okay. But I'm still sending Olivia over if she's not too busy."

Eva sighed. "Fine."

As Harvey and Abe walked across the meadow, Abe felt impending doom, as if he were walking to his own execution. It was almost not real to him, but after he shared it with his boys, it would become reality.

He pasted on a smile when Asa welcomed them in. He greeted Olivia with a hug and kissed her cheek.

"Pa wants to talk to us about some ideas he's been having," Harvey explained.

"Oh my," Olivia chuckled. "I will take my leave then. There's no telling what he's come up with!" She hurried for her coat, turning back to kiss Asa quickly.

He stood on the porch and watched until he saw the door open at Harvey's.

Abe and Harvey sat at the table waiting for Asa. He brought some cups and a pot of coffee as he sat down.

Abe declined the coffee, instead, he stood and got a glass of water.

"Pa, I didn't make the coffee," Asa laughed. "Olivia made it, so you don't have to be afraid of it."

"No, thank you, son. It's not good for me, and that's what I need to talk to you two about. In fact, we can't cover all of it tonight, so I guess I better get started."

They were all visibly upset as Abe told them what the doctor said. Taking turns at wiping their faces, pacing the room, and asking more questions, Abe asked them to pray with him.

"I have a lot of decisions to make, and I need you boys to help me keep a level head."

"Pa, you don't need to be worrying about other things. Just work on getting well." Asa choked while tears trickled down his face.

"Asa," Abe patted his shoulder. "Son, I'm not going to get well. I will have good days and bad days, and I will take care of myself as best I can, but there is no cure.

"We have to be concerned with getting things in order while my mind is clear enough to do so."

Harvey had kept quiet for the last few minutes, with his face buried in his hands. He wiped his face and shook his head to clear his thoughts. "What kind of things are you worried about, Pa? What is it you need us to do? You say it and we will take care of it."

Abe cleared his throat. It hurt him so badly to see his boys in such anguish. "I own a hundred and twenty acres, free and clear. That land is to be divided equally between the two of you. That's the easy part.

"Asa, I know you have no desire to farm or even ranch and that's fine by me, but you will always have a home here.

"Because of Mr. Farley's foresight, the contracts I have with the government about the additional land is transferable to my heirs.

"Now, hear me out before you say anything. In two and a half years, September of 1854, I will be able to purchase the farmland and in November of the same year, the ranchland. Meaning, if I transfer it to one or both of you, it will be your decision to make.

"Asa, I don't want to make you feel forced into it. Before long, you need to make the decision if you want to have a part of it. Harvey, the same for you. It won't hurt my feelings either way, but whoever decides to buy the land will be taking on quite a bit of debt. If the farm continues to prosper as it is now, it won't be a problem making the payments. But I want both of you to think about it and pray about it because once you make your decision, you need to stick with it.

"I don't want both of you starting out together then one of you changes your mind, leaving the other with all the risk, and I don't want you to start paying on something and then decide it isn't right for either of you, forfeiting all the money you have already paid on it."

The brothers looked at each other and shrugged. "Don't worry about it, Pa." Harvey looked back to Abe. "We will figure it out."

Abe smiled. "I know you will. Meanwhile, I have a request. Let's keep this to ourselves for a while. I don't want to upset the girls, especially Eva in her condition."

He started to stand. "I guess we need to make some plans to go see a lawyer sometime soon. Since we don't have one here, we will wait until after the baby comes to plan a trip. You boys need to make some decisions before then."

* *

Amy fluttered in, more cheerful than anyone should be on a dreary morning like this. "Good morning, Harvey!" She hugged him and then headed for the kitchen.

She hugged Eva and started instructing her to sit, while she tied on her apron. "I have so much to tell you, and I was hoping we could come up with something special for supper while we talk."

Eva grinned at her. "My, you do have it bad! Spill it."

Harvey walked in, interrupting briefly to say goodbye. He kissed Eva quickly, pressing his big hand firmly on her belly for a response. Smiling as he felt movement, he kissed her again and left.

"Eva," Amy swooned. "Harvey is so sweet and so downright silly about you and the baby. I do so hope Vince is the same way."

"Yes, he is a definite keeper and I'm sure Vince will be the same. Now, what's got you so cheerful this morning?"

"We picked a date!" Amy squealed, clasping her hands together. "I am hoping that you and Olivia will stand up with me. It's going to be on June 5th. Can you believe it! I am getting married in less than four months!"

Eva joined her sister's excitement, accepting the honor of being in the wedding and starting to help with plans. She even offered to have them all over for supper that night, if Amy would help her.

Abe came in for breakfast as the girls continued to chatter. Amy set his plate in front of him as Eva turned and noticed he didn't look so well. He didn't have much to say and looked a bit flushed.

Eva was about to ask him how he felt when Olivia came in the door.

"Eva, I'm running a bit late this morning, but I was wondering, do you know of anything going on around here? Asa isn't himself lately and I was wondering if maybe Harvey was the same."

Eva shrugged. "Harvey is tired when he comes in and doesn't get real lively most nights, but no, I haven't noticed or heard anything. Maybe something at work is bothering him?"

"Hmm, maybe. Well, thanks. I have to get going."

Amy hurried to her, quickly extending the supper invitation and the reason for the celebration.

Olivia hugged Amy promising they would be there for supper. Abe congratulated Amy before making his way to his room.

When Abe didn't come back to the kitchen after a few minutes, Eva grew concerned. She went to his room to find it empty. She assumed he was feeling well enough to take care of himself, shrugged, then thought no more of it.

Several times during the day, Eva complained of indigestion that just wouldn't go away. "I don't dare tell Harvey or he will be hauling me to the doctor again. We have worried that man to death!"

Harvey came in the house for lunch about that time, chilled to the bone. He kissed Eva. "Don't tell Harvey what?"

Eva blushed. "I just have a bit of indigestion but didn't want to worry you with it. I'm fine."

"Yes, indeed you are." He winked at her. "The weather is getting colder out there and looks like we may get some more snow."

He washed up quickly, then started eating. "Where's Pa?"

"I'm not sure, Harvey. He came in for breakfast this morning and then just disappeared. I assumed he felt up to working and did so. Although he did look a bit poorly."

Harvey tried to hide his alarm. No one but Asa and himself knew that their Pa was ill. "I hate for him or anyone to be out on a day like this."

He shoveled down his lunch quickly. "Sorry, sweetheart, but I need to get back on the other side of the mountain." He kissed her quickly and left.

Eva could tell something was wrong but would save her thoughts and questions for later.

Harvey was almost in a panic when he mounted his horse, wondering where his pa could have gone. "Lord, please help me find Pa. Let him be okay, Lord, please."

He looked around for any signs of tracks, movement, or anything. Nothing. Starting toward the bunkhouse, he noticed a steady stream of smoke coming from Asa's chimney.

"He went home," Harvey whispered. "Lord, please let it be that he was a bit confused and just went home."

Hurrying to Asa's, he rushed in the door, finding his pa sitting in his chair, smoking his pipe while reading a book. Relief flooded over him.

Abe looked up in surprise. "Harvey? What are you doing here this time of day? Need some lunch?"

"No thanks, Pa. I was just checking to see if you needed anything. Getting cold out there." He could tell his pa's face was a bit flushed.

"You doing okay, Pa? Not feeling bad, are you?"

Abe waved him off. "I'm fine, son. Feel a bit under the weather but nothing serious."

"Have you taken your medicine today?"

"I'm not that sick, son. I don't need any medicine. I'm just going to stay in where it's warm."

"What about the medicine the doctor told you to take every day? Did you take it?"

"Son? What are you going on about?"

Harvey didn't know what to do or say. He knew his pa was getting sick again, causing the confusion. "Oh, umm, I meant to say it wouldn't hurt for you to take a little something every day to keep from getting sick in this bad weather."

"Pshaw," Abe waved him off. "I didn't get as old as I am by taking a bunch of stuff I don't need. You go on and take care of the farm for me. I'll be back at it tomorrow. Go on now."

"Eva wants you to come over to the house. She's got a big lunch ready."

"She's such a sweetheart, and I guess I am a bit hungry. Don't want to disappoint her." He put his pipe out and stood to follow Harvey.

Harvey let him use his horse while he followed behind, hurriedly. "Now, what am I supposed to tell Eva?" he mumbled.

Minutes later, he took Eva to the side as Amy set lunch on the table for Abe.

"Eva, Pa is sick. He needs to take medicine every day for now, and if he doesn't, well, he starts to run a fever again and it causes him to be confused."

He led her to his pa's room and showed her the medicine. "Please see to it he takes this like it says on the bottle."

She nodded. "Harvey, I wish you would tell me the whole truth. I imagine it must be something you don't want me to know, so I won't press the issue. Just know that you can tell me anything." She squeezed his arm. "I will take care of him."

Harvey looked at her, noticing how tired she looked. "Sweetheart, you need to take care of yourself, too. You look so tired. Why don't you and Pa both take a nap?"

She chuckled. "Go take care of the farm, Harvey. I've got things under control here."

Moments later, he found himself mumbling about Eva being such a wonderful, yet stubborn woman, as he mounted his horse and headed toward the doctor's office.

An hour later, he returned home with the doctor in tow. Eva had talked Abe into going to bed after he took his medicine, and the doctor hurried that way. Abe was sleeping, had a fever, and was shivering. He woke him enough to get him to drink a different medicine, checked him over good, then let him go back to sleep.

Entering the parlor, he discreetly shook his head at Harvey before pasting on a smile and greeting Eva.

"Mrs. Darnell, it's your turn."

"What do you mean? I'm fine."

He smiled. "I didn't come all the way out here to hear an argument. Your husband says you aren't sleeping, you have indigestion, and you are tired all the time. All of which is quite normal, but I can help you with those things.

"Now, if you would let me examine you, please? I just want to make sure everything is still on schedule for a few weeks from now."

Eva sighed when she saw Harvey's stern look. "Alright."

A few moments later, the doctor stuck his head out the bedroom door, summoning Harvey. "I'd like to share something with you."

Harvey looked intrigued as he hurried towards the bedroom. The doctor motioned for him to stand by Eva and put the stethoscope in his ear. Pressing the other end firmly against Eva's belly, Harvey listened closely as his face lit up.

"Oh my!" was all he could say as his smile broadened.

When the doctor took the stethoscope from him, Harvey sat down on the bed, helping Eva sit up, then wrapped his arm around her and kissed her.

"It looks as though everything here is fine. I will give you two different medicines, one for indigestion and one to help you sleep. Take the stomach medicine before each meal and both at bedtime.

"While Abe is sleeping, why don't you try to do the same? There will be very little rest after this baby comes."

Harvey coaxed her into taking a dose of the stomach medicine and then a short nap. He left her cuddled up in the bed and went to talk to the doctor.

"Eva is fine. She's healthy, strong, and doesn't seem to be carrying a large baby. I'm looking for a very normal delivery.

"Your pa, on the other hand, is having another spell. This cold weather is probably bringing on cold and flu symptoms and he isn't strong enough to fight.

"With Eva living in the same house and needing to be one of his caregivers, you need to tell her the truth. She already knows he's sick."

"But doc, I don't want to upset her in her condition. I don't want to chance anything happening to her or the baby."

"Harvey, I don't think you give Eva enough credit. She may be stronger than you think. She needs to know so she can be a help, not just wonder what's really going on and start to worry. Besides, even if she went into labor soon, I have no doubt everything will be fine. I'm more concerned about your pa."

Harvey nodded. "Maybe you're right. Let me pray about it, and thanks for coming out here."

That night, after their special supper with Vince and Amy, Harvey told Asa privately about what the doctor had said. They decided it was best to tell their wives so they could all help their pa.

After Vince and Amy left and Harvey gave his pa more medicine, Asa and their wives joined him in the dining room. The two girls fell apart as they heard the news, while their husbands cried with them, holding them.

Long moments passed with no sounds but muffled cries and sniffles. When they began to regain their composure, they were able to plan how to take care of Abe.

Harvey didn't return to his rounds on the farm. He had much more important things to attend.

Abe was weak, but up and around, back in his right mind by the fourth day. Harvey told him that the girls knew and that until the weather got warm, he wasn't to step a foot out the door.

Chapter 14

"I can't believe how much better I feel," Eva enthused. "I wish I had told the doctor sooner. In fact, I feel good enough to help ma in the kitchen. Maybe I will bake a cake."

She left Harvey and Abe chuckling at her enthusiasm.

"Son, I want to thank you for all you and Eva are doing. I know it's not easy on any of you."

"You would do the same for us, pa." Harvey stood, with a twinkle in his eyes. "So, how would you feel about losing to me in checkers?"

Abe scoffed. "You know that day will never come! Bring on the game."

****

Asa and Olivia came over to check on Abe, as they did every night. Asa privately apologized to Harvey for not being able to do more to help.

"Don't worry about it, Asa. If you were your own boss like I am, you could have more time off. You have a job and a boss to answer to. I'll find a way for you to make it up to me."

"Yeah," Asa teased back. "That's what I'm afraid of."

The men heard their wives cackling in the kitchen and went to join them. Eva was a bundle of energy, drying and putting away dishes while Olivia finished tidying up. Abe was teasing with them, keeping them very entertained.

Later, Harvey walked Asa and Olivia to the door, returning to the kitchen to find his pa drinking his medicine and Eva sweeping the floor.

He reached for the broom. "Sweetheart, let me do that for you."

She jerked the broom out of his reach. "I've got it, Harvey. But if you would be so kind as to hold the dustpan, please? I can't see it and I certainly can't reach it."

When she finished, she reached for her medicine and drank it, followed by a sip of water. She got distracted, seeing the dish rag on the table. Picking it up and hanging it on the sink, she went back to the table and took her other medicine, followed by another sip of water.

Abe headed to bed, leaving them in the kitchen. Harvey pulled her on his lap and held her close. "I love you, Eva."

He put a little pressure on her belly with his hand, feeling nothing. Doing it again, he still felt nothing. "Eva, is something wrong? I don't feel the baby."

"No, nothing's wrong. Ma says the baby slows down a lot before it's born. Not enough room in there to move around."

Harvey let out a sigh of relief. "About ready for bed?"

She stood and took his hand. "Yes, I believe my medicine is already making me sleepy." She didn't realize she had taken her sleeping medicine twice, thinking one dose was the stomach medicine.

Harvey helped her to bed, noticing that she was starting to get groggy. "You've overdone yourself today, I'm afraid."

"It will make me sleep better tonight. Goodnight, Harvey. I love you."

She was asleep before he responded.

****

Harvey was awakened during the night by Eva moaning in her sleep. He shook her gently, hoping to disturb her bad dream but not wake her totally.

Soon, she was sleeping peacefully again.

Just as he was drifting back to sleep, she started moaning again. He shook her again. "Sweetheart, it's just a bad dream." He wrapped his arms around her with his hand on her belly as she relaxed and quieted.

About five minutes later, she moaned again, a bit louder.

"Sweetheart! Eva!" He shook her hard enough that her eyes fluttered.

"Wake up! You are having bad dreams."

"My stomach hurts," she mumbled before drifting back to sleep. He felt her relax.

A few minutes later, he felt her stomach tighten, moments before she began to moan again. This time he didn't have to wake her.

"Harvey, my stomach hurts."

He sat up. "Is the baby coming?"

Eva, still groggy, relaxed again. "I'm so sleepy." She drifted back off.

He was wide awake now. He propped himself on his elbow and watched her sleep. Again, he felt her stomach tighten, right before she started to moan.

Holding her hand until she relaxed again, he kept telling her she would be alright. As soon as she drifted off, he got up and pulled his clothes on. He had to send Asa for the doctor.

He stayed until she had another contraction, hoping to go out the door as soon as she went back to sleep. This time, she was uncomfortable enough that she couldn't get back to sleep.

She grabbed his hand and wouldn't let go. "Harvey, don't you leave me! Not for a minute. I'm scared and I'm hurting...oh! Harvey, don't you leave me!" she cried.

"Eva, I need to send Asa for the doctor. Sweetheart, I'll be right back, I promise." He kissed her forehead and raced for the door. Before it closed behind him, he could hear her calling for him again. His heart ached as he hurried to Asa's.

When he returned to her, she was crying, holding her hand out to him. "Harvey, please don't leave me again."

"I won't, darling. Asa has gone for the doctor, and Olivia will be here in a few minutes."

She nodded as another contraction hit her. She cried out as Olivia came through the door.

"Oh my, Eva! I have only witnessed a birth one time and didn't really help much. Here let me see if I can help you."

Harvey tried to move out of the way but Eva wouldn't let go of his hand.

Olivia rushed around getting towels, putting on some water and coffee and getting Eva situated more comfortably. "Eva, tell me what to do. What do you know about this?"

Eva panted through another contraction. When it was over, she hurriedly told Olivia all she could. "I know that the contractions get harder and closer until there is hardly any break between. I'm not supposed to push until then even though I feel like it now!" She cried out the last few words as another wave of pain hit her.

Asa was back within half an hour. "The doctor is on his way."

Abe walked in the parlor. "What's going on? Is the baby coming?"

"Yes," Asa wrung his hands and paced. "The doctor is on his way."

Abe heard Eva cry out. "Who's helping her?"

"Harvey and Olivia."

"Has Olivia done this before?"

"No, but she doesn't have much choice. Harvey can't be much help."

"Maybe not, but I can. I delivered both you boys."

"You did?"

"Who else do you think did? We didn't have anyone close by, certainly no doctor."

"Well, pa. What are you waiting for? Get in there and help Eva."

Abe squared his shoulders and entered the room. He started instructing everyone what to do. He situated Eva on the bed more comfortably and calmed her with reassurances that he knew what he was doing and that everything was going fine.

When the doctor arrived, rushing to the room, Abe shocked him. "Doc, if no one minds, I would like you to make sure everything is okay, then I would like to deliver this baby."

Harvey looked at Eva. "What do you think, sweetheart?"

She smiled between contractions while Harvey wiped her forehead. "I would be honored to have you deliver your grandbaby, Pa."

The doctor and Olivia stood by while Harvey coaxed and soothed, when at last, Abe told Eva to push one more time. The next sound was a baby crying, as Abe handed the baby to the doctor to be checked.

Abe wiped his hands before patting Harvey on the back and bending to kiss Eva on the cheek. "Congratulations, it's a boy!"

Harvey gently hugged Eva. "You did wonderful, sweetheart. Thank you for once again making me the happiest man in the world."

The doctor handed the baby boy to Harvey, then he and Olivia started making Eva more comfortable.

Harvey sat down beside Eva and put the tiny boy in her arms, holding them both. Tears of joy rolled down his face as he took turns tenderly kissing her, then the baby. "Did you decide on a name?"

"I think so. I want to name him after you and your pa. You are Harvey Abraham and your pa is Abraham Nathaniel. I would like to name him Harvey Nathaniel. What do you think?"

"Thank you, sweetheart. I like that, a lot. We can call him Nate?"

She nodded.

Everyone left them to enjoy their first private family time together. What a sweet time it was.

****

Harvey and Eva welcomed spring anxiously by having a big supper with the family, Mr. and Mrs. Farley, and the Henderson family.

Everybody thought the other silly as they teased about how they fussed over baby Nate, until it was their turn, and they did the same silly baby talk.

"What is it about a tiny baby that can turn a full-grown man into a heap of warm mush?" Asa laughed as he reached for Nate, instantly changing his voice and swaying back and forth gently.

"I don't know, dear," Olivia stole her arm around his waist, peeking at Nate. She smiled up at Asa, "I hope to find out someday soon. You will be a wonderful Pa."

He bent and kissed her forehead. "I can't wait."

Vince and Amy seemed to be in a world of their own. Vince had just rented the house and Amy was making plans on how to furnish it.

She had to constantly remind Vince that they didn't need to buy everything at once. She found herself having to be careful of what she wished for because Vince would try to find a way to make it come true. He was so sweet and doting.

They took their turns with Nate, sharing glances and blushes discreetly with each other. Amy knew how much a family meant to Vince. Growing up in the orphanage made it that much more important. She was anxious to make that happen for him.

When the men gathered outside after supper, the conversation took a serious turn. Mr. Farley was very upset about the upheaval in the nation, trying to spew quietly.

"Tariffs! Abolitionists! Extremist! Clay's Compromise! I tell you, gentlemen, this isn't good. The country will be hopelessly divided."

Asa shook his head. "I don't understand it all, but I just don't see it coming to our little neck of the woods. We all take care of our own." He kicked at a pebble. "I know things are costing us more, with tariffs and all, but I don't see where anything can be done about that."

"Asa, I wish it were that simple, that we could just brace ourselves against higher prices and be done with it. Believe me, it goes much deeper than that." Mr. Farley looked down and spoke quietly. "Mark my words, this thing will sadly and tragically touch every one of our lives."

****

Abe had good days and bad but couldn't sit around doing nothing for long. As soon as the weather allowed, he was back in his saddle, making rounds, helping where needed.

He had turned the farm over to Harvey to attend and was diligent about taking care of himself. The warm sunshine and fresh air were good for him, clearing his head, allowing him to think and have quiet time with God, as he rode slowly past each field.

Soon, he and his boys would have to make that trip to Raleigh. Harvey had decided to keep the farm going, which was no surprise. Asa had a more difficult time with his decision.

Not wanting to hurt his pa's feelings, nor let Harvey feel abandoned, he had graciously declined to be a part of the growth of the farm.

Explaining in length and very apologetically, he had his mind set on a different path for his future. "Harvey, I hope you know that I will always do anything I can to help you, but I just don't see this as my future. I hope you understand."

Harvey and Abe had encouraged Asa about his decision, and they all walked away happy.

Abe turned his horse toward town. He wired a message to the lawyer Mr. Farley had recommended, asking for an appointment.

****

The closer the wedding got, the more Amy seemed to mature and glow. She had gotten stern with Vince about his lavish spending, finally telling him, "Vince, sweetie, what I want more than anything, other than you, is for us to have a house of our own. Please, stop spending on my trivial everyday wishes and wants. That's all they are, just wants, not needs.

"Instead, save every penny you can towards our real goal, a house. Save the little extras for special occasions. Agreed?"

He hung his head for a moment, holding her hand. "I will try, Amy. I just love to see you happy, that's all I want."

She put her hand on his face, tenderly looking into his eyes. "I am happy, Vince. You loving me makes me the happiest above anything else."

Gathering her in his arms, kissing her tenderly, his whole being was filled with love for this beautiful, little woman. My, how she did make him feel like the richest man in the world.

****

May was an overwhelmingly busy month for everyone. The ladies spent every moment possible, helping prepare Amy's house, but time was limited for each of them.

Preacher Upton had gotten word about his new ministry in Oklahoma Territory. They would be leaving by wagon, carrying all their earthly belongings, on June 21st. This was bittersweet news to everyone, although Preacher and Mrs. Upton seemed thrilled.

Mrs. Upton stretched herself thin, trying to help Amy with her wedding and house, doting on her precious little grandson, deciding what to take and what to leave behind, and still making herself available to the community if anyone needed her.

Olivia was excited about finishing up the school year. She and Mrs. Powell were planning a special program for the students to perform in front of the community on the last afternoon of school. They were hoping it would draw the interest of more families, letting the children and parents see the need for education.

Eva made herself available to Amy every hour she wasn't needed on the farm. She had taken responsibility for Abe's medication, making sure he didn't miss a dose. Sometimes she had to hunt him down on the farm to give it to him, but she was diligent.

She had been learning every aspect of the farm from Harvey and Abe, wanting to do her part. Harvey had her check the women workers several times a day, making sure everyone had everything they needed, and no one was sick or hurt. This freed Harvey up to take more interest in the ranching area of the business.

Abe heard back from the lawyer and made arrangements for his boys and himself to take an overnight trip to Raleigh.

It seemed as though everything was happening at once, but all were happy and thriving. Decisions made, plans put into action, moving forward building their futures, one day at a time.

****

Amy had opted for an outdoor wedding in the park. Vince and Asa had surprised her the week before with a beautiful iron archway for her and Vince to stand under as they vowed their love to each other. She squealed in delight as she ran her hands over it.

Immediately her sisters started planning how to decorate it with ribbon and wildflowers, while Amy clung to Vince's neck, thanking him.

The day had finally arrived with everything in place. There were musicians playing their string instruments as the guests gathered. Ladies placed food for the reception on the nearby tables on their way to the ceremony.

"Amy!" Eva chided. "Please sit still, let me finish your hair. You are like a worm on a hot ash!" she laughed.

"I'm just so excited!" Amy swooned.

Olivia looked at her lovingly through the reflection in the mirror. "You are glowing, Amy. I am so happy for you! Are you nervous?"

Amy shrugged slightly. "No, not really. Why? Are you going to make me nervous like you were on your wedding day?" she teased.

Olivia giggled. "No, I was just going to reaffirm the wisdom of our oldest sister on that day."

Eva finished and had Amy stand just as Mrs. Upton came in and gasped. "Oh! My baby girl! You are such a beautiful young woman." She hugged Amy and burst into a stream of tears.

"Ma?" Eva touched her shoulder. "Ma, are you alright?"

Mrs. Upton continued to hold Amy and cry.

Olivia and Eva worked to pry her loose, filled with concern. They finally had her seated with Eva kneeling in front of her.

"Ma, what's wrong?"

Mrs. Upton shook her head, wiping her eyes with a hankie. "I'm just being a silly old woman. It's like I just woke up and realized everything that had happened so quickly over the last three years. Then I thought about the reality of leaving all three of you and that precious grandson behind." Tears flooded again. "It's about more than I can bear!"

"Oh Ma," the girls sighed in unison as they gathered around and hugged her.

"I remember sitting at the table with you, looking at that beautiful wedding dress in the catalog when you all decided to purchase it together. I never in a million years thought it would be used three times, this soon."

"But Ma," Olivia soothed. "We are all very happy. We will miss you and Pa so much but at least you will have each other and all three of us will be close together."

"Yes," she conceded. "You're right. Each of you have fine men to love you and take care of you. My job is over. I have raised you to be responsible young women, and I am so very proud of each of you."

She hugged them all. "Now, before your pa comes in here wondering what has happened, we better go. There is an anxious young groom, handsome too, I might add, waiting near the archway."

Mrs. Upton had been gone so long, Vince approached Preacher Upton with concern. "Sir? Umm, has something happened?"

He patted Vince on the shoulder. "I'm sure everything is fine, son. Let me go see what the holdup is."

189

Mrs. Upton appeared, hurrying across the park lawn, motioning for her husband. "Amy's ready," she smiled as she smoothed her skirt, patted her hair, then made her way to her seat.

Looking across, she saw Abe holding little Nate. Her heart went to her throat again. How hard it was to pull herself away from her family. Then she looked at Vince and was so aware in that moment, as all three of her sons-in-law stood there, everything would be alright. She was sure this was God's perfect plan for her girls.

The music grew louder, as everyone turned to see Olivia walking up the aisle, holding a small bouquet of wildflowers. Not far behind her, Eva followed. Both were beautiful, as they gracefully took their places.

The music stopped for a second, then loudly played the wedding march. Everyone stood, waiting for the bride to appear.

When Vince saw Amy, he gasped loud enough for everyone on the first row to hear him above the music. His knees felt weak and sweat beaded on his forehead. His eyes filled with tears, spilling down his cheeks. He quickly wiped them away, trying to get control of his emotions.

He was humbled at the thought of Amy loving him enough to give herself to him. His thoughts were filled with how much he wanted to love her and care for her in every way humanly possible.

Amy's eyes were moist as they locked with Vince's. She felt confident, radiant, and loved. She smiled at him, which she knew melted his heart, he had told her so, often.

When her pa placed her hand in Vince's, she felt him shaking. She squeezed his hand and nodded at him, her nod that let him know everything was going to be okay. "I love you, Vince," she whispered.

His heart soared as an unshed tear trickled down his cheek. He wanted to take her in his arms right that moment and never let her go, being certain that he could never love any stronger than he did right now.

The ceremony was a blur, with Vince clearing his throat several times as he spoke his vows to her, filled with the seriousness and sincerity of every word.

Her voice trembled when she began to speak her vows, love lacing her words and radiating in her eyes.

When Preacher Upton pronounced them husband and wife, Vince gathered her gently in his arms, kissing her for a long time, not wanting this moment to end. Amy was more than willing to let it continue, wishing they could magically be alone.

Asa cleared his throat, signaling for Vince to knock it off. Finally, he nudged him, breaking the spell. There was quiet laughter throughout the crowd when they finally finished, red-faced with embarrassment. Everyone started clapping and cheering the happy couple.

Chapter 15

Nate was a happy baby; there was no reason for him not to be. He went from one set of arms to another almost constantly. Eva was beginning to worry he would be spoiled. From the time Abe came in around lunch, until the time Eva or Harvey put him to bed at night, someone was doting on that boy.

At six months old, it was already easy to tell, the boy was going to worship the ground his pa and grandpa walked on. When either of them would enter the room, his little face would glow, not to mention the glow on the adult men's faces.

Eva was happy to have so many helping hands most of the time. Having Abe there with Nate, freed up her time to do chores and make more rounds at the farm.

Soon, school would resume, with Olivia going back to work, no longer able to have the much-coveted afternoon chats. Eva would really miss it.

Amy would still be working at the farm until the close of the season in November. Eva was glad of that, knowing her days would be so lonely without her sisters.

Every evening when Harvey came in, he would attempt to kiss Eva before his son got his attention. But when Nate saw or heard his pa, he would squeal in delight, to which melted Harvey's heart and he had to pick the boy up. It thrilled Eva to see it.

One night at supper, when Nate was nine months old, he was in his feeding chair between Eva and Harvey. He reached toward Harvey's knife and Eva quickly said, "No." His eyes flew to hers with his outstretched hand frozen.

He smiled at her, still not withdrawing his hand. She repeated herself. "Nate, Ma said no."

Nate turned and looked at Harvey as if to ask his opinion on the matter. Eva's first response was to smack his hand and get mad at Harvey because she knew the man would at least grin, thinking the situation funny. Instead, Harvey, looking shocked that Nate would do such a thing at such a young age, spoke to his son sternly.

"Your ma said no, Nate."

Eva was immediately proud of Harvey.

Nate's face crinkled, his lip pouted, and a loud wail followed. Eva and Harvey looked at each other, not sure what to do next. They ignored Nate for a moment and continued to eat, feeling as if they would choke on every bite.

Harvey reached over and put a bite of food on Nate's spoon. "Hush that fuss and finish your supper, boy." He spoke kindly yet firm.

Nate turned his head, refusing the food. Harvey put the spoon down and ignored Nate's slowing cries. After a moment, Nate was quiet, wiping his eyes, showing signs of being sleepy.

Eva began to stand, reaching to wipe Nate's face and hands.

"Eva," Harvey motioned for her to sit down. "Just give him a minute. He needs to finish eating or he won't sleep through the night."

She sat back down and continued her supper. They engaged in conversation with each other and Abe as if nothing had happened. Harvey picked up Nate's spoon and tried again to feed him. This time the boy opened his mouth willingly. Supper had returned to normal.

That night, Harvey and Eva talked as they cuddled in bed, quietly discussing the scene at supper. Eva let him know of her surprise at the way he handled Nate.

"I don't know why it surprises you. In fact, I'm shocked at that. Of course, we haven't talked about everything we will or won't do as far as our children are concerned, but there are some things I refuse to tolerate. Disobedience, laziness, disrespect, lying, and maliciousness, just to name a few. I figure if we start now, we won't have to be as stern with him later and may save ourselves a lot of grief along the way."

She smiled at him. "You're a good man and sometimes I think you're wise beyond your years."

He kissed her forehead. "One thing I want to be sure of Eva, and this is serious. I don't ever intend to have our children put a wedge between us. I won't tolerate it. If we don't agree, then we need to discuss it in private and come to an agreement, then approach the child with our decision.

"I don't ever want them to come to you after they have asked my permission about something, hoping for a different answer. The same for them coming to you first."

She nodded her head. "Are you sure this is your first time raising a child?" she giggled.

"With you, yes."

She punched him in the ribs. "Funny man."

He held her close. "I saw what was happening in a family that used to live around here. Sad situation. The kids were bad, the parents seemed to not care, and the situation continued to get worse until it was almost like the parents hated their children. They never looked forward to being around them.

"That's not the way it's supposed to be, and I'm not letting it happen here."

****

The holidays were bittersweet this year. The girls missed their parents being with them. They had received a few letters from them, knowing they were doing well and were settling into their new life. But they were sorely missed.

Amy cried off and on throughout the day. "I guess because I was the baby, or perhaps because I lived with them until a few weeks before they left, but I just miss them so much."

Vince tried to console her.

"I'm so sorry, Vince. You're so good and kind and here I am blubbering on our first Christmas as a married couple."

"It's alright, sweetheart. I just wish I could take your pain from you."

"Amy," Eva reached for her hand. "Come help me in the kitchen. Let's get your mind off this for a while, shall we? Let's make some fresh coffee and get the dessert ready."

While Eva kept Amy busy, she struck up a conversation that her ma had with her a year and a half earlier. Without saying anything, she made her own assessment, keeping it all to herself.

Olivia had wanted a baby so badly, and Eva didn't want to take the chance of upsetting her or misdiagnosing Amy's symptoms, but she was fairly sure that Amy was going to have a baby. She made up her mind that on Monday, she would visit her sister and take her to see the doctor.

They chattered on while they prepared dessert, with Olivia joining them in time to set things on the table. "Sorry I wasn't here to help, but I had to show Pa that he isn't the only one who can play checkers."

"You beat him?" Eva sounded shocked.

"Umm, no, but I gave him a run for his money."

They laughed together while carrying everything to the dining room.

Harvey held Nate on his lap, sharing his dessert with him. Nate looked across the table at Abe, smiling when his grandpa acknowledged him. He pointed his finger at Abe. "Um pa!"

Everything went silent. Harvey looked at Nate. "What did you say, son?" He pointed to Abe. "Who is that Nate?"

Nate smiled at Abe, who was practically glowing by now. "Um pa!"

Everyone clapped, cheered, and chattered over Nate's first word, while Harvey got up and took Nate, setting him in um pa's lap.

"Isn't that something?" Abe pulled the little boy close.

Harvey and Eva couldn't have been happier.

****

Monday morning, Olivia came over early to stay with Nate and Abe while Eva ran her errands. The three of them enjoyed their time together, with Nate being the main event.

Amy was happily surprised when Eva knocked on the door. "Eva! I'm so glad you're here. I get so lonely sometimes."

"I need to run a few errands and wanted you to go with me. Maybe we can have lunch at the diner afterward."

"That would be wonderful. Just let me fix myself a bit and I will be ready. I need a few things from Henderson's myself."

In a few minutes, they pulled up in front of the doctor's office, with Amy instantly thinking either Eva or maybe Abe was sick. "What are we doing here? Are you sick? Is Abe ailing again?"

"No, Amy. Just come with me."

Doctor Powell greeted them cautiously, thinking they needed him to come check Abe. "Ladies, how can I help you on this briskly cold morning?"

"Doctor Powell, my sister, Amy, has been feeling poorly and crying a lot lately." She winked at him and smiled before continuing. "I know we all miss our parents, but she is really taking it hard. I was hoping you may be able to help her."

"Eva," Amy chided. "I'm fine, really. Christmas without the folks was just hard." Suddenly she was in tears again.

Doctor Powell took her gently by the arm. "Please, since you are already here, just let me check a few things. Maybe you will feel better by the time you leave, just knowing everything is okay."

She nodded as he led her to another room.

A little while later, Eva heard Amy's joyful squeal. She smiled to herself and continued reading the newspaper.

****

The winter was rough on Abe. He wanted badly to go out and do what he could to help. He watched as everyone else worked constantly. Harvey would be out in the cold all day and sometimes half the night, yet still would bring in the firewood and tend to their horses. Eva would cook and clean, do laundry, feed the chickens, run errands in town and take care of young Nate.

He felt like an invalid, totally useless. Asa and Olivia would come over several nights a week to visit for a while, which was always fun, but he just felt in the way. Depression started to creep in.

Harvey and Eva noticed and talked about what could be done. They even talked to the doctor, Asa, and Olivia. They developed a plan that may work out for everyone.

Suddenly Abe was barraged with more work than he could handle. Harvey set up a corner in the big parlor for Abe to work on leather and wood repairs that were needed. His spirits picked up, feeling that he was contributing, not just doing busy work.

When Harvey saw the change in Abe's demeanor, he was relieved and saw this as his chance to talk to him about some important issues. He hadn't dared let his pa know that he was overworked and totally stressed, at least not when Abe was teetering on the edge of depression already. It would have made him feel more useless.

Now, with Abe's newfound sense of purpose, Harvey approached him with his problems. "Pa, can I talk to you about a few things? I really need your advice."

Abe put down the leather strips he had been working on. "Sure, son. What's the problem?"

Harvey chuckled sarcastically. "Which one do you want me to start with?"

Abe sat down, motioning for Harvey to go on.

"Well, pa, I don't mean to sound like, umm, a complainer, but I am just up to my ears with things to do. I thought I could handle everything, but," he shook his head. "I'm not as big a man as I thought I was. Now, I'm confused and tired.

"I'm considering hiring someone to oversee the ranching, watching over the men, settling disputes, assigning duties, and keeping track of who is supposed to be where, and when. I think if I can find someone trustworthy, with a strong enough backbone to do the job, then I will be able to handle the rest."

Abe thought for a moment. "What did your profit margin look like this year? Is it enough to cover a foreman?"

Harvey sighed, "Yes, but that brings me to my next problem. I know that I'm under a contract with the government to sell them everything I produce from that extra five hundred acres, until the fall of '54. I don't like being that dependent on a government that seems to be so shaky right now. I also don't like having all my eggs in one basket.

"I need to put my education to work, get out there and find some other contracts from private companies. That's where the money is. I have the hundred and twenty acres to start supplying at least one other contract. The government has no say over the land you own free and clear."

Abe nodded his head. "Sounds like you're on the right track, so what's the problem? You hire your foreman and start looking for your next contract."

Harvey shook his head. "Everything takes time, pa, and finding a company willing to give me a contract will take me away from home, at least long enough to meet with the owners. I can't stand the thought of leaving Eva, Nate, and you."

Abe looked sad for a moment. "You mean, you don't think we can take care of ourselves while you're out of town for a little while? I understand. You think it will be too much on Eva, taking care of Nate and me."

Harvey looked at him in disbelief. "No, that's not what I meant at all. If that was it, Asa and Olivia are right across the meadow, or I could hire someone to come in and help.

"The problem with being away from here is..." he paused and choked for a moment. "Pa, I know your days are numbered and I want to spend every moment with you that I possibly can. I don't want to look back when it's too late and wish I had done differently."

Abe was too touched to speak. After a long silence, he spoke quietly. "Thank you, son. I'm sorry I said what I did."

Harvey patted him on the back.

"So, do you have any idea who you may hire as foreman?"

Harvey smiled. "Now that you asked, maybe. I've been praying about it and I'm thinking God may have sent me an answer.

"Do you remember the Benson family that moved from here about fifteen or so years ago?"

Abe rubbed his chin. "Oh, yes. Fine man with a couple of boys a few years older than you. His wife was friends with your ma."

"Seems the younger son, Frank, has moved back to town. He asked me for a job on the ranch and started working a few days ago. I've been showing him everything myself, which is why I've been so late coming in at night. And he's a pretty good cook."

"Well, that's always a plus," Abe chuckled. "What makes you think he's foreman material?"

"He's a Christian, honest, hardworking, takes instruction and criticism well, and was working another ranch for the last eight years."

"Why did he leave? Any problems?"

Harvey stated sadly, "His wife died. He said he couldn't stand to stay around constant reminders of her."

Abe shook his head. "That's hard enough on an old man, let alone a young one. I'm sorry to hear that.

"Why don't you check with his former boss and see what kind of recommendation he gives."

Harvey stood and walked to the table beside the couch, pulling a drawer open, retrieving an envelope. "He brought this sealed envelope with him from his former boss. Apparently, he comes highly recommended. I didn't read it until I made my own assessment of him."

"Well then, what are you waiting for, son?"

Harvey smiled. "I had to run it by the boss man first. You do still run this show, you know."

Abe glowed with pride. "Thanks, son."

****

About the time Abe felt better about things, Amy announced the new arrival due in the summer.

Everyone congratulated them heartily.

On the surface, Olivia was happy for her sister. Deep down, she was happy for Amy, yet miserable for herself. Asa glanced at her and could see the sadness in her eyes, even though her smile was genuine. His heart ached for her.

That night he held her as she cried, then held her while she apologized for feeling selfish. "Asa, I just want a baby so badly. My arms ache to hold our child.

"I am happy for Amy, truly I am, but I want a baby; our baby. Is it wrong for me to feel this way?"

He soothed her. "No sweetheart. I want a baby myself, and when it's time, the Lord will bless us with one."

For the next few weeks, Olivia poured her heart out to God and energy into her students, trying to fill every moment so her mind would stay off her heartache. Finally, after much prayer, she was able to face Amy without feeling crushed, and was truly happy for her. The Lord had eased her burden, reassuring her that He was in control and heard her prayers. Whatever her future held, God was there with her, always.

****

By spring, Frank Benson was working out well as the new foreman, and he and Harvey had become good friends. Harvey had him over for supper several times, with Abe joining them to discuss business afterwards.

Mr. Farley had several businessmen come to town for visits. No one seemed to know exactly what business, but the men sure looked important.

One evening, he asked Harvey and Abe to join him and some of his friends at the diner. It seemed odd, but knowing Mr. Farley, somehow it would be to the Darnell's benefit.

They weren't disappointed. After Mr. Farley made introductions, Harvey and Abe knew exactly where the conversation was headed. One of the men owned a food processing and distribution plant in Charlotte, North Carolina and the other man owned one near Galax, Virginia.

"Harvey, I took the liberty of sharing our discussion with these men about your concern with only having a government contract. They share our views and would like to see your operation."

"That would be good. Gentlemen, why don't you ride out tomorrow morning? I can show you everything there is to see and explain my future plans."

Eva was beside herself with excitement and so proud of Harvey.

"Eva, I'm glad you're happy, but there is nothing to be proud about. Mr. Farley is the only one I spoke to about this. He did the rest."

"But you had the idea, Harvey. And I know you could have done it yourself, it may have taken a bit longer, but I know you could."

He kissed her quickly. "Thank you, sweetheart. I appreciate you having faith in me and working beside me."

Early the next morning, Harvey rode out to speak with Benson about what was going on. He was going to show the men the ranch portion also, laying out his plans for expansion. Benson assured him that everything would be running smoothly.

After the men toured the property and listened to Harvey explain his plan, they were impressed. The man from Charlotte commented, "Mr. Darnell, I am intrigued by what I see and hear. Your understanding of rotating crops for maximum yield, and especially the fact of growing food crops instead of the usual cash crops, makes you admirable.

"The irrigation system you built is ingenious, assuring a good growing season even in the driest of conditions. I would like to discuss some numbers with you, if you would make an appointment with my office at your earliest convenience."

The other man spoke up, not wanting to be outdone. "I would like to do the same. I'm sure we can come to some favorable arrangements. Please schedule an appointment with me also."

Later that afternoon, Mr. Farley sent Harvey a note by a young messenger boy.

Harvey,
Congratulations on your first private contracts! I think it's time to petition for additional land before your contract ends.
Your friend,
Samuel Farley

Once again, Mr. Farley's friendship had been a blessing. Harvey took time right that moment to thank the Lord for it.

****

Late in April, the town council called a town meeting, asking everyone to attend. They had some important issues to cover that would involve everyone.

The council had contacted Olivia and Mrs. Powell asking them to be prepared to give facts and numbers about school attendance at the meeting. They weren't told why.

Excitement grew as curious people of the community gathered at the church for the meeting. Olivia and Mrs. Powell sat with their husbands, together on the front row. They held notes of facts and figures in shaky hands as they waited for the meeting to start.

The meeting was called to order, with so many people attending, the church was full, with people standing outside near the windows to listen.

Soon Mr. Farley was called to speak. He made a plea for the council to consider building a real schoolhouse. He motioned for and introduced Mrs. Darnell and Mrs. Powell to give accurate numbers on the school's growth, along with the curriculum and progress the students were making.

One of the council members spoke up. "We have made note of your request and will get back to you after we check our finances. Next item to be discussed tonight?"

There were rumblings of discontent as the two women took their seats, filled with disappointment.

Another councilman yelled above the crowd. "Wait just a minute!" He looked accusingly at the first councilman. "I can't believe you just dismissed something so vitally important to this community. If we don't invest in our children, then we shall surely fail. There is nothing more important."

There were shouts of agreement throughout the room.

He continued for a moment, naming the advantages of the school and the disadvantages of not having it. "I think this is worthy of an immediate vote. All in favor?"

Of the five councilmen, four hands went up immediately. The fifth finally went up as he conceded that he saw their point.

The crowd cheered as the teachers hugged their husbands with enthusiasm.

The next item up for discussion was someone petitioning for permission to sell alcoholic beverages, building and opening a saloon.

The councilman who had been willing to dismiss the school so quickly, was the first to agree to the permit. An argument progressed. All five of the councilmen threw out reasons for and against.

Making no headway on a decision, one being for, one against, and three uncommitted, they agreed to have the first town vote with the matter being decided by the community. The date was set for the vote to take place by secret ballot on Friday, June 10th.

"Is there any other business for tonight?"

Mr. Farley stood. "I would like to recommend hiring more deputies for the sheriff."

The council called the sheriff, asking if he needed more deputies. The sheriff knew exactly what Mr. Farley was thinking.

"As of now, I have enough men, but if a saloon opens, I'm sure I will need to double my staff."

The room roared with laughter.

The most vocal of the councilmen looked at Mr. Farley sternly. "Mr. Farley, are you making a mockery of this council?"

"No sir, not at all. Just making sure you see there are consequences to actions."

Chapter 16

In the weeks to come, there were mixed emotions throughout the community and with the Darnells.

All the workers on the farm and ranch talked constantly about their opinions on the upcoming vote, trying to sway people to their way of thinking. Benson was beginning to have some problems with the men, having to threaten some and change shifts around with others. He certainly didn't want to add to Harvey's headaches and was able to handle it on his own.

Standing the same height as Harvey at six foot three, Benson outweighed Harvey by a good forty pounds or more, built like an ox. His deep voice mixed with his stout build, made him a force not many men wanted to mess with. Most of the cowpokes at the ranch knew not to push him too far.

The family was dealing with sorrows and joys being a part of each day. Abe was getting weaker and stayed confused more often, even without the onset of fever or other symptoms. He started complaining of pain to which the doctor immediately gave him a stronger medicine.

Eva stayed with him constantly while Harvey worked the farm. Occasionally, he would come in at lunch and tell her to enjoy the afternoon. She would take that opportunity to do her shopping and check on Amy.

Amy was progressing normally and was staying cheerful but tired. Eva knew the feeling. She did what she could to help Amy, fixed supper, and tidied up, but Vince had already hired someone to do their laundry and come in once a week to clean.

"He is just so silly about me and the baby, Eva! I can't begin to describe him."

Eva rolled her eyes and laughed. They took time to compare notes on the subject.

"This is the last week of school and Olivia is going to stay with me every day until after the baby is born. Mrs. Powell is going to join us often so they can plan things for next year's students. Oh, and guess who has put themselves in charge of overseeing the plans and building of the school?"

Eva thought for a moment. "Mr. Farley?"

"Nope, but you are so close. Mrs. Farley! She marched herself right up to that pompous councilman and announced that she was donating the property for it to be built on and that she had already hired the builders!

"Then," Amy took a deep breath, "I heard that she went on to tell him that her husband had appointed him to the council and could surely have him removed! Isn't she something?"

"Yes, she certainly is," Eva said quietly. "Ma said to be kind to her that she was just a misplaced, misunderstood soul. She was convinced Mrs. Farley has good intentions but doesn't have the patience for getting her point across with kindness."

****

June 10th rolled around with everyone crowding into town for the vote. Only the men were allowed to vote, even though several women had joined together to make banners and signs showing their disapproval. They marched through the streets singing and chanting as some men lowered their heads in shame and some others mocked them.

The sheriff and all three deputies had to keep order, with several disputes coming to blows.

Harvey and Asa were there with Benson, offering to help keep the peace. The sheriff pulled out some extra badges and swore them in.

They knew the likely outcome of the vote and hated to see it. Too many cowpokes, farmers, miners, and construction workers would like to have a drink or two after a long, hard day of work, and that was the majority of who was voting. At five o'clock the last vote was cast and at five thirty the results were announced.

Although far from unanimous, the permit was granted by an overwhelming majority.

Shouts from the winners went up as the losers shook their heads and walked away. The deputies, including the Darnells and Benson, walked through the crowd, keeping their eyes open for trouble.

That's when Asa spotted that exact thing…trouble. There, standing on the boardwalk with people all around shaking his hand and back slapping, was none other than Toby.

Asa got Harvey's attention and walked closer to see what all the excitement was about. They stood back and watched from a short distance as the crowd began to thin.

Toby looked up and grinned at the Darnells. He waved as he walked toward them. "Good to see you again," he sneered. "Seems as though we will be seeing a lot of each other from now on.

"I see you are deputies now. Well, isn't that just a fine thing! That makes me feel so much safer knowing that you have to uphold the law, not take it into your own hands."

Asa stepped forward. "And what brings your cocky self back to town? You seem to be more full of yourself than ever. Thought you would have the good sense to stay gone after what you did to my wife."

Toby smiled. "Ah yes, your beautiful wife. Let's see now, you've been married for what, well over a year now? Hmm, seems like I heard you still haven't put a child in her arms." He shook his head.

"I tried to tell her I was the man for the job…"

Benson walked up in time to help Harvey grab Asa as he lunged toward Toby.

"You pompous worm. Don't you even speak my wife's name. Don't fool yourself, you aren't safe in this town, law or no law!"

"Oh, I beg to differ. You see, I have just made very many good friends. I feel sure they will watch out for me, as the owner of the new saloon." He laughed as he turned and joined some of his new friends.

Asa shook off Harvey and Benson, straightened himself, repositioned his hat, stomping off in the opposite direction without another word. As he crossed the street, he took the badge off and threw it on the ground. "All bets are off!" he spoke loudly over his shoulder.

****

Asa drove Olivia to Amy's every morning before he went to work, then he and Vince would leave the buggy in case of emergency and ride their horses to work. Asa had warned Olivia not to go to town unless it was an emergency.

She understood his reasoning and didn't argue. She and her sisters hated that they couldn't walk freely about town without watching over their shoulders.

Mrs. Powell would take Amy and Olivia's lists to Mr. Henderson, with Asa and Vince picking up everything after they got home.

The four of them ate together every evening, with growing anticipation of the new arrival. Vince was just as silly over Amy as Harvey had been with Eva.

Olivia thought it was sweet and was very patiently waiting for her turn. She knew one day her prayers would be answered or God would give her the grace to get over it. She was truly happy for both of her sisters.

Asa seemed distant toward everything. Toby had really gotten under his skin, and he was worried about his pa. It was like the light in his eyes was dimmed; he showed no joy or interest in anything. He even seemed distant with Olivia, always protective, courteous, and kind, but quiet. He was seemingly shutting everyone out while keeping his thoughts and emotions inside.

Harvey and Benson had been keeping a close eye on Asa, making sure he didn't let his temper land him in jail. Almost every evening, Asa and Olivia would come by to spend some time with Abe, and weekends they were there almost constantly.

All four adults had been taking turns staying home from church on Sunday to be with Abe. One night Asa confided quietly to them, "I will stay with Pa on Sunday's from now on. I don't get to be with him much during the week, and I insist on having Sunday with him. I work all week and Saturday's I have some things to tend around the place. I hope you understand, I need this time with him."

They agreed, knowing but not saying, it was a deeper problem than he was admitting. Olivia's heart was breaking for her husband, yet all she could do was stay by his side and love him, until he was ready to let her back in.

****

In mid-July, Vince and Asa were on their way home from work when Vince pulled to a stop and started picking some wildflowers.

"What are you doing?" Asa laughed.

Vince smiled up at him. "Amy seems so tired lately, and I feel so bad for her. She can't even get out of the chair by herself, and her feet are swollen to the point she can't wear her shoes...I just want to do something to bring a smile to her face."

He paused for a moment. "Might not hurt for you to make Olivia smile again, either. Don't think it's been unnoticed. Sure hope you two aren't having trouble."

Asa sighed. "You're right. I haven't given my sweet wife anything to smile about for a long time. Just been too busy licking my wounds, I suppose. She deserves much better than what I've put her through lately. In fact, she deserves much better than me."

Vince looked up at him. "Poor Asa! There you go licking your wounds again. That woman adores you and is willing to stand by you through anything. But you're right, she does deserve better than what you've been doing lately. So, my friend, what do you plan to do about it?"

Asa let his words sink in for a moment. At first, he just wanted to punch him in the gut one time. Thankfully he was still on his horse and couldn't reach him. But every word Vince had said was the truth, pure and simple. Olivia was still the same sweet, beautiful, wonderful woman he had fallen in love with, and here he had brought her sadness for no reason of her doing.

He got down off his horse. "I guess I will start by picking some flowers. Thanks, friend."

They approached the house, both with flowers in their hands, finding Olivia sitting in the parlor. She rose to meet them, smiling when she saw Asa with flowers.

"Vince, Amy is sleeping but said for you to wake her when you get home. You may want to wash up a bit first. She hasn't been sleeping long."

Vince nodded, walking toward the kitchen.

She approached Asa, taking the offered flowers, shocked when he pulled her to him and kissed her with passion.

She looked up at him with tear filled eyes. "Asa, I have missed you. I love you so much."

"I love you, Olivia, and I'm so sorry for the way I've been lately. Please forgive me."

She wrapped her arms around his neck. "Please don't ever shut me out again. It's been almost unbearable, knowing you were silently suffering, not letting me share the burden."

He held her close, thinking of how wonderful she was.

"Come sit with me. Vince has quite a surprise waiting for him," she whispered. "I want to hear his reaction."

Asa smiled. "The baby?" he asked quietly.

She nodded as they sat on the couch together. She cuddled in close as he kept his arm around her.

Vince came back in, looking more refreshed and his hair wet. "Do you think I should disturb her? She needs her rest."

Olivia shrugged. "She said she really wanted you to wake her when you got home."

He nodded and went in the bedroom. He saw Amy laying there sleeping, curled on her side with her back toward him.

"Amy," he said barely above a whisper as he touched her shoulder. "I'm home darling. How's my girl?"

She turned toward him and smiled. "Which one of us?" she asked quietly, pulling the covers back, revealing a tiny bundle.

For a moment she thought he was going to faint, turning pale as his mouth gaped open. "Amy! You had the baby?"

She smiled and nodded as she picked the baby up to pass to him. "Yes, I've been quite busy today."

Placing the baby in his outstretched hands, she announced, "Meet your beautiful daughter, Sylvia."

"Sylvia," he whispered as he held her close and kissed her little head. "Oh, my darling, she is beautiful!"

He sunk down on the bed beside her, wrapped his arm around her, and kissed her tenderly. "Thank you, my love, for making us complete. We are a family."

After regaining his senses, he asked if she was feeling alright and if there was anything he could do for her.

"I am right tired, if you wouldn't mind letting me sleep for a bit?"

He kissed her gently before taking his little daughter and leaving the room.

Asa and Olivia were still sitting on the couch, cuddling and kissing when he entered. He cleared his throat before speaking.

"Good to see you two acting normal again. I do hate to interrupt but I would like Uncle Asa to meet Sylvia." He placed the baby in Asa's arms.

"Oh Vince, what a beauty she is. Congratulations!"

****

Olivia and Asa stayed with Vince and Amy for almost a week. Olivia needed to help Amy as much as possible, even though Vince didn't return to work for two days. The man spent every waking hour doting on Amy and Sylvia. He repeated her name over and again, thinking it sounded like music.

Several ladies from the community visited, bringing food and gifts for the new arrival. Eva came as often as she could, even bringing Nate once to show him his new cousin.

Eva held Sylvia on Nate's lap repeating, "Easy. This is a baby. Touch her easy." Nate nodded his little head as he reached slowly toward her face, touching her with one finger.

He drew back his hand as if she would bite him, then touched her again. "Baby!" He tried to hug her, and Eva gently moved her away.

Eva sat beside Nate, holding Sylvia as she talked to Amy and Olivia. Sylvia began to wake up. "Oh look, Nate. Her little eyes are open."

He leaned toward her and touched her face again. "Baby." Nodding his head, he touched her again about the time she let out a wail.

Suddenly, Nate's little lip pouted, and he began to cry too.

Eva handed Sylvia to Amy and started to console Nate. The rest of the day he was afraid to touch her.

****

"Asa, please take me to town and let me see the progress of the new school building," Olivia pleaded. "I haven't stepped foot in town for two months and in a matter of weeks, school will begin. I haven't even seen where the new building is."

He sighed. He had thought about asking her to quit teaching and just work on the farm, help Eva with his pa, and be content as a wife. But his motives were wrong, and he knew he couldn't keep her away from town forever.

"Alright, if it means that much to you. Go see if Harvey and Eva need anything from town while we're there and I'll get ready to go."

She kissed him quickly and took off across the meadow. He watched her bounce along happily, just like a child that had gotten the right reply from her pa. He loved her child-like qualities and her adult ones too; he just loved everything about her.

She would be starting back to work in the school and having to drive back and forth by herself. As much as he hated the thought, it was a fact. He might as well ease up on keeping her from town because it looked like he wasn't going to be able to stay with her every moment.

Something needed to be done about Toby, that was the root of the problem. The man had no fear, no shame, no morals, and knew exactly how to stay right on the edge of the law.

For now, he was going to spend a nice afternoon with his wife, perhaps even take her to the diner.

The school was located near the church and the park. When they pulled up, there were men working away on the roof.

Olivia gasped, "Asa! It's so big!"

He hurried to help her down from the buggy. Her eyes were wide with excitement, taking in everything with great enthusiasm. They entered into a big room that she supposed would be for meetings or assemblies. Off to the side were two nice rooms with blackboards already hung. Going back through the main room, there were two more rooms identical to the others.

Asa walked over and checked the stoves in each room, tapping on the pipes, making sure they were sturdy. He heard her oohing and ahhing in the other room, but he didn't see her.

"Olivia? Where did you go?"

She poked her head through a door at the front of the room, motioning for him to join her. "Look at this, Asa! It's too good to believe."

He walked through the door about the time Mrs. Farley came in.

"How do you like it, Olivia?" The woman spread her arms and slowly walked in a circle. "It's something, isn't it?"

"Oh yes, it is! It's wonderful!"

"I see you found the kitchen back here." She walked past Asa and led the way. "This room is to fill many purposes. It's to teach the young ladies how to cook, bake, set a fine table, take care of a kitchen, and such. It's also to teach the youngsters, both boys and girls, table manners and cleanliness.

"It will also be used for meetings and socials along with the big room." She pointed to a side door. When she opened it, she pointed to a large pole barn in the back. "That's for the horses during bad weather. There isn't enough room for buggies and such, but it will offer shelter for quite a few horses."

She motioned them back inside and shut the door. "You've probably seen the classrooms?"

"Yes ma'am. They are very nice." Olivia couldn't stop smiling.

"We still have to get the tables and benches built and will use what was at the other school for now. As for why there are four classrooms, we are hoping to need them, soon.

"I'm looking for another teacher in case we have more students than last year, and with that wonderful assembly you and Mrs. Powell put together at the end of last school year, I think we will have. It was quite wonderful."

Olivia blushed. "Thank you, Mrs. Farley. Thank you for all of this. I know you have put great effort into it and a lot of expense."

Mrs. Farley chuckled. "Well, it comes with a price."

Asa's brows raised, yet he stayed quiet, just thinking, *"Here it comes."*

"A price? I don't understand."

"You will have to put up with me several times a week. I will be teaching the classes in the kitchen. I call it 'Lessons of Propriety'. I am so put out with the way some older young people around here act, and if the parents won't or can't teach them at home, then someone needs to."

"I see, and I agree, Mrs. Farley, but let's not forget to teach it with loving kindness, as my ma would say." She quickly changed the subject. "Have you got any candidates in mind for the other teacher position?"

"Yes, I have a few applications. I just hate to put it off until the last minute, not knowing how many students we will have."

"The town council will do the hiring?" Olivia was getting suspicious with the overuse of "I" and "We" in the conversation.

"Yes, officially they will do the hiring, but," she got a cunning grin on her face, "I have been appointed to oversee the application process, and I have ways of getting what I want."

****

Asa had watched Olivia's excitement fade, the more Mrs. Farley talked. Now, she was fuming on the drive to the diner.

"I know Mrs. Farley was one of my ma's pet projects, and she said to be kind to the woman, but Asa, she has no business around children. She is too harsh. She will completely tear down all the effort we put into building attendance."

Asa put his arm around her. "Do you want me to talk to Mr. Farley? I'm not sure what I would say, but I will try if you'd like."

"Asa, you can't tell a man to control his wife. I guess we just make it a matter of prayer. Looks as though we have plenty to keep us on our knees."

"Don't forget, sweetheart, we have a lot to be thankful for, at least I do."

Chapter 17

Later that night, Olivia was filling Eva in on all the details of the school, the building, and Mrs. Farley, while they worked together in the kitchen preparing coffee and dessert.

The men were attempting to keep Abe's spirits up and his thoughts together. He stayed confused most of the time now, and the stronger medicine made the confusion worse. It also made him sleepy and not at all interested in anything.

He sat in somewhat of a daze as he watched Asa and Harvey play checkers. Nate captured his attention, which immediately brought a smile to his face. He reached out for the boy and pulled him on his lap.

"Baby, cy," Nate stated as he nodded his head.

"Pa, he's telling you that Amy's baby cried. Eva said it scared him so bad, he started crying."

"Amy has a baby?"

"Yes, pa. She and Vince came by the other day and showed her to you. A little girl named Sylvia."

"No, I don't know any girls named Sylvia. Don't be talking about other girls when your ma comes back in here. She gets a mite upset about that kind of thing."

Harvey and Asa looked at each other in despair. It was so hard to see their pa like this.

Abe went back to playing with Nate.

"Who's ready for dessert?" Eva asked.

"Be right there as soon as I whip Asa here," Harvey teased.

Nate squirmed down to the floor and ran toward his ma. "Me! Nate! Me!" He pointed to himself, then toward the dessert.

Olivia picked him up and hugged him before setting him in his chair. "You want dessert, sweetie? Well, Auntie Olivia will get you some."

Nate grinned and nodded, giving Olivia a hug back.

Harvey and Asa helped Abe to the table. He could still feed himself most of the time but was beginning to make a mess. The adults watched him as he tried his best, thankful that he didn't seem to notice the mess he was making. They sat with lumps in their throats and misty eyes as they watched the strong, intelligent man they all adored, deteriorate at an alarming pace.

"I hear someone coming up," Harvey jumped up and got his gun. "Awful late for visitors."

Asa joined him, getting the gun from over the kitchen door.

When he heard the knock, Harvey stepped to the side of the door. "Who is it?"

"Sheriff, Harvey. I'm looking for Asa."

Both women were alarmed but stayed seated with Abe and Nate.

Harvey opened the door and greeted the sheriff as he put his gun down. Asa did the same.

"What's this all about?" Asa asked.

The sheriff tipped his hat to the ladies.

"Care for some pie, sheriff?"

"No, thank you, ma'am. Can we step outside?"

Harvey and Asa walked out on the porch with him.

"Asa, I need to know your whereabouts today."

His mouth dropped open. "Why?"

"Someone found Toby laying on the side of the road, hurt pretty bad. He'd been pistol whipped and was about half dead. Of course, everyone seems to know your dislike of him and I'm just checking on a lead."

Asa squinted his eyes. "What kind of a lead?"

"Someone said they saw several men, one of them big, looking like you, riding in this direction, soon after this happened."

Asa looked at Harvey. "Did Toby say it was me?"

"No, he's still unconscious."

He huffed. "This afternoon I took my wife to the new school building. Mrs. Farley was with us there. Then I took my wife for an early supper at the diner. After that, we came here."

"That's it? Mrs. Farley and people at the diner could vouch for you?"

"Well sure, but I like to be taken at my word, sheriff.

"I know, and I'm sorry. How long have you been here?"

"About two hours, I suppose. You can ask our wives if you like."

"If you don't mind, I would like to do that so I can put this thing to rest. Then I won't have to take you in while I clear your name."

Harvey opened the door. "Eva, could you come here for a minute?"

The sheriff quickly asked her then she went back in to sit with his pa while Olivia went out. He asked her the same, with all giving the same answer.

"I'm sorry to have disturbed you folk. I was sure you didn't do this, Asa, but understand, this is my job."

"Not to worry, sheriff. I understand."

****

Harvey heard something that woke him up. He jumped up and listened. He thought he heard the front door open. Slipping on his pants and boots quickly, he stepped quietly across the room.

Eva stirred. "Harvey? What are you doing?"

"Shhh, sweetheart. I heard a noise," he whispered, turning to get his gun out of the top drawer.

She sat up and pulled on her robe. When he went out the bedroom door, she eased her feet into her slippers and got her gun out of her dresser. She stood by the door and listened through the crack.

Harvey made his way through the parlor and saw the front door standing open. He listened carefully as he looked around, hearing and seeing nothing. Stepping to the front door, he cautiously stepped onto the porch.

The moon was shining just enough for him to see a figure of a man, walking across the meadow towards Asa's. "Pa," he whispered.

He yelled out to Eva, "It's alright, Eva. It was pa. I have to go get him."

She stepped out and lit a lamp, watching Harvey take off after his pa. Her heart ached for him; she knew this was tearing him up.

Within minutes, they returned. Abe was crying and Harvey was trying not to. "I just want to go home! Why can't I go home?"

Harvey rode to the doctor's the next morning. After explaining how quickly his pa was failing, the doctor shook his head.

"I'm sorry, Harvey. All I can do is medicate him more. It will cause him to be bedbound, sleeping most of the time. Then one time, when he falls asleep, it will be his last."

Harvey broke down. "Doc, this is so hard, watching him turn to a weak man who doesn't even realize his wife died years ago. I don't seem to recognize who he has become."

Harvey shook himself, trying to think clearer. "I don't know what to do."

That evening, Harvey sadly sat down and talked with the family. They had to decide what was best for their pa. They cried out to the Lord to help them in their decisions and to be merciful to their pa.

One week later, Abe went to sleep, waking in the arms of the Lord.

****

School was in session again, with enough students to hire the new schoolteacher. Mrs. Farley immediately sent for her choice of applicants, taking no one else's opinion into the matter.

There were too many children to divide between the two teachers until the awaited arrival, weeks away. Olivia suggested that Eva fill in until then.

Mrs. Farley, who had taken an instant liking to Eva and her ma from the beginning, thought that was a wonderful solution.

Olivia blew out a sigh of relief. She knew Eva had a way with Mrs. Farley, and people in general, somehow bringing the best out in them.

Harvey wasn't too thrilled at first, but of course, Eva had a way with him too.

It was decided, Amy would watch little Nate while Eva taught school for a month, then everything would go back to normal...or would it?

Mrs. Farley strutted around like a proud peacock in anticipation of her first propriety class. She would have each of the three classes for one hour, two days a week.

Mrs. Powell's class was the first to attend, being the youngest children in the school. Eighteen little ones, filled with curiosity and energy, bounded into the huge kitchen. Before the hour was over, Mrs. Farley had successfully put three with their nose in the corner, smacked two on the hand with a ruler, washed one's mouth with soap, and had several six-year old's clinging to Mrs. Powell's skirt as they cried.

Olivia noticed Mrs. Powell looked disheveled and on the verge of tears as she marched her students out of the kitchen and back to the classroom. She shook her head at Olivia. "This isn't going to work. That woman is a monster."

Olivia couldn't say she was shocked, but she did expect a little better on the first day of Mrs. Farley's class. It was her turn next, and she was looking for any way to stall.

Running to Eva's class, she motioned for her sister. Telling her quickly of her observations and what Mrs. Powell said, Eva pursed her lips tightly with determination.

"Eva, she can single handedly close down this school by discouraging the children. They may not come back."

"Let my class go next," she suggested. "You go get your class involved in something that can't be disturbed, and I will take your turn. Pray for me to be able to teach Mrs. Farley something about teaching."

Olivia nodded her thanks and hurried back to her class.

Eva had the oldest group of students, ranging from thirteen to sixteen. She knew Mrs. Farley would be the toughest on them and had already prepared herself for facing this.

Unlike Mrs. Powell, who had knuckled under Mrs. Farley's authority, Eva was determinedly hands-on. Every time Mrs. Farley would bark a command, Eva would rub the woman's shoulder as she repeated in a much nicer way, instructions on what to do, getting much better results from the children. They even had a few laughs during the class.

Olivia watched as Eva's class marched back to their room, looking happy; shocked and glad of it. Then she saw Eva come out of the kitchen with her arm around Mrs. Farley, speaking quietly.

She glanced up and saw the questioning look on her sister's face. "Olivia, I have a request. It seems that everything is going so well, and with my time here so limited, could you possibly teach my class while I attend Mrs. Farley's class with your students? This woman is a wealth of knowledge and I need to learn everything I can before the new teacher gets here."

Olivia stammered a bit as she watched the pride glow on Mrs. Farley's face. "Umm, well, certainly. I would be glad to."

The next morning, several mothers of Mrs. Powell's students accompanied their children in the school, with questions about what had happened the day before. They had compared stories with each other before the teachers rang the bell and were none too happy.

Eva instructed her students to begin reading, then went to the rescue. "Ladies, I assure you, Mrs. Farley just had a rough start. I will be helping her for at least a while until she gets more comfortable in her new role."

She finally smoothed the ruffled feathers and answered the questions, then politely walked them to the door.

"Eva," Olivia sighed. "I don't know what we will do without you, and I really mean that. What's going to happen when the new teacher gets here, and you aren't here to protect us all?"

Eva hugged Olivia. "We pray, then we do a lot of thinking and planning over the next few weeks." She winked at her sister before returning to her class.

Two weeks later, Mrs. Farley came in like a lion, growling at everyone. Eva immediately took her to the kitchen.

"Mrs. Farley, please forgive my abruptness, but you cannot treat the children that way! I can see that something has upset you, but you cannot come in here and take it out on these children!

"If you would like to talk about it, I will be glad to listen. Perhaps I can even be helpful. Otherwise, I suggest that you cancel your lesson for today and go home until you feel better."

Mrs. Farley's eyes widened as she twisted her mouth into a tight grin. "How dare you speak to me like that! I will have you know that everything, and I do mean *everything* this town has is because of my husband and myself!"

Eva's eyes sparked with fire. "And I will have you know that to teach propriety and etiquette, you first have to know and practice it. I am going to the town council with my concerns and see that your class, or at least you, are removed. You have intimidated all of these children and most of the adults in town and I, for one, am sick with it.

"Now, if you would like to calm down and try to be civil, perhaps we can work something out, otherwise I ask that you leave until you do calm down."

"Don't threaten me, Eva Darnell. I know I'm not so easy to get along with at times, but I will not be threatened."

"Don't push me, Mrs. Farley. I am one of the teachers responsible for protecting these children while in my care. I take it very seriously."

When Mrs. Farley saw that Eva wasn't going to back down, her glare slowly began to soften. She turned and sat in one of the chairs, pulling a telegram from her pocket.

"Seems as though the teacher has decided not to come. Broke his leg or some kind of nonsense and won't be available until next school year."

Eva breathed a sigh of relief. Maybe the woman was going to be civil after all. She joined Mrs. Farley at the table.

"Mrs. Farley, where is your compassion? The man seems to have a good reason, not just an excuse. We can figure out a way to get by."

"Hmph," Mrs. Farley grunted. "You are the only other qualified teacher and I know how Harvey feels about you working. He wants you home, where you should be."

Eva patted Mrs. Farley's arm. "We will figure out something. Just let us pray and think. But meanwhile, I want you to think about something.

"Your conduct toward the children is not tolerable. Please tell me, what good did it do to strike out at them, making

226

them scared and upset? Did it solve your problem at all? Why do you have such a problem showing kindness?"

"Hmph, kindness is a sign of weakness, you have to be firm in this world to get what you want. The sooner you show people your firmness, the less they try to take advantage of you."

Eva shook her head as she stood. "That's a sad way to live, Mrs. Farley. I feel so sorry for you if that's what you truly believe." She turned and left the room.

****

"Mr. Henderson?" A nicely dressed man had entered the store and approached Gerald.

"That's me," the older man smiled as he extended his hand. "How can I help you?"

"I was told that you own the empty building on the other side of the street near the sheriff's office. I may be interested in renting it."

"Well now," Gerald's smile widened. "Yes, I do own it. What kind of a business are you thinking about?"

"Law. My name is Zeb Watley, attorney at law."

Gerald looked shocked. "You don't say! We've been needing a lawyer around here. Let me get the key and I will show you the building."

****

"Eva, I'm not sure I like this idea. I wasn't thrilled about you going back at all, but permanently? I need your help around here. You don't realize how much I count on you to keep all the records straight for the farm and ranch."

"Harvey," she rubbed his shoulders as she stood behind him. "The children need me. You know it doesn't take that much time to keep track of the books, especially during most of the school year. At the end of next month, there won't be another entry until March. By then, the school year is almost over. I'm sure I can do both."

"What about Nate? Chores? All you need to do around here every day?"

He stood and took her in his arms. "And what about feeling up to taking care of me?" He kissed her softly.

She put her arms around his neck. "That, my dear husband, is certainly not a chore. That is definitely my pleasure. Everything about being your wife is my pleasure. Have no fear of that changing."

When he finished kissing her again, he realized she had wrapped him tighter around her finger, again. "You do know how to get your way, Mrs. Darnell."

She smiled cunningly. "I know how to keep my man happy. You just let me know if you have any complaints."

Harvey came back to his senses, clearing his throat. "Yes, well, maybe we can give it a try for this school year, but in September, I will be purchasing that land and having more contracts. That's going to take more time and more bookwork. I'm already a bit nervous about it and I need you beside me."

"I will be, I promise. Let's just get through this school year and pray for another teacher."

****

Mrs. Farley had handed the responsibility of teaching propriety over to the three schoolteachers, saying that she had other, more important matters to assist with.

She had met her new best friend, Mrs. Smith, the preacher's wife, and had thrown herself wholeheartedly into doing volunteer work for the church and the community.

Mrs. Farley found that Mrs. Smith could be easily manipulated into giving up secrets about people. She didn't mean to gossip, but Mrs. Farley had a way of weaseling information out of the woman.

The latest item of interest was why the banker had taken his family and moved away. His young daughter had gotten in the family way, and he refused to let her marry the young man responsible.

"That is such a shame," Mrs. Farley said with mock compassion. "We must keep that family in our prayers. I do hope the young man isn't a permanent resident here, taking advantage of other girls. Tsk, we need to keep a closer eye on our girls, I suppose."

"Yes, we certainly will," Mrs. Smith agreed. "But he is so tied up in his new business, hopefully, he won't have time to be attentive to any of our young ladies. Besides, not many of our girls would dare step foot in a saloon."

Mrs. Farley continued with her needlework, looking down as she smiled. She had gotten the information she had hoped for, and Mrs. Smith didn't even realize how much she had said.

Mrs. Farley started thinking, putting pieces together. *"Maybe it wasn't Asa that beat Toby so badly. Hmm."*

****

Progress brought the good and bad with it. The population had grown, and the town expanded. It was good for the economy, with everyone working and buying everything they needed right in their own town.

There were quite a few drifters that would come through, stay for a while, and then move on, but now they tended to stay longer, causing concern for the sheriff and deputies. Most of them were professional loafers or conmen.

The sheriff's office was starting to have a low tolerance and advised these men to get jobs or move on.

To add to their headaches, the saloon was scheduled to open on New Year's Eve with a big party lasting until after midnight. As soon as the announcement went out, the sheriff asked the town council for extra deputies.

Harvey heard about it and had a talk with the sheriff. "The farm is shut down with nothing much to do until the first of March. I could use something to do and make a little bit of money."

"You have made my day, Harvey." The sheriff immediately slapped him on the back and went to his desk. He pulled out a badge and swore him in again.

When he told Eva about it that night, she wasn't so happy. "What about your safety? Are you trying to get hurt, Harvey?"

"No, my love, I am trying to keep innocent people safe."

She couldn't argue with that.

"Besides, you know I'm trying to save all the money I can to pay off this land I'm getting ready to purchase."

"I know, and I admire you for it. Every penny of my teacher's pay will go to it too."

He took her hand. "No, you need to save that for you and Nate, whatever you may need."

"Harvey Darnell, just what is it you think we need? We are almost self-sufficient. Almost all the money we make is able to go back into the farm. I appreciate you feeling the way you do, but we work together for everything."

"I never need to wonder why I love you, Eva."

Chapter 18

The holidays passed with Harvey picking up as many extra shifts at the sheriff's office as possible. Several deputies wanted time with their families during the holidays, and Harvey was glad to see it. He wouldn't be full time until the saloon opened, and he wanted the hours.

On New Year's Eve, all the deputies were on duty, prepared for that night's party. The saloon opened its doors at six o'clock and arrests were being made by nine. Public drunkenness, shooting firearms within town limits, drunk and disorderly, and fighting were the main offenses.

Before the night was over, they had arrested twenty-two men, keeping some handcuffed at the doctor's house. Mr. Watley entered the jail the next morning hoping to earn some business. He asked each of the men if they had been treated unfairly, roughed up, or anything. The sheriff and deputies took offense by the man's pointed questions and his views of right and wrong, yet said nothing.

Only a few of the drifters wanted to speak out against the deputies, but even they didn't hire the lawyer.

Most of the men were allowed to leave as soon as they sobered up and paid their fine. The ones shooting firearms had to stay an extra two days. The ones fighting had to pay their fine and the doctor bill of the one they were fighting.

Mr. Farley came in later and was appalled to find out the lawyer was wanting to defend the criminals against the sheriff and his men. "Sounds like I need to write to a few people about an honest lawyer." Then he laughed, "If there is such a thing! I know they all have a tendency to stretch things quite a bit to suit their need to win."

****

The town council was pleased with the way the saloon was causing the general fund to grow. Toby was upset that he was starting to lose customers because of it. He hired Mr. Watley to go against the sheriff's office saying they were standing watch over his establishment, waiting to arrest anyone who left the premises.

He took it before the town council and lost, knowing it probably wouldn't stand up in front of a judge either. That's when Toby came up with another idea. He sectioned off a portion of his building for his customers to rent a room, cheaper than a fine, to sleep it off and not get hauled to jail. Business began to pick back up.

He started building a two-story addition on the back of the saloon, hired some women to cook and others to entertain. Now, his saloon would be open from morning to midnight. He figured he would get rich while he showed this town not to mess with him.

****

At the end of February, Harvey turned in his notice and his badge, heading back to the farm until late November. He had to get the fields ready for the workers and start ordering supplies. Now is when he needed Eva, and true to her word, she was right there for him, every afternoon and evening.

By April, the workers returned, and everything was going well. Planting was taking place and hoes were in every hand available. The ranch was doing well also, with Benson handling every aspect just as Harvey would.

Eva, Olivia, and Mrs. Powell were starting to plan their end of the year program, with all of the students having a part. Three of the students would be finishing this year, and they knew of at least six that would be new for the next year.

With the town council's permission, the teachers were allowed to pursue finding another teacher to take Eva's place.

****

Vince, Amy, and little Sylvia would visit every weekend at the farm. Vince and Asa would usually tinker with the machinery, helping Harvey keep everything in good shape, then they would have a nice supper together and create memories.

Olivia had caught a cold and had a hard time getting over it. She missed a few days of school, staying at home in bed. Finally, her fever passed and her sneezing and coughing subsided, but she couldn't shake the fatigue.

Several evenings, Asa found her asleep on the couch when he got home, with concern for her growing.

"Asa, I'm fine. We have been working so hard on the program at school and I'm afraid it may be interrupting my sleep at night. I guess I'm just excited."

"Sweetheart, maybe you need to see the doctor and let him give you something to either sleep better at night or give you more energy during the day."

"And maybe you need to get something for your hearing, Asa!" she yelled as she marched toward the bedroom. "I told you I am fine!" She slammed the bedroom door after one last glaring look at him.

He ate supper by himself, thinking she would calm down and join him at any minute. Then he put away the food and washed up his dishes. He tried to think if he had said anything wrong but couldn't come up with anything. "Maybe she just fell asleep again," he mumbled to himself as he blew out the lamp and went to the bedroom.

She was asleep, fully clothed and on top of the covers. He woke her gently, asking if she was ready for bed.

"Asa, I'm sorry I yelled at you." She hugged him around his waist as she began to cry.

He rubbed her back. "All is forgiven, sweetheart, now let's get to bed."

The next day was Saturday. As usual, the three men worked on equipment while the women, cooked, visited, and played with the two babies.

Olivia didn't say a word about her outburst to her sisters, but Asa said plenty to Harvey and Vince.

Harvey stopped working after Asa said Olivia had yelled at him. He stood and grinned. "Vince, does any of this sound familiar to you?"

Vince thought for a minute. When he saw the grin on Harvey's face, he knew immediately what he was thinking. "Yes, now that you mention it, it does."

"What?" Asa asked cautiously. "Will one of you grinning possums tell me what it is?"

Harvey walked over to him and slapped him on the back. "I think maybe you should insist that she go to the doctor, whether she wants to or not. Perhaps you should just mosey on into town now and take care of it."

"Now? Why? You think she's that sick?"

Vince started laughing. "Nothing that a few months won't clear up, I'm thinking."

Finally, he caught on to what they were suggesting.

He threw down his tools and ran to the house. A few minutes later they laughed and back slapped as they watched him help her into the buggy and head towards town.

When they went in for lunch, Eva and Amy asked about Asa's strange behavior.

"He came in here and just ordered Olivia to get in the buggy! When she asked why, he just repeated himself. He didn't look mad, in fact, he almost looked amused or happy." Eva shrugged when she finished.

"From what he told Vince and me, we think Olivia may be getting her prayers answered. He says she is tired and sleeping in the afternoons and that she about snapped his head off last night."

Eva and Amy looked at each other and smiled as they hugged each other, jumping up and down.

Later, Asa and Olivia arrived back at the farm, quickly sharing the good news with the family. For a little while, they celebrated with hugs, back slaps, and bellows of congratulations.

Asa got their attention. "Thank you, everyone." He pulled Olivia close as she glowed with excitement. "Don't think we are ungrateful, but we really want to go home and have some private time together. My wife and child need a nap too." He put his hand on her belly and bent down and kissed her cheek.

Eva motioned them toward the door. "We understand, now go! We have plenty of time for celebrating and planning. When is this little one due?"

Olivia swooned, "Late October or early November." She looked lovingly at Asa.

He turned her toward the door and carefully led her to the buggy.

When they arrived home, they held each other as they prayed together, thanking God for this blessed, answered prayer.

****

More news about the unrest in the country came weekly. It seemed there was no compromise that would fix this problem.

People in the town started mentioning they had caught glimpses of black people on the outside of town, walking through fields and on the edges of the woods. A lot of people around here had never even seen a black person before.

One day, Harvey came up on one of the families, camped in the woods on his property.

The man looked terrified when Harvey approached on his horse. Harvey dismounted and walked to him with an outstretched hand. "I'm Harvey Darnell."

The man timidly took Harvey's hand while keeping his eyes downcast. "I'm Grady, and this is my family, sir. We don't mean you no harm, sir. We will move on, sir."

Harvey noticed they looked tired and underfed. "You don't have to move on, Grady. You look as though you could use some rest and a good meal."

Grady just stood still, looking downward. "We don't want to cause you trouble, sir. We will be on our way."

"It's no trouble and my wife is a good cook. In fact, she will be home soon and starting supper. You and your family are welcome to join us."

Grady looked at his wife who was standing with her arms around three children ranging in age from young teen to toddler. Her eyes looked sad and pleading, as she nodded.

"Thank you, sir. My children are hungry."

"Come on to the house with me."

"Oh, sir, we can't come out in the open while the sun is shining." Grady swallowed hard. "We don't want to cause you trouble, sir. You seem like a kind man."

The enormity of the situation suddenly became clear, knowing right then he was dealing with runaway slaves. He had to proceed with caution, but he wouldn't turn his back on this family in need. "I understand. You will be safe here. Just let me go get my wagon and I will take you to the house. No one will see you, I promise."

Grady nodded. "Thank you kindly, sir."

Harvey hitched up the wagon with the steel sides, Asa had made for their pa. Soon he returned for Grady and his family.

Eva was surprised when Harvey met her on the porch. He took Nate from her and kissed her quickly. "Sweetheart, we have guests for supper. I hope you don't mind, and I need you to stay quiet about this. We can't tell anyone."

She nodded and turned very serious.

She was shocked when she entered her house to find a family huddled together in the parlor. She knew in an instant what kind of trouble this could bring them. They could lose everything and possibly go to jail. Her compassion overrode the caution when she looked at the desperation in their faces. These people were just as human as she was, with the same emotions and physical needs as herself.

She smiled and extended her hand to the woman. "I'm Eva Darnell, it's a pleasure to have you join us."

The woman, Wanda, joined Eva in the kitchen and helped prepare supper, while they began to chat a bit. The girl, looking to be about eight years old, was incredibly skilled in kitchen work, for her age.

When Eva called the men for supper, she saw Nate sharing his toys with the toddler who was three years old, noticing he was smaller than Nate, who had just turned two a few months back. She was sure the child hadn't been fed properly and her heart ached for him.

As they sat, talking quietly over supper, Asa suddenly bounded in the door. No one had heard him walk up until he was already on the porch, opening the door.

"Hey, Harvey, I need..." he stopped abruptly when he saw the guests.

Harvey had already stood, trying to make his way to the parlor before anyone saw their supper guests. He put his arm around Asa's shoulder, turning him back toward the door, walking him into the parlor.

"What was it you needed?"

Asa pulled from him, putting his hands on his hips and looking stern. He spoke barely above a whisper, while he really wanted to scream. "Just what do you think you're doing, Harvey? Do you know how dangerous this is and what kind of trouble you could be in?"

"Asa, all I'm doing is extending Christian kindness to a family that is tired and hungry."

"Yeah, you make it sound so simple. What if it was the sheriff and those bounty hunters that had come bursting in? What then Harvey? You are putting your family in jeopardy!" He shook his head. "I thought you were smarter than that. I'm really disappointed. I guess I will take on your family while you rot in jail."

"No one is going to jail. You just keep your mouth shut, don't even tell Olivia, and let me handle this, you hear?"

"What are you going to do Harvey? How long will they be here? How do you plan to get them away from here?"

"Asa, I didn't say I had all the answers, but I'm praying about it. I hope you will do the same."

****

Eva and Wanda made up the bed Abe used to sleep on and made pallets on the floor for the children.

"I wish I had better to offer your family, Wanda, but this is the best I can do."

"Ma'am, your kindness is medicine for my wounded soul. I thought all whites were evil," she paused and swallowed a lump in her throat. "You've shown me how wrong I was."

Harvey made sure all the curtains were pulled tight before he sat down to talk with Grady. "I'll be honest with you,

Grady, I don't know what to do next. I want to help you and your family, but these are such dangerous times for all of us."

"I understand, sir, and believe me, you have already been a great help. We don't want to bring you trouble. We will be on our way before the sun comes up."

"Where will you go? How will you live?"

Grady smiled. "I'm grateful for your concern, sir, but I can't tell you. We've been told of places to go where we can get help getting to the North, maybe even Canada. We just get one piece of information at a time, that way, if we get caught, we can't tell more than we know."

Harvey nodded. "I understand. Do you mind if I ask why you would take such a chance with your family? Was it really all that bad?"

Grady looked sad. "It was worse than bad." He closed his eyes and shook his head. "Things happened that will never leave my mind. I had to stand by and watch my wife and oldest son suffer punishment for something I had done and couldn't do a thing to protect them." A tear ran down his cheek. "Their screams will haunt me forever."

Harvey thought of how he would be willing to die for Eva and Nate, not able to imagine the torture of watching them suffer.

"I'm not making any promises, Grady, but if you could tell me at least the area you need to get to, I will see if I can help."

"Sir, you are most kind, but we don't mean to cause you trouble."

"Just let me worry about how much I think I can do for you. If I think it's too much or too dangerous, I will let you know."

Grady shook his head with a smile. "We need to be gettin' in the direction of Allegheny County."

Harvey rubbed his chin, deep in thought. "You know, I have been needing to pick up some equipment from that direction. Might need to take a load of feed as I go." He stood. "It's about time to bed down for the night. I will speak to my foreman in the morning, get him to get the wagon ready for my trip. We could leave at first light the morning after?"

Grady stood to his feet. "Yes sir, that would be just fine, sir. Thank you and may God bless you and your family."

****

"Benson, I have a project for you." Harvey walked toward the corral to greet the man.

"I need a sturdy second floor built in the bottom of this wagon. I need it to be two feet off the floor and sturdy enough to hold a load of grain and hay on top. And I need it by tonight, ready and loaded."

Benson thought it was an odd request at first, especially coming from Harvey, who was always practical and level-headed.

"So, what you need is a false bottom?"

Harvey's head jerked up in surprise. "Umm, well, of sorts, I suppose."

Benson looked around and spoke quietly. "How many are you fitting in there?"

"I'm not sure what you..."

"Darnell, I'm not stupid. You are hauling something or someone that you intend to keep hidden. You don't have to tell me anything. I will tell you that I have made a few special trips before, and if there is risk involved, I would rather do it for you. You have a family to worry about."

"Thanks, Benson, but I can't involve anyone else in this."

"Seems as though I've already involved myself. So why don't you tell me what I will be hauling and to where."

After a bit of prodding, Harvey finally gave in. "You just take care of this, and I will talk to you tonight."

Eva was relieved when Harvey told her about Benson's offer.

"But Eva, if something happens to him, I will be to blame. I don't know if I can live with that."

"Harvey, you didn't ask him to do it, he volunteered. He would blame himself if something happened to you if he didn't insist. He's a good friend."

That night, Eva, Wanda, and the children worked on a mattress to pad the floor of the wagon. They packed plenty of food, along with a few clothes and a little bit of money.

The next morning, before the first rays of light, Grady shook Harvey's hand and Wanda hugged Eva before they crawled in the bottom of the wagon with their children.

"If you ever are able to return to the South as a free man, be sure to come here to work on my farm."

Grady chuckled. "I appreciate the offer, sir, but if I ever get out of the South, I ain't never comin' back!"

Harvey drove the wagon to the bunkhouse where Benson was waiting. "Benson, I can do this. It's not your responsibility."

"Darnell, just be ready to give me a raise when I get back!" He laughed as he hoisted himself to the driver's seat.

"You've earned yourself more than that, my friend."

****

Benson returned five days later with Harvey's new equipment in the wagon.

"No problems to report, boss, and it just so happens, I knew exactly where I was going. I've been to the same place several times."

"I never knew that Benson. Apparently, I have a lot to learn about you."

"Na, there's not that much out of the ordinary. I just went a little crazy after my wife died, figuring I didn't have anything to lose. Just took a few chances, trying to help people, while I came back to my senses. Other than that, I'm just a normal old cowpoke."

****

The program on the last night of school went without any problems, with record numbers of people packed into the room. The teachers had spread the word to the entire community, announcing there would be a social afterward. They wanted to catch everyone's interest, and they did. Before the night was over, they had seven new, older students enrolled and five younger. All the present students were returning the next year other than the three that were finishing that night.

The teachers announced the starting date for the new semester in September and told about the new teacher that would arrive by August. What they didn't announce was that they were suddenly short one teacher, now that Olivia was going to be home with a new baby. They had to see if they could find one more teacher because Eva hadn't planned on returning either.

Harvey needed her more than ever and she wouldn't disappoint him or make him worry. She promised him this school year was her last, and she had to stick to her promise.

Ever since they had helped Grady and his family, Harvey couldn't get his mind off the impending doom of the country. Mr. Farley had warned them years before about hanging on to gold, and they had. Abe, Asa, and he had hidden their gold in case there was an emergency. It wasn't going to be touched until then or until the country was more stable.

He had overheard some of the soldiers that had come to get some horses from the ranch, talking about what they had been instructed to do if the war broke out. One thing they said almost terrified him. They had been told that if and when the time came, they were to confiscate all the food from farmers, under the name of the government, so they could feed the troops. This included produce and animals for slaughter.

This thing was getting serious fast. He needed to come up with a plan to keep his family and this community, safe and fed. Maybe he should talk to Mr. Farley and Asa.

Chapter 19

Asa was silly over Olivia, doting on her anytime he was home. He couldn't get her to give up working on the farm but did get her to agree to work just a few hours in the mornings. With the heat of July coming on, she was more than glad to comply.

July also brought another birthday for Eva. They usually had a special supper with cake and a few presents, but with all the deep-thinking Harvey had been doing lately, he wanted to get her a special gift that he knew she would love and put to good use.

The two of them sat at the table one night, playing with Nate as he finished a cookie, talking over the numbers for the business.

"The land has been offered to me for four thousand dollars, one thousand acres of prime farmland and five hundred acres of partially wooded area. How much cash money do we have for purchasing it?"

Eva looked through her book. "We have three thousand seven hundred fifty dollars in savings. We also have the money paid in advance on the crops, from this year's contract, but that is to pay the workers and all expenses until the end of the growing season. With expenses so far, and calculating wages and expenses for the rest of this season, that brings the total to one thousand three hundred twenty, not counting our savings."

Harvey bowed his head. "I wish Pa was here. He was so looking forward to being able to purchase that property."

He stood and reached for Nate. "It's about time for bed, son. Let's get you washed up a bit, while your ma tries to magically find some more money in those numbers."

"But Harvey, I thought you would be pleased. We can squeeze out enough to buy the property, and without any extra expenses, by the end of October we should have a good amount left over, not to mention the final pay out for the last of the crops."

"It looks good on paper, Eva, you know that. I can't cut us back to the last penny and we can't count on crops until they are out of the fields. So many things can happen.

"But you're right, I am pleased. We have scrimped and saved for seven years. Now that we have the private contracts for next year, out from under a shaky government, yes, I am pleased."

He grinned as he left the room. He was going to get Eva that surprise for her birthday, knowing now what their finances looked like.

****

"Rise and shine, sleepy head."

Eva awoke to Harvey opening the curtains, while Nate had his face within inches of hers, smiling. Before she said a word, she smelled bacon.

Harvey walked over to the bed. "Happy birthday, darling!" He bent and kissed her. "Nate and I have a surprise for you."

She sat up and took Nate in her arms. "You have a surprise for your ma?" She tickled his belly.

He laughed and nodded his head.

"Well, let me get up from here and see what it is."

Harvey led her to the kitchen table and motioned for her to sit. He put Nate in his chair and then started setting breakfast on the table.

"Oh my!" Eva exclaimed. "This is wonderful! Thank you, Nate and my dear, sweet, thoughtful husband."

"This is your day, sweetheart. Your every wish is my command."

Her eyes twinkled with mischief. "Watch what you say, my dear. You don't want to regret your words."

He leaned in close. "Do I look scared to you?" He chuckled before kissing her nose. He took her hand and led them in the blessing over the food.

"Your sisters tell me that you are meeting them for lunch at the diner and then supper tonight at Asa's."

"Yes, I'm really looking forward to it. We're going to spend some time together in town and then Olivia and I will be coming home together, with Nate of course.

"I just love being around Olivia. She is practically glowing. I'm so happy for her and can't wait for her to have this baby. She says Asa is more silly than you were, which I find hard to believe."

****

Harvey rode the farm, making sure everything was going well with the workers, then headed out to the bunkhouses. He needed to get Eva's surprises from Benson and get everything set up while she was gone.

"You got it all done?" Harvey grinned from ear to ear.

"Yep, come take a look. Got the boys to load it in the wagon and I have a couple of men ready to help unload it for you. Just say when."

"A little after noon should be good. I'll be watching for you." Harvey shook Benson's hand. "Thanks, Benson. You're a good friend. I hope you are joining us tonight?"

"Nah, I have a few pressing matters around here I'm having to keep my eye on. Think one of the boys is developing quite a taste for drink. He's been hanging out at the saloon every day off, I've heard, and I just need to make sure that's the only place he's drinking."

"I hate that, but I appreciate you saving me the headache. We will miss you being there, but I'll save you some cake, maybe."

****

The girls were joined by Mrs. Powell at the diner, where they enjoyed chattering as they ate. None of them were prone to gossip but couldn't help but be intrigued by what Mrs. Powell told them.

"Guess who got married recently?"

All eyes were on her.

"Toby! Can you believe someone would marry him?" she barely whispered.

The girls shook their heads. "I, for one, pity her," Olivia spouted. "Who is she? Do we know her?"

"No, she's new around here. Apparently, he met her when he was living elsewhere, and she was waiting for him to send for her. She's a beautiful girl but," Mrs. Powell looked around and lowered her voice. "I hate to say it, but she's dumb as a rock."

"She would have to be to marry him," Eva spat quietly.

"No, I really mean it. I've met her and I don't think she's quite all there."

"Why would he marry someone like that?" Amy asked. "He is handsome enough to catch a girl's eye, but why would he marry someone that isn't quite right?"

"That's exactly why he married her. No one else would put up with him. Plus, I heard that her father fronted Toby the money for his saloon on the promise he would marry her."

"He's such a rat!" Olivia snarled. "Sounds just like something he would do, and I say shame on her father."

"Anyway, I just wanted to let you know that he's married now, and hopefully will leave everyone else alone."

"Somehow, I don't think that will slow him down much." Olivia sighed. "Poor girl."

****

When Eva returned home, she found Harvey in the house, which was unusual for this time of day. He looked full of mischief as he met her at the door.

"Harvey? What's going on? Why do you look like I caught you with your hand in the cookie jar?" She looked past him at something covered with a sheet.

"That's because you almost did." He followed her eyes. "Don't be looking at that, it's a surprise for your birthday, and you can't see it until tonight."

"Harvey, you really shouldn't have bought anything. We are grabbing for every penny to put towards the land next month. I appreciate your thoughtfulness, but I would have rather had you owe me. I like it when you owe me. I can play you more easily."

"Ahh, now I see how you do it. How you get me to do whatever you want. Shame on you! I feel so abused!" he teased.

She put her arms around his neck. "Poor man. Maybe I can make you feel less abused and more appreciated." She kissed him as Nate ran up to them, hugging both their legs at once.

"Hold that thought for later," he winked as he reached down and picked Nate up to join them.

The birthday supper celebration went well, with lots of chatter and bantering. When they finished eating, they all walked to Harvey and Eva's to watch the unveiling of her birthday gift.

She lifted the corners of the sheet and carefully pulled it off to see a brand-new sewing machine and a beautiful, tall armoire. She gasped, turning to Harvey, squealing while throwing herself around his neck.

"Thank you! I love it!"

"Don't just thank me. Look inside the armoire and see the rest of what we did."

She threw the armoire doors open to find it loaded with fabric, thread, buttons and snaps, a new pair of scissors and several patterns.

"Oh my! This is the most wonderful birthday ever!" She turned back to the group and started hugging and thanking each of them.

Within minutes, the crowd left, wishing her one last, "Happy Birthday!"

Harvey picked up Nate and had him kiss his ma goodnight, then turned to Eva before taking Nate to his room. "Umm, I seem to remember you saying you needed to make me feel more appreciated?"

She shot him a cunning grin. "Yes, maybe I do."

****

Harvey shouted with glee as he entered the house after signing the papers on the property. "Hallelujah! It's ours! And for a better price than I had hoped!" He picked Eva up and twirled her around.

"Oh, Harvey! I am so happy for you!"

"I offered them thirty-five hundred, thinking they would either say no or come back with another offer, but they accepted it, Eva! They accepted thirty-five hundred! That puts another five hundred dollars toward the ranchland. This is a wonderful day!"

"Harvey, I'm so proud of you. Your pa would be too."

He held her close. "Somehow, I think he is."

After a moment of quiet, he looked down at her. "I guess it's time to get the books back out and see what we have for the ranch. They made the offer today and want three thousand for the full thousand acres. That's a good price for some good land."

She looked at him exuberantly. "I don't need to get the book out. I have the number burned in my memory. After seven years of the allowance they gave you, and what you actually had to pay out, plus the savings from you and your pa, you have four thousand three hundred sixty dollars."

"Woo Hoo!" he shouted as he twirled her around again. "Oh my, Eva! This is wonderful. Now I will have enough to buy some livestock of my own." He kissed her quickly then held her close. "I can't believe it. After all these years of hard work, sometimes feeling as if I had held my breath, I finally made it. We made it, and it is wonderful."

****

Harvey almost felt guilty as he told Asa about the deal he had gotten. "All along, Pa and I both were thinking I would be in debt for a long time. Now, I almost feel as if you've been cheated out of it somehow.

"Don't you want to reconsider and jump back in with me?"

Asa shook his head. "I thank you, but no. I got paid for the work I did on the farm and ranch. Then pa gave me his house, all it cost me was building that little shed for him. You and Eva took care of him until the day he died, so no, don't feel like you owe me anything, Harvey. If anything, I owe the farm, living here for free and all."

"I don't see it that way. Half of the original farm is yours free and clear. You have as much right here as I do. But I'm telling you, there is room for both of us in this farm and ranch business and all you have to do is jump back in."

"No, this is your dream, not mine. I see myself happy with a few acres, a house, a small garden, maybe a cow, some chickens, and a few horses. I have no use for a bunch of land."

"Alright then, if you're sure about it and you're happy, then I'm happy."

Harvey lowered his voice, leaning forward. "I would like to talk to you about a few things in private though. Maybe take a walk with me?"

"Sure, let me tell Olivia I'm going to ride on your rounds with you."

A few minutes down the road, Harvey began. "I've been hearing scuttlebutt about if and when a war breaks out, the government is going to have the right to confiscate produce and livestock from farmers and ranchers, to feed their armies."

"They going to pay for it?"

"From what I heard, no. They confiscate it saying it's our duty to help the army."

"What about feeding your own family?"

"That's what I want to talk to you about. I have an idea you may be able to help with."

He led his horse toward the wooded hillside, and soon was pointing to the base of a foothill. "See that area there, Asa? The side of that hill? I want to dig it out, have you build a steel room of sorts, in the hill, with good solid walls, roof, and door. We could store lots of food in there for a good long time. Canned goods, salted meat, everything we may need to get by on for as long as it takes, I hope."

Asa dismounted. "I could do that, and it would be back here where no one would be likely to find it. Harvey, you do use your head sometimes. I think it's a good idea.

"So, you think it's going to get bad, huh?"

"I'm afraid it may. All we can do is hope for the best and prepare for the worst. I've already ordered more canning jars than I care to admit. I hope we don't need them, but just in case."

****

October was a gorgeous month. The sky was blue, the weather warm during the day and crisp at night, and the fields were emptying of this year's harvest.

Harvey had shared his thoughts with Eva about planning ahead and she immediately started canning at least double of everything they had left in the garden. She was working on filling their cellar until Asa and Vince got the steel room ready, determined that her family wouldn't go hungry.

On the last night of October, they were awakened by Asa banging on their door, crying out in panic.

"Harvey get the doctor quick! Olivia is in pain and there's blood everywhere. Please, Harvey, hurry! I'm so scared I'm going to lose her and the baby! Oh, God! Please be merciful! Don't take my wife and my child!"

"Asa!" Eva yelled. "Get a hold of yourself! You need to be strong for Olivia right now. Go back to her and I will be there in a few minutes."

Harvey rushed by them, headed for the barn. Within a few moments, he took off down the road.

"Thank you, Eva," Asa called over his shoulder as he ran back toward his house.

Eva quickly and gently bundled Nate, whispering, "Everything is alright Nate. We are going to Aunt Olivia's," as she hurried out the door and across the meadow, holding him tightly.

She sat a sleepy-eyed Nate in the feeding chair and gave him a cookie, knowing there was no way the child could sleep with all the screaming going on. She just hoped he wouldn't start screaming too.

She rushed to her sister, trying to tamp down her own panic when she saw the horrific scene before her, hearing the constant cries of agony. There was nothing she could do except try to console her sister and try to stay brave, while in a constant state of prayer.

Harvey was back with the doctor in tow in less than an hour, which seemed an eternity to Asa.

He rushed to Olivia, soon asking Asa to leave the room, and Eva to stay and help.

He quickly gave Olivia some laudanum, beginning to check her and listen for the baby. He gave a quick smile that the baby seemed okay for now.

"Eva, I'm going to have to do a cesarian. I will need your help. Are you up to it or do you think you will faint?"

"The Lord will give me the strength to help Olivia."

He pulled a bottle of chloroform out of his bag, pouring some on a cloth, instructing Eva to hold it over Olivia's mouth and nose for a few seconds.

Within seconds, Olivia was unconscious, and the doctor prayed as he began. "Eva, be ready to take the baby and clean it up quickly, clearing its mouth and making sure it's breathing. I'm going to have my hands full with stopping your sister from bleeding to death."

Eva quickly grabbed a towel to wrap the baby in, standing by the doctor, watching in horror and then amazement as the baby appeared.

She took the tiny baby and immediately got it breathing. It wasn't until she started washing it that she noticed it was a little girl.

"Are you alright, Eva? You still with me?"

"Yes, doctor. Everything is fine here. We have a precious little girl."

"Wonderful, now, take her to her pa and come back and help me, quickly, please."

Eva took the baby and placed her in Asa's arms. "Meet your daughter, Asa." She turned quickly to go back in the room.

"How is Olivia? Please tell me she's alright."

"The doctor is doing surgery on her now. Just pray. He needs me back in there."

Asa sank to the couch, clutching his daughter to his chest as he cried out to God to keep His hand of safety on his wife. His tears fell freely as his heart felt torn from his chest. He couldn't feel the joy of his newborn for the heartbreak of his wife.

An hour later, Harvey sat on the couch holding Nate as he slept, while Asa cuddled his daughter, kissing her cheeks and her head covered with downy soft blonde hair, just like her ma.

The doctor came out of the room, covered in blood, wiping his hands. "Asa, Olivia is going to be sore for a while, but she will be alright. I will keep a check for infection, but I think she will be okay."

Asa started thanking the doctor and the Lord, simultaneously.

"Asa, you're going to need to find something to feed the baby with. Perhaps Eva can help you. Olivia will be sleeping for quite a while, I'm sure. And, I hate to tell you this, but there will be no more babies. I'm so sorry."

Asa's face went blank. He seemed to be in a trance momentarily. Finally, he spoke. "Thank you, doc. If this is the only child the Lord sees fit to bless us with, then that's fine with me. She is truly a blessing. I'm just so grateful that you saved them both. I was so fearful of losing them."

Eva came from the room, her arms loaded with laundry stained with blood, looking so tired. "Asa, I have something you can feed the baby with. It's in your kitchen so I will get it ready for you."

"Thank you, Eva. You don't know how much I appreciate all you've done tonight."

She patted his arm and peeked at the baby. "She's precious and perfect. Does she have a name?"

"No. I'm going to let her ma name her."

The next day, when Olivia woke, Asa was beside her with his arms around her and the baby, sleeping.

She stirred and winced in pain, waking him up. "Oh Asa, our baby!" She reached to touch her. "Is it a boy or a girl?"

Asa smiled and kissed her cheek. "It's a precious baby girl. How are you feeling?"

"I'm right sore. What happened? The last thing I remember is panicking when I saw blood and feeling excruciating pain."

Asa cleared his throat. "The doc said you have to be careful how you hold her because you have stitches in your belly. He had to cut her out to save you and her. But both of you will be fine."

She reached for the baby as Asa helped get her situated.

"She's precious, Asa." Tears of joy streamed down her face. She unwrapped her and touched her fingers and toes, the softness of her skin. "She's perfect."

"And she's a blessing." He choked for a moment. "Olivia, darling, the doctor said there won't be any more babies, and after I saw you going through what you did, I'm glad. I couldn't stand to see you go through that again."

She looked into his eyes. "I'm so sorry, Asa." She started to sob as he pulled her to his chest. "I can't give you any more children, I've failed you."

"Shh, don't you say such things. You have blessed me beyond measure. I have my whole world right here and I am one very blessed man. Now, what would you like to name this little angel?"

Olivia looked down at their tiny daughter, kissing her head gently. "Ruth."

Chapter 20

Within days after Olivia had Ruth, Eva knew without hesitation that she was with child again. Even though Olivia and Asa seemed to have accepted the news about never having another child, Eva wished her timing was different.

She went to town with Harvey the day he met the men at the lawyer's office to sign the purchase of the ranchland. He hoped the men would also present him with a contract to lease the land from him, with him still overseeing the livestock kept there.

Eva told him she was going to run some errands and would meet him at the diner. As soon as she saw him disappear into the lawyer's office, she turned and quickly headed for the doctor. He confirmed her suspicions within minutes, then she slipped out of his office, quickly heading for Henderson's store.

Clint Henderson greeted her, which took her by surprise.

"Good morning, Clint. What are you doing here? I hope your pa isn't feeling poorly."

"Well, he doesn't seem to ever feel good anymore, so he asked me to take over the store for him. I have been learning it all my life, it seems, and he said he thinks it's time."

She smiled at him. "Welcome to the world of being a businessman. I hope you enjoy it."

"I think I will, ma'am, thank you. Now, what can I do for you today?"

She handed him a list. "I need to get these things and I'm going to look around a bit. My sister just had a baby and I need to pick up a few things for her."

Clint nodded as he looked over the list. "Umm, are you sure you wrote this right, Mrs. Darnell? That's an awful lot of sugar, salt and vinegar."

She laughed quietly. "Yes, it's written right. We have a few projects going on at the farm."

"Alrighty then, I will get it loaded in your wagon."

He went in the back storage room and started hauling sacks to her wagon. Harvey came in and helped him.

Soon they were finished at Henderson's and sitting at the diner. Harvey was quietly telling her how well everything had gone, and that the government was continuing to lease the land from him.

He looked at her and noticed her smile. "You look happy. Are you just smiling about my news, or do you have something to add?"

She reached and took his hand. "Harvey, I am so proud of you. Seeing you happy means everything to me. I'm just wondering if you could be any happier?"

He looked at her, intrigued. "Oh, I don't know. It would certainly have to rate up there pretty high. You want to give it a try? See if you can top my good news?"

"Oh, my dear husband, I can definitely top your news. You're going to be a pa again!"

He smiled and kissed her hand. "You just wait until I get outside of town. I'm going to shout with joy! When did you find out?"

"I've suspected for a few weeks, but the doctor just confirmed it. Please don't make such a fuss, Harvey. I know Asa and Olivia are hurting and this may be like rubbing salt in a wound."

He hung his head. "You may be right. We will keep this quiet for a while, not that it's going to be easy."

****

Mr. Farley rode out to the farm one Saturday afternoon in mid-November. He noticed there were still a few workers milling about, getting the fields cleaned from the end of harvest. Everything looked good and he was very proud of the job Harvey had done.

He saw Harvey, Asa, and Vince near the barn, tinkering on some machinery. They stood and greeted him as he approached.

Harvey walked toward him. "You're just in time, Mr. Farley. I have a wrench over there that will fit your hand just fine." He stretched his hand toward the man, helping steady him as he dismounted.

"Good, good! I would love to be put to work on something with my hands for a while. I haven't been able to tinker on anything in a long time. What are you working on?"

"Everything seems to be in good working order, we just like to make sure it stays that way." Asa turned to tease, "Harvey is quite the task master. He won't feed us unless we finish the work, and I'm smelling something good coming from the house."

"What brings you out this way, Mr. Farley? Nothing wrong, I hope."

"No, Harvey, nothing wrong except a little bit of boredom. Agnes is out of town visiting her ailing sister, and I thought I would spread my wings a bit while she's gone.

"Thought maybe I could catch up on things around here, see what all is going on. Hope you don't mind."

"Not at all," Harvey waved his arm for the man to join them. They fell into a conversation filled with news of Asa's daughter, how the land purchase went, the contracts for the next growing season, and then, of course, it turned to the probability of war.

Without telling Mr. Farley specifically about the steel room they were building, they talked about having a community meeting, discussing how each family could start preparing to take care of themselves if necessary.

"I hope you boys have stocked up on some gold, as well as food." Mr. Farley sighed. "But I didn't come out here to dowse cold water on your spirits. I came to just enjoy spending time with you, like we used to before…" he paused. "I'm sorry, I miss your pa sometimes, something fierce. He was a good friend, a good man."

"Thanks, Mr. Farley. We miss him too, and he thought very highly of you." Asa patted the man's shoulder.

Harvey changed the subject. "Why don't you join us for supper? My stomach is telling me it's getting about that time."

"If you're sure it won't be an imposition, I would love to."

Vince chuckled. "I hope it doesn't give you a good case of indigestion. It does get quite noisy with three babies around."

"I will cherish every minute, I assure you."

****

Eva stayed busy at her sewing machine, repairing, mending, and fashioning new clothes for Nate, who was growing like a weed. She also made gifts for each of her family members. Lovingly touching the tiny folds and ruffles on the little dresses she made for Sylvia and Ruth, she started hoping she would have a girl this time.

She looked over at Nate, playing in front of the fireplace, whispering, "Lord, another fine boy would be alright too. I will love whatever you bless me with."

Nate glanced up, seeing her look at him. He gave her a winning smile that melted her heart. She opened her arms to him. He jumped up, and ran to her, hugging her tightly.

"You are such a good boy, Nate." She kissed his head and enjoyed the embrace while it lasted, which never was long enough, it seemed. The boy was too busy building with his blocks or exploring, and every few minutes running to the window looking for his pa.

Harvey had gone back to work with the sheriff for the winter, and his family missed him. He worked mostly nights, which meant he slept during the day, and they saw very little of him. Sometimes he wondered if it was worth missing his family to work this extra job. They didn't really need the money; they didn't spend that much, they had everything they needed, and Eva was the most thrifty person he had ever known.

About the time he was thinking about turning in his badge, the sheriff would remind him in some way, how grateful he was for him helping out and how appreciated he was. That would cause him to look at this job through a different set of eyes. He had always tried to help people and that was the driving force behind this decision.

So, he would quietly keep his badge, give the other deputies some much needed time off, and do his best to protect, help and serve the people of the community.

****

Christmas was a joyous occasion, each one of them feeling blessed beyond measure. The babies were passed around, conversations were light and cheerful, and Nate was the center of attention.

Harvey and Eva had bought him a pair of boots, Asa and Olivia gave him a stick horse, and Vince and Amy gave him a tool belt with a rubber hammer. He really put on a show for them, riding his horse around the house, 'fixing' every door and table with his hammer along the way.

263

As the evening progressed, the conversation turned to making preparations, as always, in case of war. Eva took them down to the cellar, showing them her progress. She had shelves lined with jars filled with beans, greens, pumpkin, and apples.

"I didn't know we were doing this in time to get the early summer crops done." She pointed to the potatoes in the bin. "I will start on those before they go to seed. Harvey says he will buy seed potatoes this year instead of using these, so I can add them to our collection."

Everyone was impressed.

"I started on some of the same," Olivia ran her hand over some jars. "I haven't done near this much, though. Now that I've had Ruth, come summer, I will get more serious about it."

Amy agreed as she looked at Vince. "I need to buy a lot more jars and do our part. I admit I haven't gotten a good start yet, but I will."

"Do you really think it will come to this?" Vince almost scoffed. "We are in the backwoods of nowhere really, we don't own slaves, there are no plantations around here..." he shook his head. "I think we are overreacting."

Asa started leading everyone back up the steps as he spoke. "Use your head, man. First of all, it's not just about slavery. I'm against the things I've heard about it, and don't think any man should 'own' another man; it's just not right. But this goes so much deeper.

"It's about state's rights. The north needs the south and the south needs the north, but the north is buying our raw materials for nearly nothing, using their big industries to turn those materials into things we need, and charging us more than we can afford to pay. They are breaking our backs and it's not right."

They sat down at the table while Eva and Amy got dessert and coffee, motioning for Olivia to sit.

Harvey cut into the conversation. "Vince, it is serious and seems to be getting more so every day. I'm convinced we need to be prepared for the worst, just in case. I mean, what will it hurt? If it doesn't happen, and I really hope it doesn't, then we are stocked up for a while. No harm in that."

Vince sighed, "I suppose. I'm just weary with it."

****

By February, Eva could no longer hide the fact she was going to have another baby. Olivia hugged her and sobbed in her arms.

"You are such a sweet sister. You had no cause to keep this from me, I am happy for you, truly I am. I appreciate you trying to spare my feelings," she pulled back from her and wiped her face. "I have been blessed with a beautiful little girl and a wonderful husband. I couldn't ask for a better life and I am truly happy and blessed. Don't you feel bad because God has another path planned for you."

Eva joined with her own tears as she cupped Olivia's face tenderly. "I love you, Olivia."

The two women fussed around the kitchen, preparing supper while Ruth slept in the cradle and Nate 'helped' the men at the barn.

Nate was absolutely a daddy's boy, worshipping the ground Harvey walked on, mimicking his every move. When Harvey hammered, Nate hammered, when Harvey laughed, Nate laughed. Harvey was suddenly aware he had to be very careful of everything he said or did, making sure he only instilled good in his boy.

"There's been talk at work about new opportunities available in the steel and iron industry. Seems with all this talk about war, the nation is wanting to ramp up supplies of all sorts and build more trains and tracks than you could imagine."

Harvey stopped hammering, Nate stopped too, and they looked at Asa. "And? Seems there is more on your mind."

"Well, you know that Vince has always had his heart set on working with the railroad, and he's been excited about the talk he's been hearing."

Harvey waited a moment. "Asa, don't play games with me. If there is something you want to say, then say it."

"He talked to the big boss this week and got a list of places he may consider working. The boss is really encouraging him because he gets some kind of fee for finding skilled workers to fill the positions."

"Hmm." Harvey thought for a moment. "Can't say I'm surprised. He's always talked about it, and everyone should be able to pursue his dreams. I did, you did, now it's his turn. Hopefully, he can work close by."

"That's just it Harvey, it's nowhere near close by. The list he has, is for companies that are states away. Some are up north and others down south. The closest one is in Georgia."

"I see." Harvey tossed his hammer down. He instantly turned with surprise when Nate did the same, forgetting that the boy was right by his side, as usual. He chuckled, reaching down to pick the boy up. He put Nate up on his shoulders.

"Vince has to make up his own mind what's best for his family. I sure would hate to see them move away, knowing it would break the girls' hearts, but each of us has to do what we feel is best."

Asa looked quizzically at Harvey, putting his hands on his hips. "You really feel that way, Harvey?"

Harvey chuckled. "Sure, I do. I may not like it, but what else do you propose we do? Lock him in his house? Tie him down? He has to make up his own mind."

Asa looked down, and Harvey got an empty feeling in his gut. "Asa? There's more, isn't there?"

Asa nodded his head. "Yeah. I've been looking at some things too. But before you say anything, the only place I may be interested in is just over the Virginia line in Wythe County, so it's not that far away."

Harvey didn't say a word. He walked out of the barn and into the house. "Eva, I have to get ready for work, sweetheart. I need to go in early tonight."

"You won't be here for supper?"

"No," he kissed her quickly, turning to see Asa come in the door quietly. "Sorry, sweetheart. Just save me a plate for tomorrow. I will get something from the diner tonight." He shook his head at Asa as he walked out of the room.

****

By spring, Ruth was sitting up by herself, unless she laughed, then she would fall over and wait for someone to sit her back up. Sylvia was busy trying to follow down behind Nate, carrying her doll every moment, while Nate continued to 'fix' everything he could find.

Eva was uncomfortable often, feeling as if she would burst. Olivia doted on her when Harvey wasn't home and enjoyed doing it. Eva would sit at her sewing machine most days, creating all kinds of treasures for her house and family.

There had been no mention from anyone about taking a new job or moving. Harvey finally mentioned it one Saturday afternoon to the men while they were working outside.

"You mean, neither of you has told your wives?"

Both men shrugged, then Vince spoke. "No need to tell them before we've made a decision."

"What about them being a part of the decision and perhaps praying with you about it?"

"Harvey," Vince reasoned. "God gave me a good brain and I think He expects me to use it. You and I just see things a little differently, I suppose. I adore my wife and my daughter and want what's best for them. Having a good job will enable me to give them everything their hearts desire."

"Except for being around family." Harvey shook his head, knowing there was nothing else to be said. Vince had his mind wrapped around material things, always had.

"I promise you, Amy will be happy once we get settled in our new lives, and we can always visit each other."

Harvey looked at Asa. "And what about you? Do you feel the same way?"

Asa looked sheepish. "No, not entirely. I'm going to talk to Olivia, but I know it will upset her at first, and will also upset Eva. I thought I would wait until after she has the baby. Besides, we aren't talking about leaving tomorrow."

Nothing more was said about it. They started working again, each caught in their own thoughts.

****

Harvey rode up to the house at lunchtime, surprised to see Eva and Olivia about to get in the buggy with Nate and Ruth.

"Whoa! Where do you think you're going?"

"It's such a beautiful day, Harvey, we are going to take a ride to town." Eva kissed his cheek as he settled her in the buggy.

"Do you think that's wise? You sure you feel up to it?"

She giggled as he put his hand on her belly. "I feel fine."

Three-year-old Nate asked if he could stay with his pa.

Harvey grabbed him up out of the buggy. "Sure, you can, son. That should make it a bit easier on your ma. You ladies be careful, there's a lot of precious cargo in this buggy." He winked as Nate waved, when Olivia snapped the reins and moved the buggy forward.

They stopped by Amy's, inviting her to join them, then enjoyed the afternoon together, until Eva had her first few labor pains.

"I think I'm going to see the doctor for a moment. You two just go on about your shopping and I will return soon."

After an hour, they went looking for her. She was just coming from the examining room when they entered the office.

The doctor looked exasperated. "I need you ladies to get your sister home, carefully. I will be out there shortly. She is in labor and should stay here but insists on going home. My, what a stubborn woman."

"Doc," Eva scolded. "You said it would be hours. I have plenty of time to get home."

"Then go, Mrs. Darnell, and I will see you in a bit."

Olivia and Amy helped her in the buggy, carefully getting her settled before riding toward Amy's. By the time Amy got out with Sylvia, and Olivia was driving them home, Eva was wishing she had stayed with the doctor. She was holding little Ruth and having a hard time doing it.

Olivia yelled out for Harvey as they passed by the fields. He was sitting on his horse having a conversation with Benson at the time. When she motioned for him, he knew something was wrong. He handed Nate over to Benson and arrived at the house at the same moment Olivia stopped the buggy.

He needed no explanation as he looked at Eva. She pushed him away when he tried to move her, raising a finger for him to hold on a moment.

"Okay, help me quickly before another pain starts."

She had barely got up the porch steps and to the door when another hit. She stopped, holding onto the door facing until it subsided.

When she nodded it was over, Harvey picked her up and carried her to their room, where Olivia was already preparing everything. He sat her on the bed and started helping her into her gown, when she screamed out.

"The baby is coming now, Harvey!"

In the next few moments, they had her on the bed and the baby was indeed coming, doctor or no doctor.

Harvey delivered his precious little daughter, Caroline, over an hour before the doctor arrived.

Eva held Caroline with Harvey propped up on the bed beside her, holding both in his arms. Eva called to Olivia, "Look, Olivia. She looks so much like Sylvia and Ruth; they could be mistaken as sisters instead of cousins."

"They sure could, and all three of them as beautiful as I've ever seen."

Olivia then turned to Harvey. "Why don't you take Caroline and introduce her to Nate while Eva gets some sleep."

"Nate!" Harvey exclaimed. "I left him with Benson hours ago! Olivia, can you stay long enough for me to go get him?"

Laughing at his apparent state of embarrassment, she nodded and motioned for him to go.

****

Vince surprised Amy one evening with flowers and train tickets. "I want to take my beautiful wife and daughter on a vacation."

"Oh Vince, that would be wonderful! Where are we going, and when?"

"Alabama, my dear. We will be leaving on Monday, October 15th, and will be gone for two weeks. It will be a wonderful trip to a place I've heard is like Heaven."

He went on to describe it being warm almost all the time, with flowers and trees blooming constantly, cities with theaters and fancy dining, tree lined streets filled with big,

Victorian houses, "and fancy carriages that make our buggies look like buckboards."

"It sounds wonderful, but what is the special occasion?"

He wrapped his arms around her and kissed her. "I just wanted to do something special with my girls."

Amy was over-running with enthusiasm when they went to the farm Saturday afternoon. She went on about what Vince had told her to expect, then asked Eva if they could possibly work on a few new dresses for her trip.

"I have four weeks to get ready and I have to find something to fill the hours, or I shall surely burst with excitement. I will go to Henderson's Monday and buy some new fabrics, and perhaps look in a catalog for some of the latest fashions." She squealed with excitement.

A different kind of conversation was taking place in the barn between the men.

"Yes, Harvey. I am taking her down there to let her fall in love with the place. I'm sure she will. Then I will tell her about my new job, and we will start looking for a house."

Harvey snarled at him. "Good to know she has so much say so in her future. Hmph, well maybe she will get to pick her own curtains; maybe."

"I resent that, Harvey. I'm the man of the family, the head of the family."

"Yes, you are, but you are supposed to treat your wife with love and respect, not bribes and demands." Harvey shook his head. "Forget it, Vince. I just don't agree with how you've gone about this. What's done is done, and I hope it works out well for you."

Harvey caught a glimpse of Nate, standing with his hands on his hips, looking stern at Vince, just like he was. "Nate, get back to work." Nate immediately started back to work, pulling nails out of a board.

When the men came in for supper, Eva and Olivia could tell something wasn't right. Amy was so excited, in her own little world, she didn't notice anything amiss.

Vince made excuses for them to leave soon after supper, with Amy still rattling on about preparations for the trip.

As soon as the door closed behind them, Eva and Olivia motioned for Harvey and Asa to join them at the table. Both babies were asleep, and Nate climbed on his pa's lap.

"Alright," Eva started. "Which one of you cares to tell us what's going on here?"

Asa shrugged and looked at Harvey.

Eva looked from one to the other. "I promise there won't be any sleep until someone does some explaining."

Harvey cleared his throat. "Eva, sweetheart, it's not for us to say. It's really not our business."

"Harvey Darnell, don't you hang whatever it is on a technicality. Something has you two upset and so it does make it our business."

He knew he was fighting a losing battle, but he had to be careful not to say enough to let Asa's secret out, or he would really get a scalding from Olivia.

"Sit down and I will tell you." She sat immediately. "Vince is thinking about taking a job down in Alabama, that's why he's taking Amy down there to show her the place."

After the initial shock, and the tears that followed, they talked about it for a while until both wives were calm.

"I would appreciate it if neither of you said anything to Amy. Vince needs to be the one to tell her."

Asa cleared his throat and summoned all his courage. "Umm, Olivia. I might as well be completely honest, while the subject is open. I have been offered a really good job, right over the state line in Virginia. We won't be that far from home and could come for a visit maybe once a month or so, and Harvey and Eva can…"

He was interrupted as Olivia started to cry and ran from the room.

Eva stood and gave Asa a look that made him cringe. Then she followed down behind Olivia.

Harvey looked down at Nate. "It's about time for bed, boy. Let's go get your pajamas on."

Suddenly Asa felt very alone, almost like he was the enemy.

Chapter 21

Vince had certainly guessed Amy right. She loved Alabama so well, she didn't want to wait to move there, at least until she got back home and realized how much she would miss her family. She was so excited, yet so torn.

In April 1856, Vince started his new job, leaving Amy and Sylvia behind until he could find a house. In June he sent Amy a telegram saying he had everything ready for their arrival.

Harvey, Eva, Asa and Olivia helped her pack everything to be shipped to her new home. After a tearful goodbye, not knowing if they would ever see her again, they waved from the platform as Amy and Sylvia waved back through the train window until they could no longer see her.

Asa's new job was to start in September. He and Olivia took a trip to Virginia, looking at all they would be surrounded by. It wasn't much different from home except in the industrial district.

Olivia had consoled herself to the fact that Asa and Ruth were her family now, and if this was what Asa really wanted and felt was best for his family, then that's what they would do. Unlike Vince, Asa and Harvey were brothers and would always share a bond. She felt sure they would stay in close contact with visits back and forth.

They found a house on a small piece of land, just like Asa had wanted. With the money he had saved over the years by living on the farm, he was able to purchase it. A nice little farmhouse with two bedrooms, a nice parlor, and big kitchen, sitting on five acres of land, thirty minutes ride from where he worked and twenty minutes in the other direction, to town.

Ruth would be turning two on November 1st, and Harvey agreed that would be a good time for them to come see their new place and visit for a few days.

After another tearful goodbye, Eva had never felt so empty and clung to Harvey and the children closer than ever. The field workers were starting to finish up for the season, leaving even more emptiness. She worked harder than ever, cooking, canning, sewing, and taking care of her family, anything to fill the void in her broken heart.

Nate rode the farm with his pa for several hours every day. Sometimes he would protest when Harvey would bring him home at lunchtime, but Harvey made it clear that he wasn't to back talk or be disobedient. Nate was always easygoing and seemed to strive for his parents' approval. Harvey and Eva never had to do more than scold him, and he would immediately straighten up.

Caroline, on the other hand, seemed to be more independent with a bit of a stubborn streak, even at the age of sixteen months. Harvey and Eva could tell, this one would be a handful.

****

Eva and Olivia clung to each other and chattered until their voices were about gone. The week-long visit had been wonderful, seeing where Asa worked, where they lived, the town, and everything there was to see.

"Olivia, I must say, you seem happy. This place isn't too different from home."

"It certainly isn't home, though. I miss all our visits back and forth, but Asa is so happy with his new job." She glanced lovingly through the window at him as he walked through the yard with Harvey and the children.

"I will get used to it. Ma had to pick up and start over many times for pa, never begrudging him for it. She always made the best of the situation and I want to be like that."

Eva wrapped her arm around her sister's waist, standing beside her as they watched their families through the window.

Asa was busy filling Harvey in on all the responsibilities he had at work, being hired as a foreman. "The boss said I could climb the ladder of success quickly. Says I have the drive and determination for it.

"But listen, Harvey, this war stuff is becoming more real every day. I get orders for wartime machinery and ammunition headed for the...well, I can't say, I've been sworn to secrecy. But the location doesn't matter. My point is, I want to work out something with you, making sure that if anything happens to either of us, we will see to it our families are taken care of."

"Asa, you know that goes without saying. I know I would take care of your family and I assumed you would do the same for me."

Asa nodded. "I want to show you where I've hidden a few things around here, you know, like we did at your place. And yes, I've been keeping my eyes on gold. Seems Mr. Farley could almost see into the future.

"It may seem odd to you, and I'm not trying to be dishonest, but even Olivia doesn't know how much money I make. I bring home enough to live on with a bit left over, she handles that money and always saves back a bit.

"The rest goes into a secret place in case a real emergency comes up. That, my dear brother, is only for you and I to know about. It's not much yet, but I add to it every month."

They walked into the woods, carrying Ruth and Caroline, while Nate used a stick to beat back the weeds and sticks in their path. Stopping near an incline, Asa set Ruth down and rolled a dead log from in front of a rock. Harvey set Caroline down and instructed Nate to show the girls a frog that had jumped on the path.

Harvey helped Asa roll the big rock a few inches, just enough to let Harvey see a good-sized metal box, tucked into a hole in the side of the hill. Harvey nodded and helped him replace the rock and log. They dusted their hands and called the children back.

Asa handed Harvey a key. "You and I are the only ones that know or have a key. Agreed?"

Harvey assured him with a nod and pat on the back, before noticing Caroline was missing.

"That girl," he mumbled. "Nate, where's your sister?"

Nate pointed, "Catching the frog."

Harvey followed the sound of squeals and giggles, off the path farther than he would have guessed her little legs could carry her. Finally, he caught up with her. "Caroline Darnell, what in the world do you think you're doing?" He picked her up, seeing she had ripped her dress, messed up her hair, and had dirt smudged on her face from her filthy hands.

"Fog!" she shouted with glee as she pointed and nodded. She squirmed to get down. "Fog, pa, fog!" she patted his face as if to get his attention.

"No, Caroline. We need to get back to your ma." Oh, how he regretted those words a moment later when her lip trembled, and she pouted one last choked word, "Pease."

He immediately choked, trying to think of a diversion, quickly. He hugged her close and whispered, "Aunt Olivia has cookies!"

He headed back to the path, thinking she was over the frog, when the tears and wails began. Asa came running with concern etched on his face.

Seeing the dirty, tattered little girl, and hearing her cry, made him even more concerned. "What happened, Harvey? How bad is she hurt?"

Harvey chuckled. "She's not hurt. This is the true Caroline. Tough and tomboy already, stubborn, but such a tender heart."

****

The visit had done them all good. It reassured them that they could still see each other, just not as often.

Christmas time, Asa, Olivia and Ruth visited with Harvey's family. Asa left the day after Christmas, leaving Olivia and Ruth for a couple of weeks. With Harvey working for the sheriff at night, it suited everyone well.

They shared Christmas greetings from Vince, Amy and Sylvia, with cards and letters they had received. Amy went into detail about everything. They could almost imagine her squeals of delight over all the sights and events she described.

"She seems to be very happy," Eva sighed with a smile as she put the last letter on the table. "I'm happy for her."

"Vince seems to be as doting as always. Can you imagine buying a piano when no one even knows how to play it?" Olivia scoffed.

Eva shrugged. "She says they entertain guests quite often and some of them play, and of course she intends to have Sylvia take lessons in a few years. That will be a good thing."

"Leave it to you, Eva. Always finding the good in everything, Which reminds me, how is Mrs. Farley and what is her project for now?"

Eva laughed. "As far as I know, she is keeping her hands off the school and is still keeping the sheriff informed of everything. Don't misunderstand me, I agree with men and women conducting themselves properly, but I don't agree with her sneaking around attempting to make something out of nothing.

"Apparently, she is really on a rampage about Toby's conduct, although he keeps it all well hidden from the public and inside his saloon."

"What do you mean? He's married and getting ready to be a father. I assumed he had settled down."

"Don't you tell a soul I told you, because I'm not supposed to know."

Olivia nodded.

"Toby has some rooms upstairs in the saloon, dedicated to 'special entertainment'. His wife has come in several times over the last year looking for him, finding him in very compromising situations in one of those rooms."

Olivia gasped. "How horrible! How can she live like that?"

Eva shook her head in disgust. "I don't know. My heart breaks for the woman. I know she isn't very smart, but she still has feelings. I'd like to string Toby up myself. He will never change, and his wife will continue to suffer."

Within a few days, Olivia had no need to be sworn to secrecy any longer.

Harvey was late getting home one morning and looked very upset when he came in. He was quiet, refused anything to eat and didn't go to bed.

"Harvey," Eva soothed as she massaged his shoulders. "What has happened to upset you so?"

His eyes misted as he took her hand and kissed it. "Eva, it's the most horrible thing I've ever witnessed and I'm not sure you should hear about it." He thought for a moment.

"Maybe it will be better coming from me. Everyone will know soon enough." He cleared his throat and motioned for her to sit.

"I should leave you two alone." Olivia started to stand when Harvey motioned for her to stay.

"Toby's wife went in and found him being unfaithful again last night. From what the few witnesses say, he just laughed and scoffed at her, telling her to go on home where she was supposed to be.

"She was hysterical, crying and screaming. Then she pulled out a gun and shot herself right through the stomach, killing the baby first and then herself."

Everyone sat quietly. No sounds were heard except the children playing in the other room, and sniffles around the table.

"What about Toby?" Eva asked. "Surely he has to be held responsible for this."

"He's responsible," Harvey growled. "Once again, he is inside the boundary of the law, and it's a dern shame. There is nothing the law can do about it. He already talked to us at the office, claiming his innocence, saying she was mentally ill.

"I imagine her father will be in town soon. We'll see what he has to say and how he feels about Toby then. We still won't be able to arrest him, but some people have been known to take the law into their own hands. I just hope I'm not called on to protect him."

****

The day before Asa came back for Olivia and Ruth, the ladies made a trip to town, treating the children to candy sticks from Henderson's. They looked at the yard goods and picked up a few packs of flower seeds.

"Eva, let's both plant these flowers around our front porches. Every time we look at them, we can think of each other."

"Yes, I like that idea. Why don't we send a pack to Amy also?" She picked up another pack as Olivia agreed.

They heard a disturbance outside and went to the front window. Several men had gathered in the street and were taking turns punching someone. They couldn't see who, until the wounded man was thrown on his horse, and someone slapped the horse's rump, sending him out of town.

"Was that Toby?" Eva gasped.

Clint Henderson had been standing behind them, watching the same scene, without them knowing. "Yes, ma'am. Seems he's been caught cheating on more than his wife and his customers are fed up with it. There has been talk about running him out of town, and I guess that's what they did. Can't say I'm surprised or sad about it."

"Oh, my goodness Olivia, we left the children unattended. Caroline can't be trusted for a moment." She hurried to find Caroline sitting behind the counter, sharing her candy stick with a puppy.

She giggled as the puppy continued to lick her face, hands, and then take a bite of the candy. Eva laughed at the sight, then picked Caroline up, taking her to the basin.

Clint poured some fresh water for her while taking an opportunity he saw open up. "Umm, Mrs. Darnell and Mrs. Darnell. Seems I have a few pups I need to find homes for. Would either of you be interested?"

The sisters looked at each other, seriously at first, then both broke into a grin. They turned to him and spoke in unison, "Yes!"

He took them to the back room and let them have their pick of six pups. The women let the children play with them for a few minutes, seeing which interacted best. Before they knew it, they had Gerald load four of the six in a crate and put them in the back of the buggy.

They wanted them all because they couldn't decide, but Clint said he would like to keep two. They let him take his picks and then thanked him.

They had experienced so much excitement, Eva almost forgot her real purpose for coming to town. "Olivia, I need to see the doctor."

Olivia looked at her and knew, without another word, why. "You go on. It's such a nice day, I'll take the children to the park and wait for you."

When Eva returned, her glow told everything. Olivia hugged her tightly. "Eva, I am so happy for you. Let's go home and make a special supper to celebrate!"

****

Eva heard Harvey stirring around in the bedroom. "He's awake, Olivia. I'm going to slip in there and tell him the news."

Olivia grinned and waved her on.

Eva slipped into the room, finding Harvey half dressed, laying back on the bed. "Harvey? Are you feeling bad?"

He sat up. "No, not at all. I just kept having dreams, and when I woke up, I figured out they weren't dreams at all. Do I hear a puppy?"

"Oh, well, yes you do."

"Henderson. I had the feeling I would end up with one of his puppies. He sure makes a lot of noise for one puppy. Guess the children are keeping him excited."

"I'm sorry they disturbed you, Harvey, but, umm, there is more than one puppy. Olivia and I...

He laughed and pulled her to him. "It's fine, Eva. Every farm needs a dog. I'm sure Asa won't mind that Olivia got one too. In fact, it will probably make both of us feel better knowing the dog will warn of danger and such."

"I'm glad you feel that way, Harvey because we did get two...each." She cringed, looking impishly happy.

He looked up at her while he stayed seated, hugging her close. "That's fine."

She noticed his head was pressed against her belly. "Umm, Harvey?"

283

"Yes, sweetheart? Another surprise perhaps? Did you happen to find a litter of kittens too?"

"No, I just wondered if you could hear anything while you've got your head where it is."

"No, why? Are you hungry? Is it time to eat already?"

"No, I'm not hungry. I'm…" she paused, letting it sink in.

He looked up and smiled. "You're…?" He pulled her down on the bed with him, laying back with her in his arms.

"Eva, you continue to make me the happiest man in the world. I love you so much." He kissed her passionately then held her for a few moments before they heard Olivia scream.

"Get that puppy off the table!"

"I guess she needs our help." Eva laughed as she jumped up and hurried to her sister's aide.

****

Vince and Amy were blissfully happy. He had landed a good position with the railroad, working in the manufacturing of engines and cars. He was foreman over an entire department and was thrilled when his boss told him he was the youngest and most promising foreman he had ever hired.

He had found a nice house, in a nice neighborhood, not far from the hub of the city and about two miles from his job. Amy loved the house, the city, the weather, everything. Vince had insisted on her and Sylvia having the best of everything and begin to enter into the social groups. They entertained often, with Amy being an absolute perfect hostess. Vince was so proud of her and loved showing her off.

The only problem he and Amy had was the same as it had always been. She complained that he spent too much money on things they could do without. Feeling it was doing no good to say anything, Amy finally gave in except for one promise she made him keep. He gave her a certain percentage of his pay every week to put aside as savings. Every Monday morning on her way to the ladies auxiliary meeting, she would stop at the bank and make a deposit.

During the evenings they didn't have guests, the three would take a nice stroll through town and into the rich neighborhood beyond. They loved to look at the mansions and wonder what the inside looked like. Vince would point out some, telling her who owned them, and what they did for a living.

"Perhaps one day, we will be invited to some of these homes. Who knows, maybe we will own one."

"Vince, we have a beautiful home. Why would you want more? Why can't you be happy with what we have?"

He kissed her cheek. "I am very happy, Amy, but there's nothing wrong with ambition, is there?"

"I suppose not, but it shouldn't be an obsession."

He squeezed her waist as they continued to stroll. "The only obsession I have is with you, my love."

****

Eva closed the books and wiped her forehead. The heat from cooking supper had been unbearable. The humidity outside was stifling and not a breath of wind was blowing. She walked out on the porch and sat in the swing. It was a little cooler than in the house, but not much.

She adjusted a pillow behind her back and rested her hand on her bulging belly, looking at her ring glisten in the last rays of the sun. Her finger was so swollen, she couldn't get her ring off, making a mental note to try again in the morning.

"There you are," Harvey beamed as he stepped out on the porch.

"Thank you for putting the children to bed, Harvey. I'm just tired out tonight. I can't get comfortable and it's so stinking hot." She fanned herself with her hand.

"I'm sorry, sweetheart. You had the other babies before it got so hot, and I guess that doesn't help matters. Hopefully, you don't have much longer." He sat beside her and rested his hand on her belly.

He started to put his arm around her when she stopped him. "Harvey, it's just too hot. Please, no cuddling right now."

He sat back straight. "That's fine. I wish there was something I could do for you. How about a nice bath? I will fix you one and you can lay back and soak as long as you please."

"I must say, that sounds nice."

He kissed her cheek and went in the house, returning a little while later, helping her to the bedroom. After helping her into the tub, he turned to leave her in peace.

"I'll be right here in the parlor if you need me. You call when you're ready to get out and I'll help you."

"Thank you, Harvey." She blew him a kiss then stretched out in the tub and enjoyed every minute. This being the greatest pleasure of the day, she soon found herself dozing, then woke with a start.

"Harvey!"

In less than a minute he entered the room. "Finished already? I figured you would sleep there tonight."

"Umm, I can't be completely sure, because I dozed off and I'm sitting in a tub of water, but I think my water just broke."

He reached down and helped her up, wrapping a towel around her. "How do you feel?"

"Fine, so far. Let's just wait a few minutes and see what happens." She started getting dressed for bed, then started getting things together in case she was about to go into labor.

Suddenly she stopped and gripped the blankets she held in her hands. "Harvey, I need you to help me get the bed ready. I am in labor for sure."

"Do we have time?" he asked nervously.

"I'm sure we do. This will only take a minute, then I will get in bed while you go for the doctor."

"No, I've already talked to Benson. You don't have Olivia or Amy this time, and I'm not leaving you alone with two children sleeping except long enough to ride to the bunkhouse. He will get the doctor and he even volunteered to keep the children calm and occupied."

"He's a good friend. Ohh!" She winced and grabbed her stomach then her back. Harvey went to her and gently rubbed her back. In a minute she was feeling better.

"The bed is good enough, Eva. I'm going for Benson."

She nodded and watched him race out the door. By the time he returned she had gotten in bed and had three more severe pains.

"I guess each one is different, but I have never had my back and hips hurt like with this one."

"What can I do for you, sweetheart?" He was holding her hand as another pain took over her body.

She turned on her side and had him rub her back. "That eased the pain through the last one."

"Then I will stay right here and continue." He bent over and kissed her forehead. "You know, I have been blessed to be right with you with all the babies, even got to deliver Caroline, which scared me to death."

He could feel her tense again, even though she tried to keep her cries to herself, not wanting to wake or scare the children.

"I thought you would have appreciated coming home like Vince did. He missed the labor, delivery, and everything. Just walked in to find a baby."

Harvey chuckled. "Nope, I like being here with you and for you. I just wish I could take your pain."

They heard footsteps approaching from the parlor. The doctor opened the door and immediately went to work. "Well, Eva, seems you are doing another fine job. Are you actually going to let me deliver this one? Your pa delivered the first, Harvey delivered the next, I was beginning to wonder if you trusted me enough to do it."

He saw her tense. "You don't have much longer." He timed the length of the contraction and the time between.

Within a few hours, he told her to push one more time, and a screaming little boy entered the world.

Eva and Harvey glowed as the doctor placed the tiny, yet loud baby boy in their arms. Harvey swallowed hard while unwrapping the blanket and getting a good look at his son.

"You want to name him Charles, after your pa?"

Eva nodded. "Yes, we can call him Charlie."

Chapter 22

"Asa! Eva had a boy! I know she and Harvey are overjoyed. Oh, how I would love to get my hands on that new little one." She looked at Asa mischievously, as she held up the letter from Eva.

"I know you would, sweetheart, but we can't leave right now, you know that. We have the garden to tend, and I can't miss work right now."

Olivia tried to hide her disappointment. "I know, I just miss them so much sometimes. I know we will go sometime soon though, right?"

Asa pulled her into his arms. "You know we will."

He looked in her eyes and took in her face. "Olivia are you alright with being here? Do you want me to go back to the refinery and move back home?"

She looked away. "Asa, I'm happy being right by your side, wherever you are. I do miss Eva something fierce sometimes, but you being happy is the most important thing.

"Most days I'm very happy with where we are, it's just when I'm missing out on wonderful occasions such as a new baby, I get a bit homesick. I love you with all my heart, my darling, sweet, thoughtful man." She wrapped her arms around his neck and pulled him into a very convincing kiss.

Ruth came out to the porch with the two dogs following her. The light-colored dog, she had named Sugar, the brown one she named Cinnamon; two of her favorite things.

Asa bent and picked her up. "You look just like your ma and are almost as sweet." He winked at Olivia, stepping off the porch with Ruth on his shoulders and the two dogs swarming around his feet.

Olivia watched him mount his horse and tuck Ruth right in front of him. The man adored his daughter and she loved him.

She looked around at all she had to be thankful for. Asa had worked to get a garden broke for her and helped when he could. He had fenced in an area for a couple of cows and even built a chicken house. They had yet to buy the cows and needed a few more chickens, but he was looking at some horses right now and everything just took time.

Amy had written a few weeks earlier and seemed thrilled with her busy life. Olivia was glad her sister was happy but couldn't imagine living that lifestyle. Entertaining guests so often, being involved with so many groups and organizations, had no appeal to her.

She would love to see her house though and have a visit with her, Sylvia and Vince. Sylvia had just turned four and that was hard to believe. "Things will just never be the same," she mumbled, turning back to the house.

****

As soon as the garden harvest was over and Olivia canned the last of it, she marched straight to Asa. "I'm finished and will be ready to go as soon as I can get packed."

He laughed at her. "Well, alright then. I promised and I will stand by my word. Let me arrange for a few days off and we will be on our way." He kissed her nose.

She almost danced away from him, so excited about the trip. "I will do laundry tomorrow to make sure we have everything we need."

The next evening, Asa dreaded getting home. He knew Olivia would be upset, but nothing could be done about it.

Meeting him as he came in the door, she threw her arms around his neck. Ruth ran to join them in a hug.

"My, what a welcome!" he exclaimed. He picked Ruth up. "How's my little darling?"

She pointed to the dogs. "Bad dogs! Bad!"

He looked at Olivia. "What happened?"

"They were just overly interested in the laundry hanging on the line. I had to do a few pieces over. At least they didn't destroy anything; this time."

He put Ruth down. "Supper smells good." He reached out and pulled Olivia to him. "And you look wonderful," he whispered against her hair.

She blushed. "Thank you, kind sir. Your supper will be ready soon." Breaking away from him, she hurried into the kitchen.

Over supper, he quietly broke the news. "Olivia, I hate to tell you this," he sighed. "I can't get any time off from work right now. But you and Ruth can still go and have a great time. I will miss you both, but I promised you could go and I really want you to. I know how much it means to you."

"Asa," she whined. "I don't want to go without you!"

"I know, but it won't be any different than when you stayed while I returned home before. I wish I could, and I hope maybe at Christmas I can. But this time, I just can't.

"I will buy your tickets tomorrow and send a telegram for Harvey to pick you up. I insist."

Reaching for his hand with tears in her eyes she whispered, "Thank you, Asa. I love you and will miss you something fierce."

The last thing Asa said to her as the train pulled away a few days later, "Don't bring home any more puppies!"

****

It was like Christmas all over again when Olivia and Ruth arrived. She hugged everyone and then took little Charlie. "I'm your Auntie Olivia and this is your cousin Ruth."

Ruth couldn't remember seeing a baby before and was amazed, but not for long. Caroline and Nate got her attention, and she ran off with them to play.

Olivia looked around. "Something seems different."

Eva took her by the hand and led her toward Nate's room. When she got close, she noticed another door at the end of the hallway.

"This is your bedroom while you're here." She swung the door open. "It's not much, but we are drawing plans to expand the house come spring. This probably won't stay as a bedroom, but for now, it's yours, and when you go home it will be Caroline's."

Olivia listened carefully as Eva explained their plans for the house. "Harvey wants to put four bedrooms upstairs."

"Oh my! How many more babies do you plan to have?"

"Not that many I assure you. But we want to have room for anyone that comes for a visit, hoping you will come more often." She hugged her sister. "I have missed you so much!"

****

Spring 1860

Between the farm and having three children, Harvey and Eva didn't get to visit Asa and Olivia except for maybe once a year. But Asa always made sure that Olivia and Ruth, with or without him, visited the farm at least four times each year.

Amy wrote often but hadn't come back for a visit in the nearly four years she had been gone. She was active in the community, Vince was making a name for himself, Sylvia would soon be seven, taking piano and voice lessons, and they were enjoying life to the fullest.

In May, Eva and Olivia received telegrams from Amy announcing she, along with Vince and Sylvia, would be arriving for a visit on Friday, June 1st.

As Eva was jumping for joy at her house in North Carolina, Olivia was doing the same in Virginia. They were finally going to see their baby sister again.

A few days later they both received letters explaining that Vince would only stay a few days, but she and Sylvia would like to stay a bit longer if it wasn't an imposition.

Eva immediately started arranging and rearranging the bedrooms in the new addition. She made a list of things for Harvey to attend to, such as buying or building two new beds for the empty bedrooms.

She made a list for herself of purchases to be made at Henderson's, including some extra sheets and blankets, chamber pots, basins with pitchers and stands, and extra baking and cooking supplies.

Olivia arrived the day before Amy, helping Eva get all the last-minute things done. They worked well together cleaning and cooking while Harvey and Asa did their bidding and played with the children.

At last, Asa and Harvey were pulling up in the buggy with Vince, Amy, and Sylvia. The first thing they heard was Amy's excited squeal. It was good to know, that some things would never change.

Sylvia was a bit timid at first, not remembering anyone, but hearing plenty about them. She was intrigued by the cousins, how Caroline and Ruth would take off running and climb a tree just like Nate did. She had never seen a girl do that before. She followed at a distance, until Ruth, who was almost six, came and took her by the hand.

"We can play dollies if you want to."

Sylvia smiled warmly. "Yes, that would be nice."

The men sat on the porch and talked as they watched over the children. Vince was finally believing war was imminent and talked non-stop about it.

"The army in Alabama has already started guarding places that may be targeted by the north if we do go to war. One unit is surrounding our area constantly. Most of the major railroads meet there and it is filled with industry and commerce. It would be a major disaster to lose our city."

"Do you think you should move back here? Or at least move Amy and Sylvia back here?" Asa was truly concerned.

"No, I think we will be alright. As I said, the army has us heavily guarded. But I appreciate the offer and will definitely send them here if things do get bad."

Eva stepped out on the porch. "I know something I should have purchased in town."

"What's that, sweetheart?" Harvey quizzed cautiously when he saw the teasing look on her face.

"A dinner bell! There's no way I can yell loud enough for all those children to hear me. What a ruckus they make! Isn't it wonderful?"

She turned to go back in, "Supper is ready. Can you call the children and get them to wash up?"

"Yes ma'am." Harvey stood and whistled, immediately drawing everyone's attention. "Supper! Get washed up!" He motioned for everyone to come on.

"I wish all her wants were that easy to handle!"

"I heard that, Harvey Darnell." Eva peeked out the door, grinning.

****

"My ma is working here today, and I was wondering if you wanted to go fishing or something, Nate." Seven-year-old James Russell fidgeted while he waited for Nate's reply.

"That sounds like fun. Let me ask my ma." He turned, hurrying to the house.

A few minutes later, Nate hurried back out, motioning for James to come with him. They ran to the barn and started getting Nate's fishing pole and bucket for worms.

"We need to get going quick! Caroline heard me ask Ma, and now she's having a fit to go." Nate peeked out the barn door, hearing Caroline all the way from the house, but didn't see her.

"Come on James, let's get out of here." Both boys took off running toward the creek.

"Caroline, not another word. You have Ruth and Sylvia to play with, now just hush," Eva scolded her disappointed daughter.

Caroline knew the matter was closed. She stomped her foot as she turned to leave the kitchen. Suddenly she got a swat on her backside.

"Young lady, I will not put up with your attitude. You straighten up right now, or I promise you will be sorry."

"Yes ma'am." Caroline left the room quietly and was soon back to playing with her cousins.

"That girl," Eva shook her head as she chuckled. "She should have been a boy. I've never in my life seen a girl so bent on catching frogs and lizards, climbing trees and such, yet in the next minute, she will be cuddling on Charlie and playing with dolls."

Olivia joined her sister. "I'm afraid that Ruth is about as bad. Asa takes her around with him and teaches her everything he would have taught a son, and I try to teach her about being a lady. I guess they are just stuck being tomboys."

"I must say," Amy chirped, "I don't have that problem with Sylvia. She is constantly in a club or group that gives her so much social training. In fact, she's not really around very many boys except in school."

"Well, maybe she can rub off some of those social graces on our girls while she's here," Eva smirked. "I wish her luck."

A few hours later, Nate and James returned with a string full of fish. When he took them to his ma, he was shocked to have her put a knife in his and James' hands.

"Come with me. I will show you how to clean them, then it's up to you two to get it done."

Harvey, Asa, and Vince rode up in time to see the spectacle of a mess the boys were making.

Harvey approached and was about to take over when Eva called through the window. "Teach or stay out of their way. They need to learn there's more to it than catching the fish."

He and Asa took turns showing the boys what they were doing wrong until at last, they got the hang of it.

Nate proudly held up a nice clean filet and yelled toward the kitchen window. "Look Ma! I did it!"

Eva appeared at the window and beamed with pride. "I knew you could, son. Good job!"

Caroline had been watching while perched in a tree, somewhat relieved she didn't have to clean fish. She determined that she could, and would certainly do as good a job, if not better if she had to.

Harvey saw her and motioned her down.

"Uncle Vince is leaving tomorrow, so we are going to make tonight a special night. You girls go get washed up and maybe get Sylvia to help you look extra special tonight."

Caroline huffed. "Pa, do we...?"

"Yes, Caroline. You have to. Just be a good girl. It won't hurt you to act like a little lady at supper after being so rough and tumble all day. Now go on and do as I say."

"Yes sir."

Sylvia was happy to help them dress up for supper, she even helped fix their hair with pretty ribbons of her own. When they stepped into the dining room, Sylvia was beaming with pride while Caroline and Ruth felt uncomfortable. When they saw that Nate had to dress nice for supper too, they felt much better.

The ladies had fixed a wonderful supper with several desserts. There was food on the table and the buffet, with platters and bowls brimming full of everything they could imagine.

Before everyone sat down, Harvey called for quiet while he said the blessing, first saying a few words to Vince, about how glad everyone was to see him again and that they hated he had to leave so soon.

Finally, they bowed their heads, having no idea as they all gathered around the table, holding hands while the blessing was said, this would be the last time they would all be together as a family.

Chapter 23

Vince had some very important things to attend while Amy extended her family visit. He had come up with the surprise of a lifetime for his beautiful wife. He adored her more than anything and loved his daughter more than life itself. All he wanted was to make them happy.

In May, before they left on vacation, one of the smaller mansions, the one Amy always said was her favorite, had come up for sale. He had secretly inquired about it and put a deposit on it. Now, while she was out of town for another month, he had to sell their house, finalize the paperwork and get everything moved.

The morning after he arrived back home, he went to his new mansion and walked through each room, reveling in how wonderful it felt and how far he had come since his childhood days at the orphanage. He thought of how surprised Amy would be and about her being the lady of the mansion.

His thoughts wandered to Sylvia, his little princess, and imagined her sitting in that huge parlor with twelve-foot ceilings, playing the piano for their guests. "Perhaps I should trade our piano in on a grand piano," he mused.

He walked past the smaller parlor which would make a fine office, and on into the dining room. He marveled at how spacious it was with floor to ceiling windows on one side, looking out over a beautiful yard. From there, he wandered into the kitchen, noticing a door he had paid no attention to before.

Assuming it was a pantry, he opened it to find a separate, smaller kitchen, which he immediately realized its purpose. "A summer kitchen to keep the heat out of the house, and a place for the servants to eat," he mumbled to himself. "How nice."

There was a utility porch for doing laundry, with steps leading to a secluded area of the yard where there were clotheslines strung.

Completing the tour of the downstairs, he walked through both large bedrooms and stood in amazement at the huge water closet. "Amy will absolutely love this!"

Hurrying up the staircase, he walked through all six nice sized rooms. There was a big foyer at the top of the stairs, centrally located to each of the rooms. Another water closet was on the backside of the foyer.

He continued to the third floor, realizing they would probably not even furnish that far. It was more beautiful than he remembered. There were three big rooms, each with nice views of the city, and another water closet. Reconsidering, he thought, *"This is too nice to waste. We will have to furnish this nicely and comfortably."*

As he exited the house, he walked around the back and side yard, breathing in the aromas of the beautiful flowers. The yard was surrounded by a white picket fence, with a big gazebo sitting near the back, complete with a swing. He could envision his Amy sitting there, content, reading a book, like the lady of leisure she should be.

Walking back through the downstairs quickly, he realized that their furniture, although nice and practically new, wouldn't suit this house at all. "I must get busy! I have so much to do!"

By the time Amy and Sylvia were within days of coming home, he had successfully sold their home along with most of the furniture, moved the special pieces he decided to keep, and furnished the most used rooms in their new mansion. He couldn't wait for her to see it.

He was waiting on the platform for them at the station when they stepped off the train. "Oh, my darlings! I missed you so!" he exclaimed as he hugged them both at once. Then he picked Sylvia up in one arm and wrapped the other around Amy, in a tight embrace and long-awaited kiss.

"I hope you enjoyed your time with the family because I don't think I can live without you again." He glowed as he took in Amy's smile and beautiful face.

He motioned for the porter to collect their luggage and pointed to their buggy. Tipping his head at him, he slipped a coin into the man's hand.

"It's so good to be home! I have missed you too, Vince," Amy almost squealed with delight.

"I'm so glad you're both back. I've had to stay extra busy to keep myself from falling into despair of loneliness. Now, I can show you what I've kept myself busy with. You are going to love the surprise."

"Vince, I've told you repeatedly, you don't have to buy things to show us how much we are loved by you." She squeezed his arm and cuddled in close. "I have been dreaming about having your arms around me again. That's all I need."

When he turned in the opposite direction of home, Amy sighed. "Vince, I know you are excited, but we are tired from traveling. I would really like to go home."

He patted her hand. "I promise, I will have you home in no time." Grinning, he turned into a driveway.

"Vince, whose house is this? I really don't feel up to visiting." She looked at him seriously. "Can't this wait until tomorrow?"

He jumped down and reached for her hand. "Come, my darling. Trust me. I know who owns this house, and so do you. I know it's your favorite around here and I thought it was time for you to see the inside."

She sighed again and let herself be led up the walk and steps of this beautiful house. She had always wanted to see the inside of it and felt herself getting a bit excited. She smiled at him.

"Thank you, Vince. You know I've always loved this place. You are so very thoughtful."

Stepping to the door, he swooped Amy up in his arms. "Sylvia, would you open the door, please?"

"Vince! Have you taken leave of your senses? You can't act like this around people!"

He stepped into the house with her and spun around. "Welcome home, my darling! The house is yours!"

"What?" Amy felt elated and upset at the same time. "Vince, what have you done?"

He set her down and grabbed her and Sylvia by the hand, leading them through the house, showing and telling them all he had been doing during their absence.

Amy sent Sylvia to look around the place, then she turned to Vince, looking upset. "Vince, we can't afford something like this, and you know it. What have you done?"

"Amy, darling." He reached out to touch her face with her pulling away. His heart sank. "I got a very good price for our house and a very good deal on this one. I will have you know; we can afford it. We may not have servants and such luxuries, at least for now, but we can certainly afford it.

"I have talked extensively with the banker. We have ten years to pay it off. We are both young and strong and can afford to take this step. I don't want to wait until we are too old to enjoy life to have such pleasures."

Amy was trying not to let him know that she was seething. The man had no sense when it came to being frugal. They had been around this issue many times, just never with this large a purchase. She stood in thought, beginning to look around.

What would be the point to continue arguing? The damage is already done...again," she thought as she shrugged her shoulders.

"Which did you say is our bedroom? I am in need of a short nap."

"Yes, darling, let me show you." He led her by the arm through the parlor, to a huge bedroom.

She stopped him before he entered, putting her hand on his chest. "Please, stand right there for a moment."

He smiled, knowing she would be alright with this for now, and thrilled about it by tonight. His heart was crushed a moment later when suddenly, she slammed the bedroom door as hard as she could, right in his face.

Amy woke a few hours later, after crying herself to sleep. She couldn't believe that Vince would take on something like this without even discussing it with her. Now, the bank owned them for the next ten years. Thank goodness she had put a good amount in savings. At least that would hold them over for a while in case they needed it.

As she opened the bedroom door, she heard voices and laughter coming from the direction of the dining room. She quickly went into the water closet, splashing water on her face and tidying her hair.

She entered the dining room, seeing an older couple sitting there with Vince and Sylvia.

"Oh, darling. I do hope you're feeling more rested now. Come, I want you to meet our neighbors." He pointed to the man, who was now standing, and then to the woman. "This is Mr. and Mrs. Blakely. They live right next door."

"Nice to meet you," Amy said quietly.

"Darling, they brought supper for us as a welcome to our new home."

"That was so kind and thoughtful. Thank you so very much."

Mrs. Blakley motioned to her husband before she spoke. "My dear, I look forward to becoming acquainted in the near future. For now, we need to leave you be. We know how exhausting travel can be, and you need the chance to settle into your new home. We shall visit with each other again, soon."

"Yes, ma'am and thank you, for being so attentive to our needs. I look forward to a visit soon."

They said goodbye to their guests at the door, then Amy quietly turned, making her way to the kitchen to serve supper.

Sylvia was granted permission to explore the house again, as Vince continued to follow down behind Amy.

"Amy, please. Don't be mad at me. Please look at me."

She turned to face him. "Vince, I'm not so mad anymore, but I am upset. It will take me some time to get over this."

"Why, Amy? What is so wrong with having a beautiful house?"

"Vince! There is nothing wrong with having things, but there is something very wrong with living above your means. I'm upset, yes, but I'm more scared than anything. I'm not used to living like this, owing someone, especially owing so much! I am scared to death!"

He reached for her, and she shrugged away. "Vince, listen to me. We have had this conversation so many times over the last eight years, and apparently, you haven't been listening. You save your money first, then you buy things. I have never known my parents to do any other way. That's how I was taught. It's too risky to think that all of this could be taken away if we happen to fall on bad times."

She reached for his hand. "Sweetheart, I love you with my entire being. All I want is for us to be together and happy. But happiness isn't measured by the material things you lavish us with. You say that you give us all these things because you love us, and I know you mean that. I see a deeper, hidden reason that perhaps you won't even admit to yourself. You somehow have confused yourself into believing that these gifts are a measure of your self-worth. That really concerns me. You are the sweetest, most kindhearted man I've ever known, and you still would be, even if you never brought me another surprise. Don't you understand I love you, because of who you are, not because of what you can buy me?"

He wrapped his arms around her. "Darling, you don't seem to realize how much you mean to me. You are my life. You and Sylvia are all I live for. I love you so much."

She pulled back from him. "I love you, Vince. Now, let me get used to this new kitchen of mine and get supper on the table."

She started opening the gifts of food from the neighbors. "I'm sure we will survive, Vince. I feel much better knowing that we do have enough savings to carry us through a rough patch if it should come."

Looking at him when he didn't respond, she saw his face turn white.

"Oh, Vince, no! Please tell me you didn't use our savings!"

"Now, darling, you know that we always said our savings were for a house. That's what I used it for."

Her knees buckled as she reached for a chair. She sat down, put her head on the table and sobbed.

He wrapped his arms around her. "Darling, it's really not as bad as you think. Please come with me and let me show you the finances I have worked out."

For the next hour, food was forgotten, and serious talks were taking place in Vince's new office. He showed her all the numbers and was able to convince her they would be fine, at least as long as nothing serious happened.

****

Asa was finally able to get four nice horses and six cows. Olivia was thrilled that they now had a farm of their own, with a small garden, enough chickens to keep them supplied with eggs, milk from their own cows, and of course, two loud, lively dogs to warn them of everything, including frogs, butterflies and anything else that moved.

Ruth was a delightful, highly intelligent child. Asa and Olivia were able to enroll her in school a few weeks before her fifth birthday, and she loved going to school. Not only did she love to learn, but she also enjoyed the chance to make some friends. Olivia loved watching her every morning as a group of children would gather around her upon arriving at school.

She had thought several times during Ruth's first year of school, about going back to teaching and had finally talked to Asa about it over the summer. After inquiring where to fill out the paperwork, she immediately got it taken care of. School wouldn't begin for another few weeks, leaving enough time for them to consider hiring her if there was an opening.

It didn't take long for her to get a reply that the school needed her. She was thrilled and so was Ruth.

Asa came home that evening to see both his girls beaming with joy. He had some news he needed to share with Olivia that she wouldn't take very well but decided not to ruin the joyous occasion.

Olivia and Ruth hugged Asa, with Olivia lingering around his waist, looking up at him, smiling radiantly. If she only knew how much it meant to him to have her look at him like that. The love and pride he took in knowing she was his, and completely happy, made him stand a bit taller, as if on top of the world.

"I got the job, Asa! Isn't that wonderful? Ruth and I will begin school together in a few weeks."

He held her close. "That is wonderful news, sweetheart. Congratulations." He kissed her before she hurried back to the kitchen.

"Your supper is almost ready. Get washed up and I will get it on the table."

How he would approach the subject was constantly going through his mind. He knew he would wait until Ruth was bedded down, but he knew, no matter how he said it, it wasn't going to end well.

After supper, Asa continued to teach Ruth how to play checkers until Olivia joined them after cleaning the kitchen. He motioned for her to sit beside him on the couch, lovingly wrapping his free arm around her.

"You are my good luck." He kissed the top of her head then rested his head against hers. Suddenly, he looked shocked as Ruth wiped out all his checkers in one move.

"Did you cheat, young lady?"

"Nope, I just have a good teacher who doesn't play as good when Ma comes in the room."

They all laughed. "Yes," he admitted. "She is quite the distraction."

When Ruth went to bed, both Asa and Olivia said her goodnight prayers with her, then hugged and kissed her goodnight, as they always did.

Asa cuddled up on the couch with Olivia, basking in the joy of having such a wonderful family. He needed to talk to her and give her a bit of notice about what was happening.

"Sweetheart, I, umm, I need to talk to you seriously about something."

She turned and looked right in his eyes. "Asa, this doesn't sound so good."

He shook his head. "It's not good, but I need you to hear me out and hopefully you will see my reasoning."

She nodded solemnly.

"I enlisted in the Army today." He felt her tense as she gasped. Her hand went to her mouth and tears filled her eyes.

"It's almost certain we are headed for war. Every man between eighteen and thirty-five is to serve three years. I've been talking to some of the men at work and we have come to a conclusion.

"The men who sign up before the war starts will get more training for when we have actual battles. The ones who come in afterward, well, they will most likely be sent straight to battle.

"We want to be prepared, so we all signed up today. We leave in three weeks."

Tears flowed freely down Olivia's cheeks. He pulled her to his chest and held her. She never said a word.

"I need to know what you want to do. Do you want to move back to the farm and stay close to family? Do you want to stay here? I just need you to think about it and tell me what you want to do. There are a lot of preparations to be made either way."

She nodded and spoke through her sobs. "I will pray about it and let you know." Another wave of sobs hit her. All she thought was how could she live without this man for one day, let alone months or possibly years? What if something happened to him? Her heart literally ached as she sobbed against his chest.

He held her, rubbing her back and kissing the top of her head until her crying subsided.

****

Eva walked in the dining room, just in time to see Caroline pull the chair from under Nate as he began to sit down. Caroline doubled in laughter as Nate sprawled on the floor.

"That's alright, little sister. I've got something coming for you." Nate chuckled as he stood.

Eva shook her head in amusement. Her two oldest were constantly pulling pranks and teasing each other. They never fought, taking it all as a challenge to out do each other, and they absolutely adored each other.

"Alright, you two, straighten up. No more pranks at the table." Eva mumbled as she went back to the kitchen, "Lord help anyone that you both go up against at the same time."

Harvey came to the table and sat down quickly, standing back up just as quickly as he shouted, "Oww!" He looked down in his chair to see where he had just crushed a half dozen pinecones.

"I know better than to ask who did this," he laughed. He pointed to Nate and Caroline. "Clean it up, both of you. Hurry up and get back to the table."

Nate and Caroline giggled to each other while cleaning up the mess.

Harvey leaned toward three-year-old Charlie. "Did you see who did this?"

Charlie nodded and grinned. Nate and Caroline held their breath.

"Secwet!" Charlie laughed.

Harvey looked shocked, then amused. "You two are teaching him well," he laughed as he looked over at the two older ones, who were grinning from ear to ear.

Eva joined them and they had a good supper with lively conversation. They all listened as Eva told them about school starting in a few weeks and all that had to be done beforehand.

"Nate, you have done well in school so far, and I expect you to continue. Caroline," she shook her head, "I just don't know about you. This will be your first year of school and you don't know how to sit still. I pity Mrs. Powell with you. You better behave."

"I like Mrs. Powell, Ma. I promise I will be good for her."

Harvey began to tell of some new things happening in town, most of which the kids had no interest in and were barely paying attention to. "Mr. Farley sure is excited today. He rode out here and told me that tracks are being built to bring the trains right to our town. He has been working on that for thirteen years now. I'm glad he's finally seeing it happen.

"That's not all he's happy about. He finally got the town council to sell him the old saloon. The building has been abandoned for four years, without anyone being able to find Toby. Taxes haven't been paid on it, so the council is going to set back the amount of the purchase price in case Toby ever does return. Says he's going to turn it into a nice hotel, with a diner on the first floor."

"That sounds nice. It will be a pleasure to see it used for something good, instead of being an eyesore sitting there with the windows and doors boarded up."

"Nate, Caroline, help your ma get the table cleared, then come ride with me to check everything for the night."

Harvey had given each of them a pony and was teaching them how to care for it, saddle it and do everything for themselves. They both loved to ride, and it made them proud when their pa would ask them to join him, even when he asked them to work. He and Eva had instilled something in them that had made them willing workers, always doing their best, wanting to make their parents proud.

Every night, Harvey and Eva gathered the two older ones in the parlor after Charlie was asleep. They would listen to Harvey read from the Bible, then they would join hands and pray before going to bed.

Caroline blew out the lamp in her bedroom and hopped into bed. "Oww! Nate!" Caroline screamed out.

Harvey and Eva smiled at each other before Harvey called, "Nate, help clean up whatever it is. Make it quick."

"Those two," Eva snickered while shaking her head.

The next morning, Harvey and Eva rode to town to pick up supplies for the farm and the house. They were surprised to see a somewhat unfamiliar face behind the counter at Henderson's.

"Good morning Mr. and Mrs. Darnell. How can I help you?"

"We came in to pick up some supplies we ordered and do a little shopping. Where is Henderson?"

The young man leaned toward them and spoke quietly. "Mr. Henderson's pa isn't doing well. The doc is with him now."

Harvey nodded solemnly. "We will keep him in our prayers." He handed the young man his list.

"Henderson has quite a big order ready for me to pick up. It should be in the back with my name on it. I also need these things on the list."

Eva walked to the yard goods and fingered some of the fabrics, thinking of what she could do with each one.

"See something you like, sweetheart?"

"Oh, yes. But every time I imagine how sweet Caroline would look in a dress made from a pretty fabric, I also imagine the tail end of the skirt hanging from a tree limb. I tell you, she should have been a boy. Sometimes I'm tempted to put her in some of Nate's old pants."

Harvey grinned. "I know what you mean, dear, but she is much too pretty to have been a boy. I like her being tough, makes my job easier."

"How so?" Eva looked up at him in confusion.

"Well," Harvey rubbed his chin. "I don't have to worry about boys giving her a hard time. I imagine she will be able to take care of herself."

Eva elbowed him in the ribs.

"Oww, I see where she gets it from!"

Harvey helped the young man load everything in the wagon as he checked the list of what he was supposed to have. "Seems everything is right. Now, I need to order a few things for next week."

"Yes sir." He went behind the counter and picked up his pad and pencil, beginning to write it all down.

"That's a lot of stuff!" he exclaimed. "Oh, and before I forget, there is a letter for Mrs. Darnell and a telegram for you, sir."

Eva took her letter. "If you would cut three yards of each of those fabrics I stacked there?" She pointed. "I'm going to stand over here and read my letter while I wait."

Harvey interrupted her before she got the envelope opened. "I don't know what's going on, Eva, but it looks as though Olivia and Ruth are coming back here to live. They will be here Saturday."

"What? What about Asa?"

"I don't know. It doesn't say."

"That's odd. I hope nothing is wrong." She turned back to her letter. "I guess we will find out Saturday."

The letter was from her baby sister, Amy. For three pages she spewed and ranted about what Vince had done and how worried she was. Next, there were three more pages filled with how nice the house was.

When Harvey finished settling the bill, he walked to Eva. "I'm ready to go if you are. Is everything alright with Amy?"

"Yes, everything is fine. Vince bought her a mansion with eleven bedrooms, three parlors, two kitchens, and three water closets. That's all," she stated matter of factly.

Harvey stood in shock. He would have considered the news from Amy happy, perhaps even a bit humorous, if he didn't have a growing concern and nagging feeling about what was going on with Asa and Olivia. What would be bringing his brother, or at least his brother's family back home? Was it something good or not?

They would find out soon enough, they were about to meet with more heartache and devastation than they ever knew existed.

The War Was Coming

Continue the journey with the Darnell family as they face hardships they aren't sure they can survive...

Whirwinds Of Turmoil
Darnell Farms Book 2

War was imminent...
Before the war was over, every life would be touched by sorrow and tragedy...
If only they knew how much devastation would be suffered...
The life they knew and loved would soon be nothing but a memory...
The war took more than they could stand to give...
Some of the family wouldn't live to tell it...
How could they go on?
Had God forsaken their country? Their town? Their family?

Cut off from the rest of the world, the dwindling community pulls together trying to survive, wondering if they had the strength.
Protecting their children prodded them forward as they continued crying out for mercy from God.

If you have enjoyed this book, please leave a review on Amazon.com or Goodreads, or any of your favorite book hangouts!

Be the first to know about
new releases, cover reveals,
exclusive contests and much more,
when you sign up for my newsletter at

LynneLanning.com

Follow me on FaceBook at Lynne Lanning Author

Dear Friend,

I hope this book has been an inspiration and a joy to read. If you are perhaps looking for a church, or for spiritual help, please feel free to contact our church. Other than traditional church services, we also have online services and radio broadcasts.

Trinity Baptist Church

2722 U.S. Hwy. 601 South
Mocksville, NC 27028
336-284-2404

Trinitybaptistchurchnc.org

Preacher Darrell Cox

Made in the USA
Columbia, SC
15 October 2022

69514304R00174